STAR WARS

X-WING

ROGUE SQUADRON

IN THE EMPIRE'S SERVICE

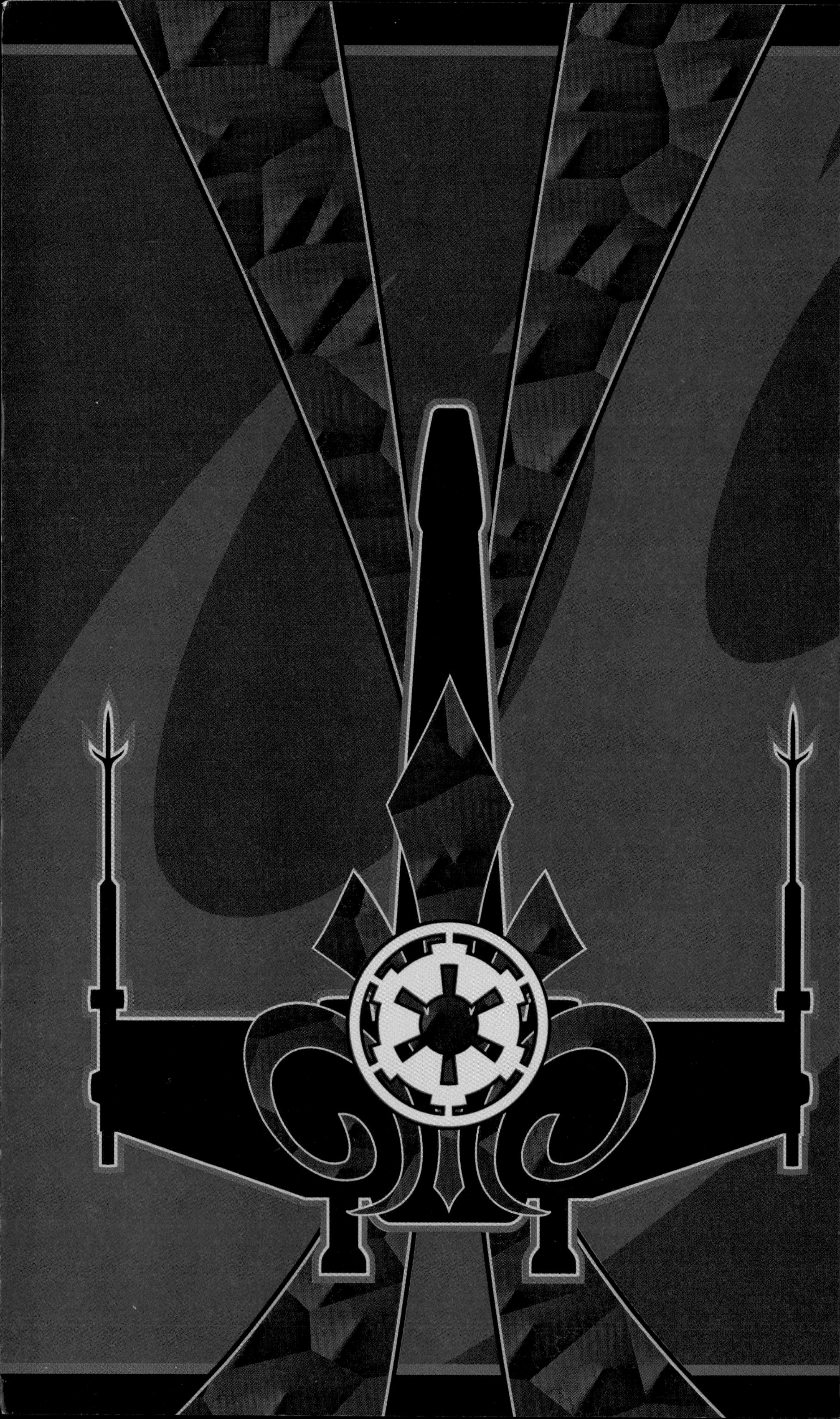

STAR WARS

X-WING

ROGUE SQUADRON

IN THE EMPIRE'S SERVICE

Michael A. Stackpole
story

John Nadeau
pencils

Jordi Ensign
inks

Dave Nestelle
colors

Vickie Williams
lettering

Timothy Bradstreet and **Grant Goleash**
cover

TITAN BOOKS

Mike Richardson
publisher

Peet Janes
series editor

Chris Warner
collection editor

Kristen Burda
collection designer

Mark Cox
art director

Special thanks to Allan Kausch and
Lucy Autrey Wilson at Lucas Licensing.

This book collects issues twenty-one through
twenty-four of the Dark Horse comic-book series
Star Wars: X-Wing Rogue Squadron.

Published by
Titan Books Ltd.
42-44 Dolben Street
London SE1 0UP

First edition: June 1999
ISBN: 1-84023-008-8

1 3 5 7 9 10 8 6 4 2

Printed in Canada

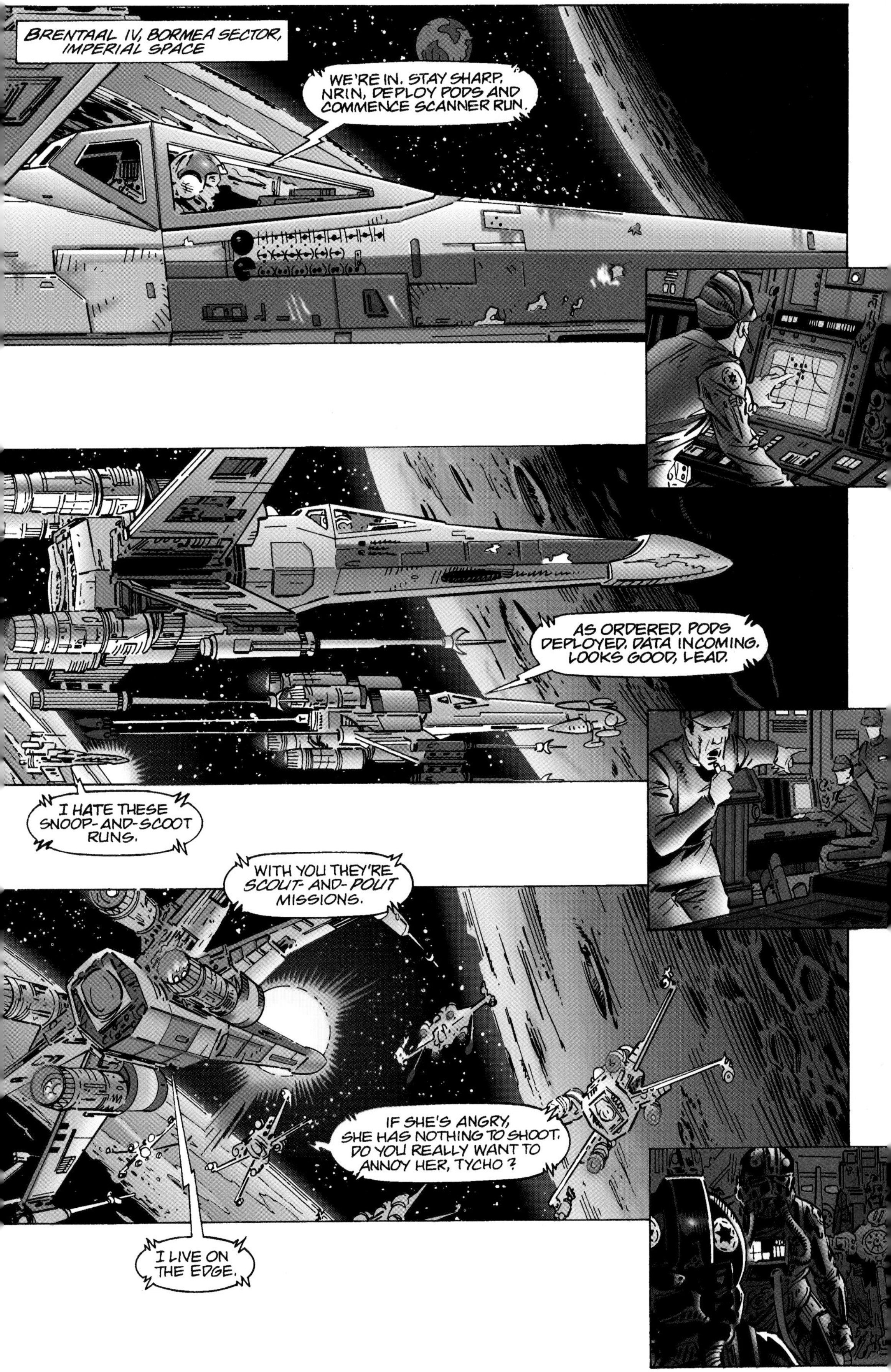
BRENTAAL IV, BORMEA SECTOR, IMPERIAL SPACE
WE'RE IN. STAY SHARP. NRIN, DEPLOY PODS AND COMMENCE SCANNER RUN.
AS ORDERED. PODS DEPLOYED. DATA INCOMING. LOOKS GOOD, LEAD.
I HATE THESE SNOOP-AND-SCOOT RUNS.
WITH YOU THEY'RE SCOUT-AND-POUT MISSIONS.
I LIVE ON THE EDGE.
IF SHE'S ANGRY, SHE HAS NOTHING TO SHOOT. DO YOU REALLY WANT TO ANNOY HER, TYCHO ?

YOU CAN DIE THERE, TOO, TYCHO.

LT. PLOURR ILO

SAVE THE IDLE BRAGS FOR SIMTIME, PLOURR.

LT. TYCHO CELCHU.

ALWAYS THE GLUTTON FOR PUNISHMENT, EH, TYCHO?

LT. WES JANSON

CAN IT, ROGUES, NRIN DOESN'T NEED TO FILTER YOUR CHATTER FROM HIS DATA.

CAPTAIN WEDGE ANTILLES

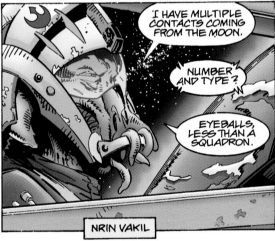

I HAVE MULTIPLE CONTACTS COMING FROM THE MOON.

NUMBER AND TYPE?

EYEBALLS, LESS THAN A SQUADRON.

NRIN VAKIL

JUST AS WELL, WE'RE SOMETHING LESS THAN A SQUADRON RIGHT NOW...

LEAD, THEY'RE IN ATTACK FORMATION ECHO-3.

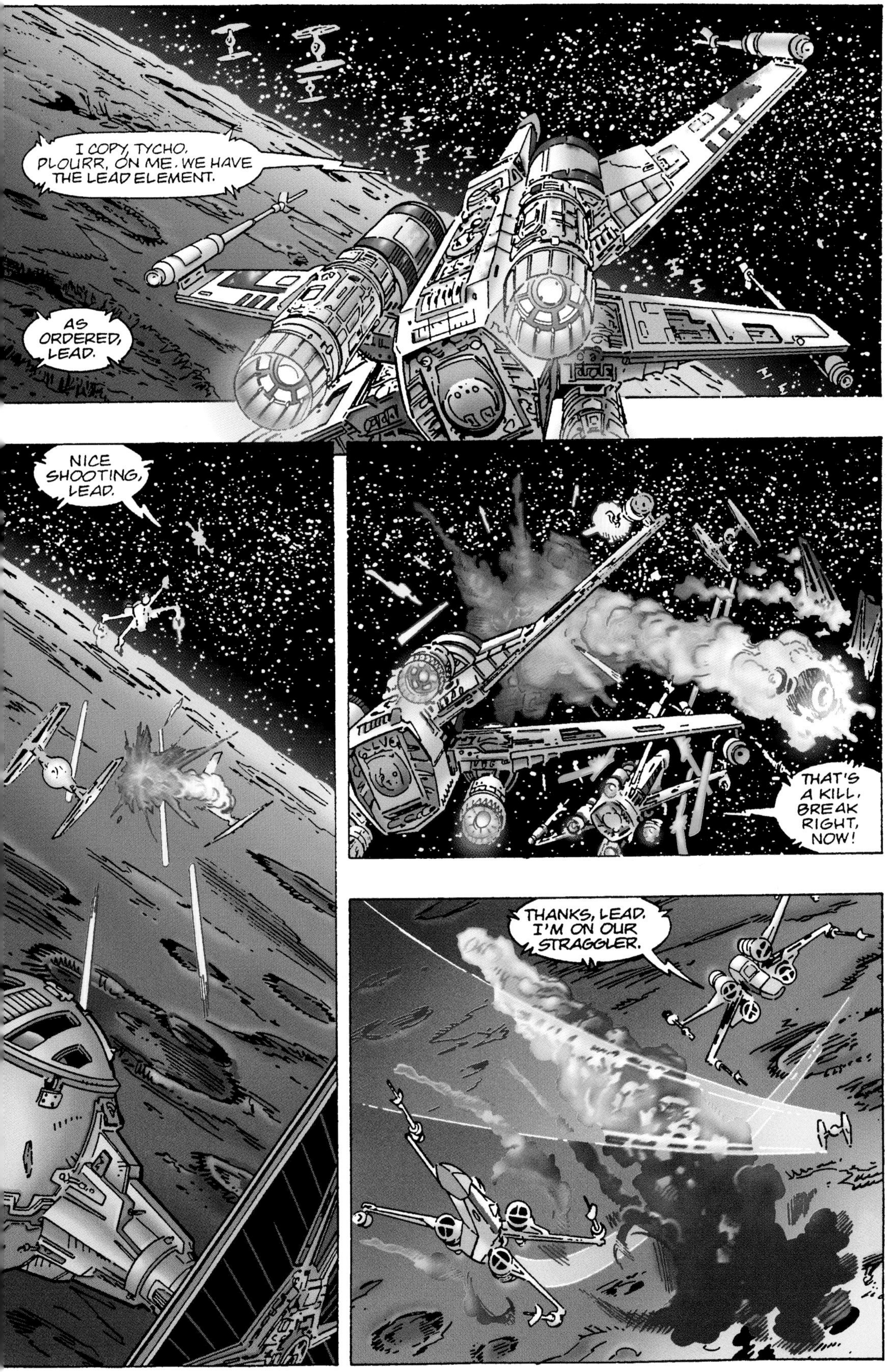
I COPY, TYCHO. PLOURR, ON ME. WE HAVE THE LEAD ELEMENT.
AS ORDERED, LEAD.
NICE SHOOTING, LEAD.
THAT'S A KILL. BREAK RIGHT, NOW!
THANKS, LEAD. I'M ON OUR STRAGGLER.

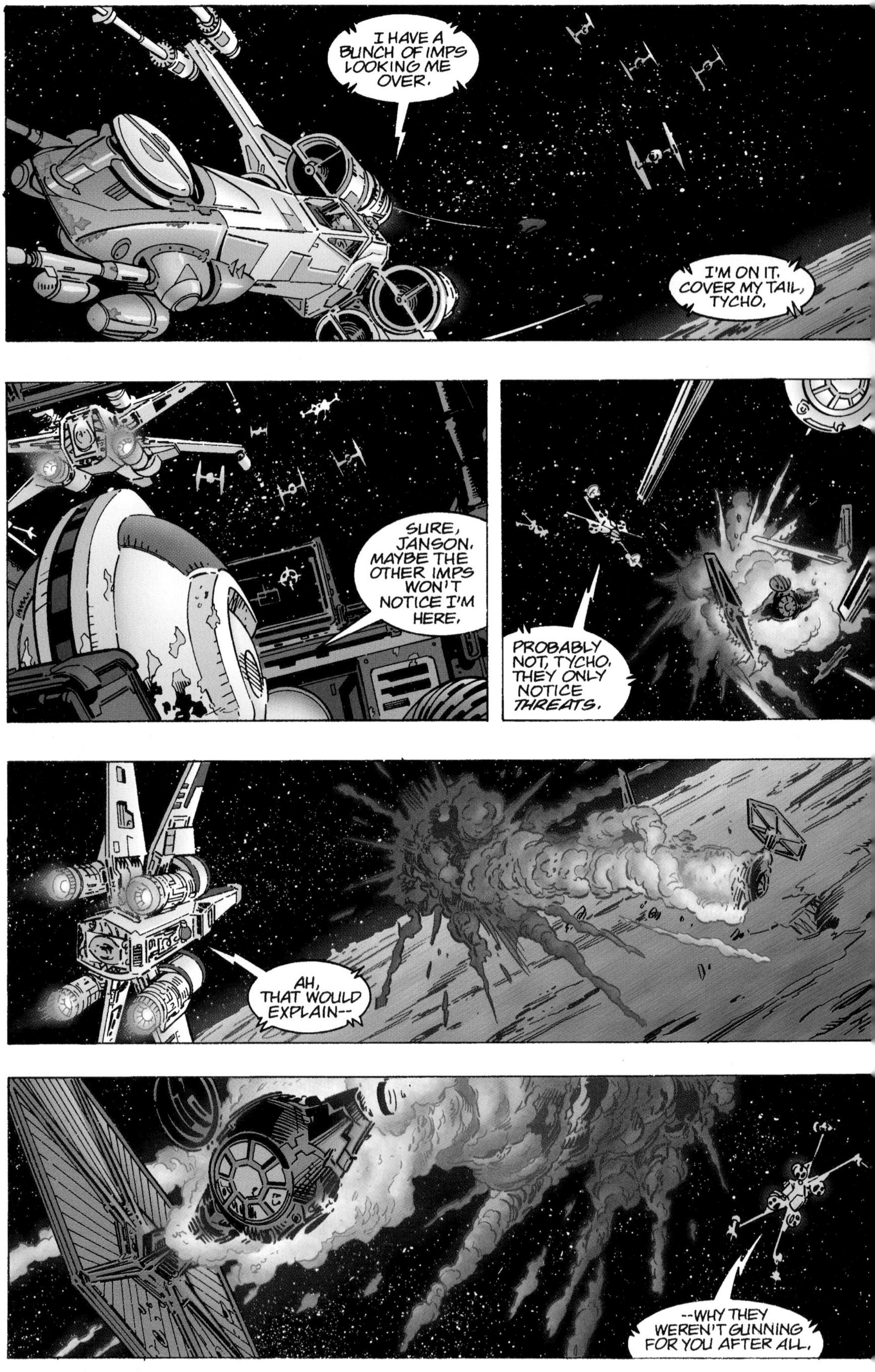
I HAVE A BUNCH OF IMPS LOOKING ME OVER.
I'M ON IT. COVER MY TAIL, TYCHO.
SURE, JANSON. MAYBE THE OTHER IMPS WON'T NOTICE I'M HERE.
PROBABLY NOT, TYCHO. THEY ONLY NOTICE *THREATS*.
AH, THAT WOULD EXPLAIN--
--WHY THEY WEREN'T GUNNING FOR YOU AFTER ALL.

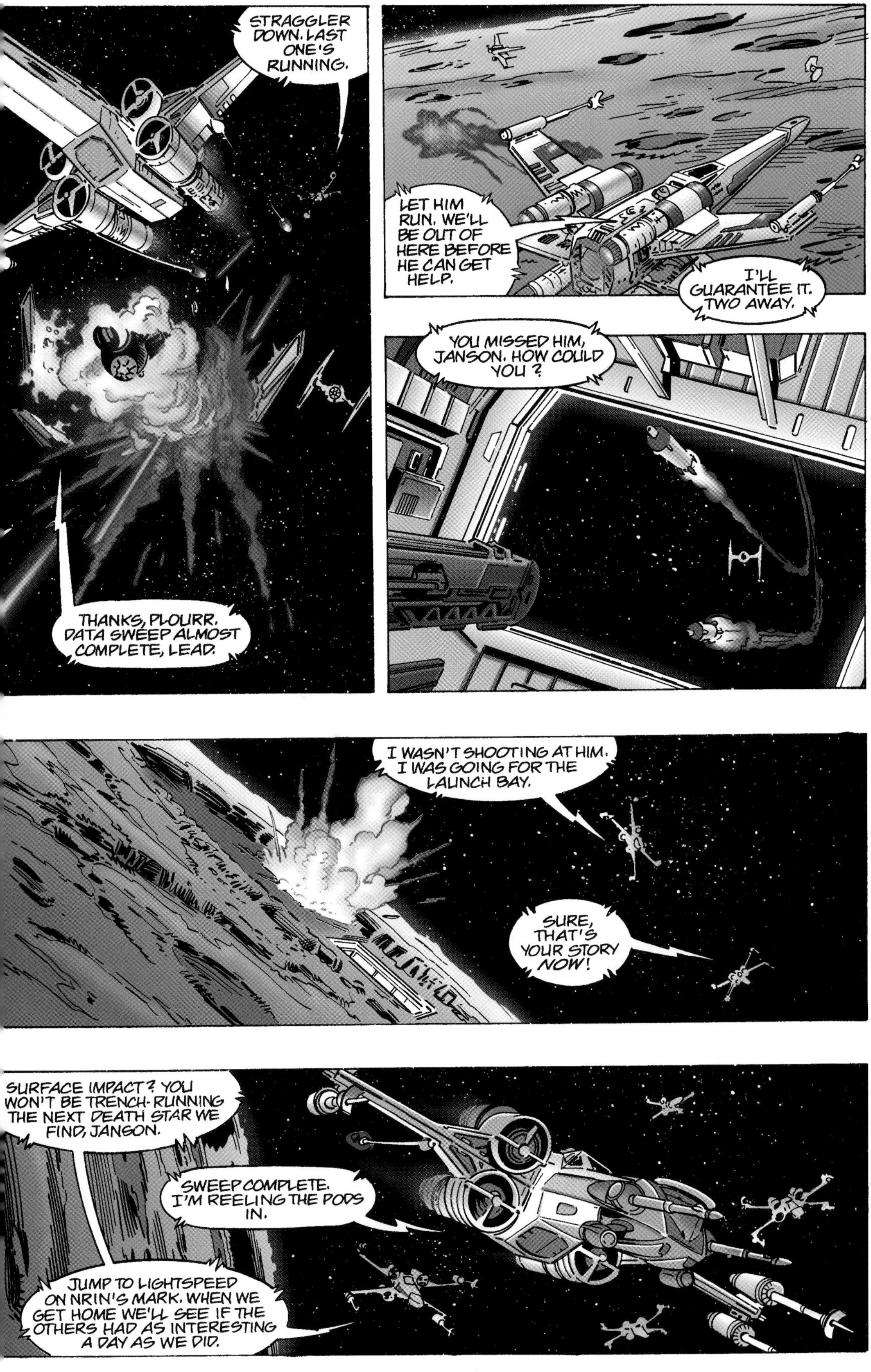
STRAGGLER DOWN. LAST ONE'S RUNNING.
THANKS, PLOURR. DATA SWEEP ALMOST COMPLETE, LEAD.
LET HIM RUN. WE'LL BE OUT OF HERE BEFORE HE CAN GET HELP.
I'LL GUARANTEE IT. TWO AWAY.
YOU MISSED HIM, JANSON. HOW COULD YOU ?
I WASN'T SHOOTING AT HIM. I WAS GOING FOR THE LAUNCH BAY.
SURE, THAT'S YOUR STORY NOW!
SURFACE IMPACT? YOU WON'T BE TRENCH-RUNNING THE NEXT DEATH STAR WE FIND, JANSON.
SWEEP COMPLETE. I'M REELING THE PODS IN.
JUMP TO LIGHTSPEED ON NRIN'S MARK. WHEN WE GET HOME WE'LL SEE IF THE OTHERS HAD AS INTERESTING A DAY AS WE DID.

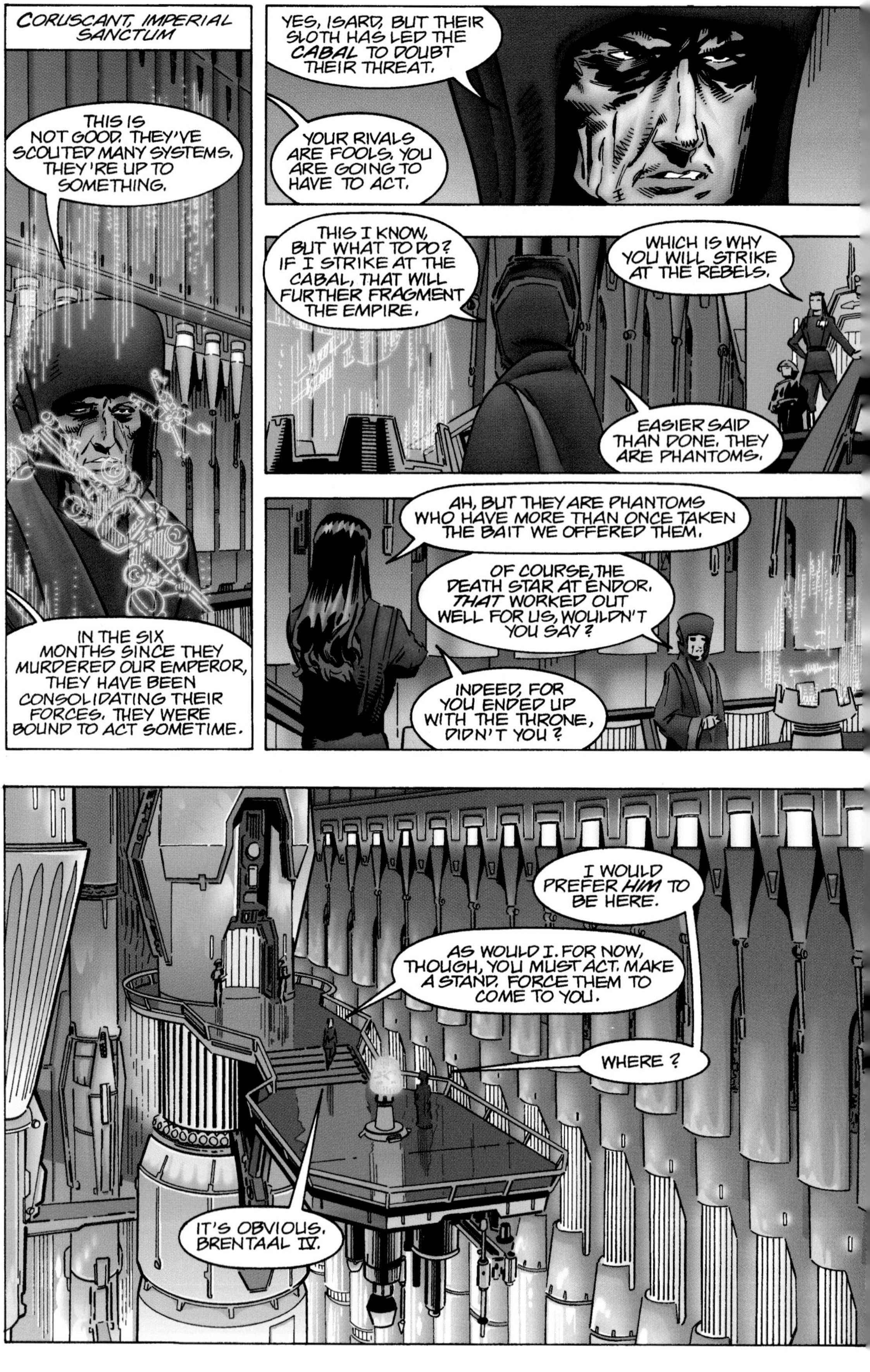
CORUSCANT, IMPERIAL SANCTUM
THIS IS NOT GOOD. THEY'VE SCOUTED MANY SYSTEMS. THEY'RE UP TO SOMETHING.
IN THE SIX MONTHS SINCE THEY MURDERED OUR EMPEROR, THEY HAVE BEEN CONSOLIDATING THEIR FORCES. THEY WERE BOUND TO ACT SOMETIME.
YES, ISARD, BUT THEIR SLOTH HAS LED THE CABAL TO DOUBT THEIR THREAT.
YOUR RIVALS ARE FOOLS. YOU ARE GOING TO HAVE TO ACT.
THIS I KNOW, BUT WHAT TO DO? IF I STRIKE AT THE CABAL, THAT WILL FURTHER FRAGMENT THE EMPIRE.
WHICH IS WHY YOU WILL STRIKE AT THE REBELS.
EASIER SAID THAN DONE. THEY ARE PHANTOMS.
AH, BUT THEY ARE PHANTOMS WHO HAVE MORE THAN ONCE TAKEN THE BAIT WE OFFERED THEM.
OF COURSE, THE DEATH STAR AT ENDOR. THAT WORKED OUT WELL FOR US, WOULDN'T YOU SAY?
INDEED, FOR YOU ENDED UP WITH THE THRONE, DIDN'T YOU?
I WOULD PREFER HIM TO BE HERE.
AS WOULD I. FOR NOW, THOUGH, YOU MUST ACT. MAKE A STAND. FORCE THEM TO COME TO YOU.
WHERE?
IT'S OBVIOUS. BRENTAAL IV.

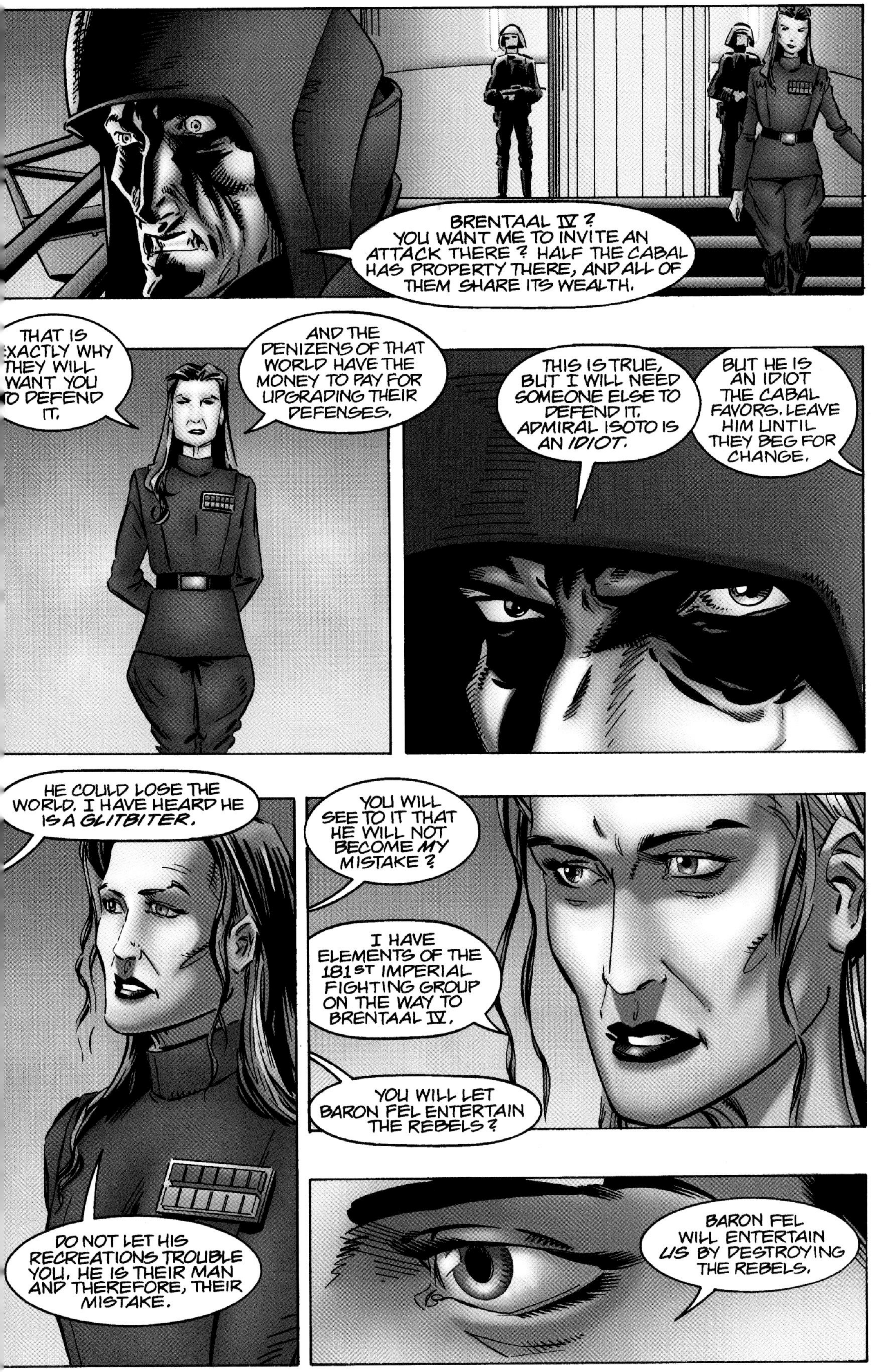
BRENTAAL IV ? YOU WANT ME TO INVITE AN ATTACK THERE ? HALF THE CABAL HAS PROPERTY THERE, AND ALL OF THEM SHARE ITS WEALTH.
THAT IS EXACTLY WHY THEY WILL WANT YOU TO DEFEND IT.
AND THE DENIZENS OF THAT WORLD HAVE THE MONEY TO PAY FOR UPGRADING THEIR DEFENSES.
THIS IS TRUE, BUT I WILL NEED SOMEONE ELSE TO DEFEND IT. ADMIRAL ISOTO IS AN *IDIOT*.
BUT HE IS AN IDIOT THE CABAL FAVORS. LEAVE HIM UNTIL THEY BEG FOR CHANGE.
HE COULD LOSE THE WORLD. I HAVE HEARD HE IS A *GLITBITER*.
DO NOT LET HIS RECREATIONS TROUBLE YOU, HE IS THEIR MAN AND THEREFORE, THEIR MISTAKE.
YOU WILL SEE TO IT THAT HE WILL NOT BECOME *MY* MISTAKE ?
I HAVE ELEMENTS OF THE 181ST IMPERIAL FIGHTING GROUP ON THE WAY TO BRENTAAL IV.
YOU WILL LET BARON FEL ENTERTAIN THE REBELS ?
BARON FEL WILL ENTERTAIN *US* BY DESTROYING THE REBELS.

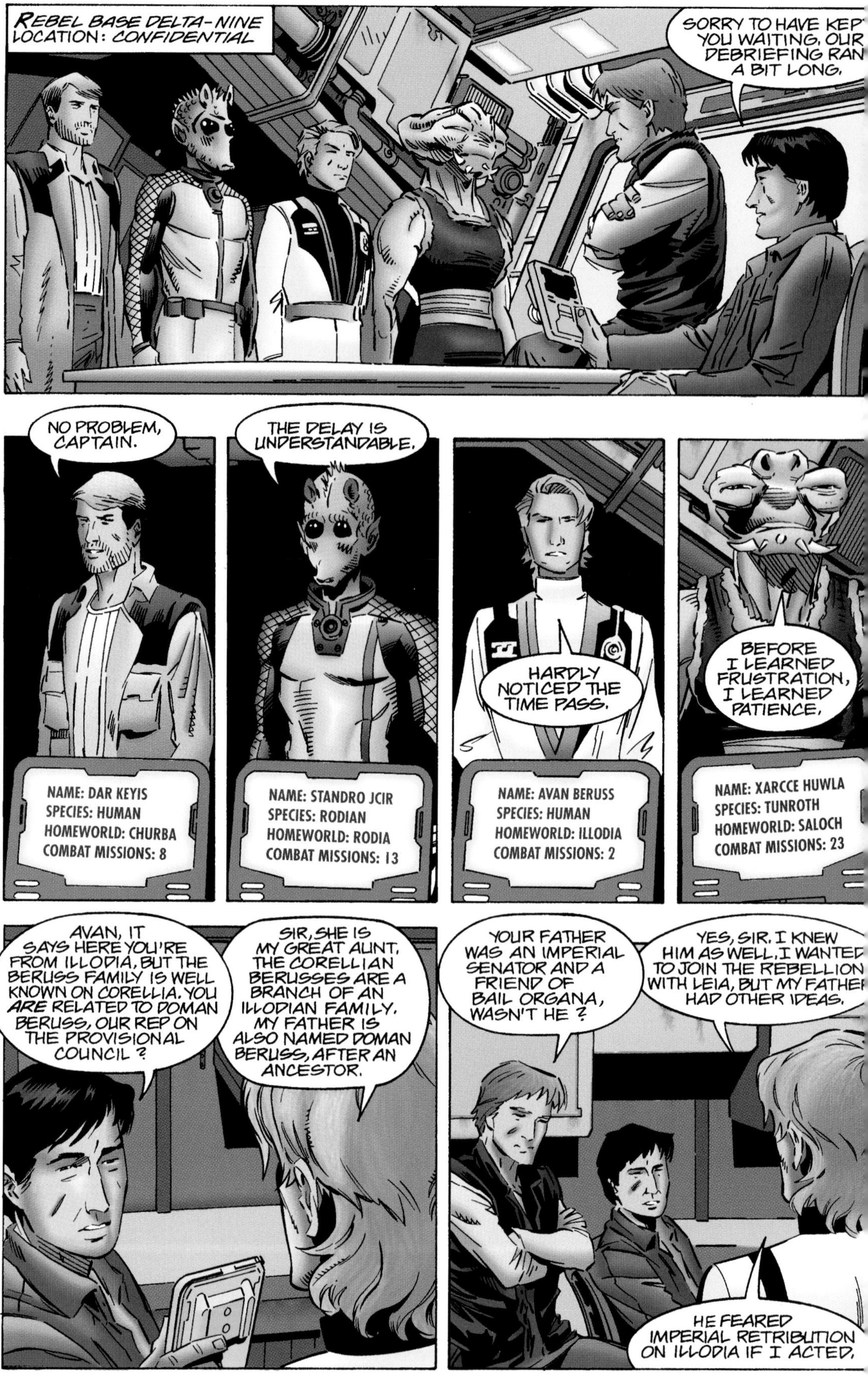
REBEL BASE DELTA-NINE
LOCATION: CONFIDENTIAL
SORRY TO HAVE KEP YOU WAITING, OUR DEBRIEFING RAN A BIT LONG.
NO PROBLEM, CAPTAIN.
NAME: DAR KEYIS
SPECIES: HUMAN
HOMEWORLD: CHURBA
COMBAT MISSIONS: 8
THE DELAY IS UNDERSTANDABLE.
NAME: STANDRO JCIR
SPECIES: RODIAN
HOMEWORLD: RODIA
COMBAT MISSIONS: 13
HARDLY NOTICED THE TIME PASS.
NAME: AVAN BERUSS
SPECIES: HUMAN
HOMEWORLD: ILLODIA
COMBAT MISSIONS: 2
BEFORE I LEARNED FRUSTRATION, I LEARNED PATIENCE.
NAME: XARCCE HUWLA
SPECIES: TUNROTH
HOMEWORLD: SALOCH
COMBAT MISSIONS: 23
AVAN, IT SAYS HERE YOU'RE FROM ILLODIA, BUT THE BERUSS FAMILY IS WELL KNOWN ON CORELLIA. YOU ARE RELATED TO DOMAN BERUSS, OUR REP ON THE PROVISIONAL COUNCIL ?
SIR, SHE IS MY GREAT AUNT. THE CORELLIAN BERUSSES ARE A BRANCH OF AN ILLODIAN FAMILY. MY FATHER IS ALSO NAMED DOMAN BERUSS, AFTER AN ANCESTOR.
YOUR FATHER WAS AN IMPERIAL SENATOR AND A FRIEND OF BAIL ORGANA, WASN'T HE ?
YES, SIR. I KNEW HIM AS WELL. I WANTED TO JOIN THE REBELLION WITH LEIA, BUT MY FATHER HAD OTHER IDEAS.
HE FEARED IMPERIAL RETRIBUTION ON ILLODIA IF I ACTED.

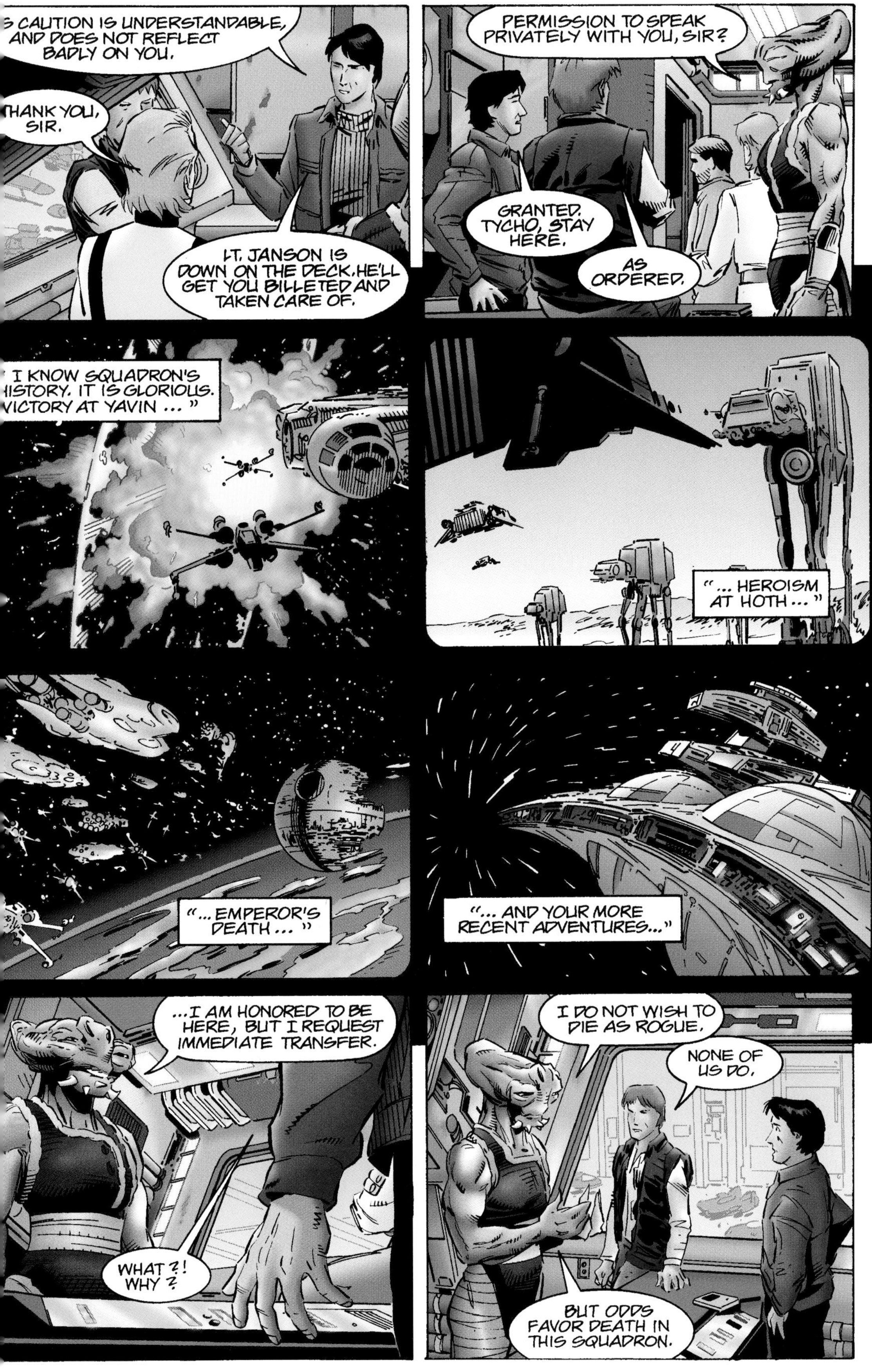
S CAUTION IS UNDERSTANDABLE, AND DOES NOT REFLECT BADLY ON YOU.
THANK YOU, SIR.
LT. JANSON IS DOWN ON THE DECK. HE'LL GET YOU BILLETED AND TAKEN CARE OF.
PERMISSION TO SPEAK PRIVATELY WITH YOU, SIR?
GRANTED. TYCHO, STAY HERE.
AS ORDERED.
I KNOW SQUADRON'S HISTORY. IT IS GLORIOUS. VICTORY AT YAVIN ... "
"... HEROISM AT HOTH ... "
"... EMPEROR'S DEATH ... "
"... AND YOUR MORE RECENT ADVENTURES..."
...I AM HONORED TO BE HERE, BUT I REQUEST IMMEDIATE TRANSFER.
WHAT?! WHY?
I DO NOT WISH TO DIE AS ROGUE.
NONE OF US DO.
BUT ODDS FAVOR DEATH IN THIS SQUADRON.

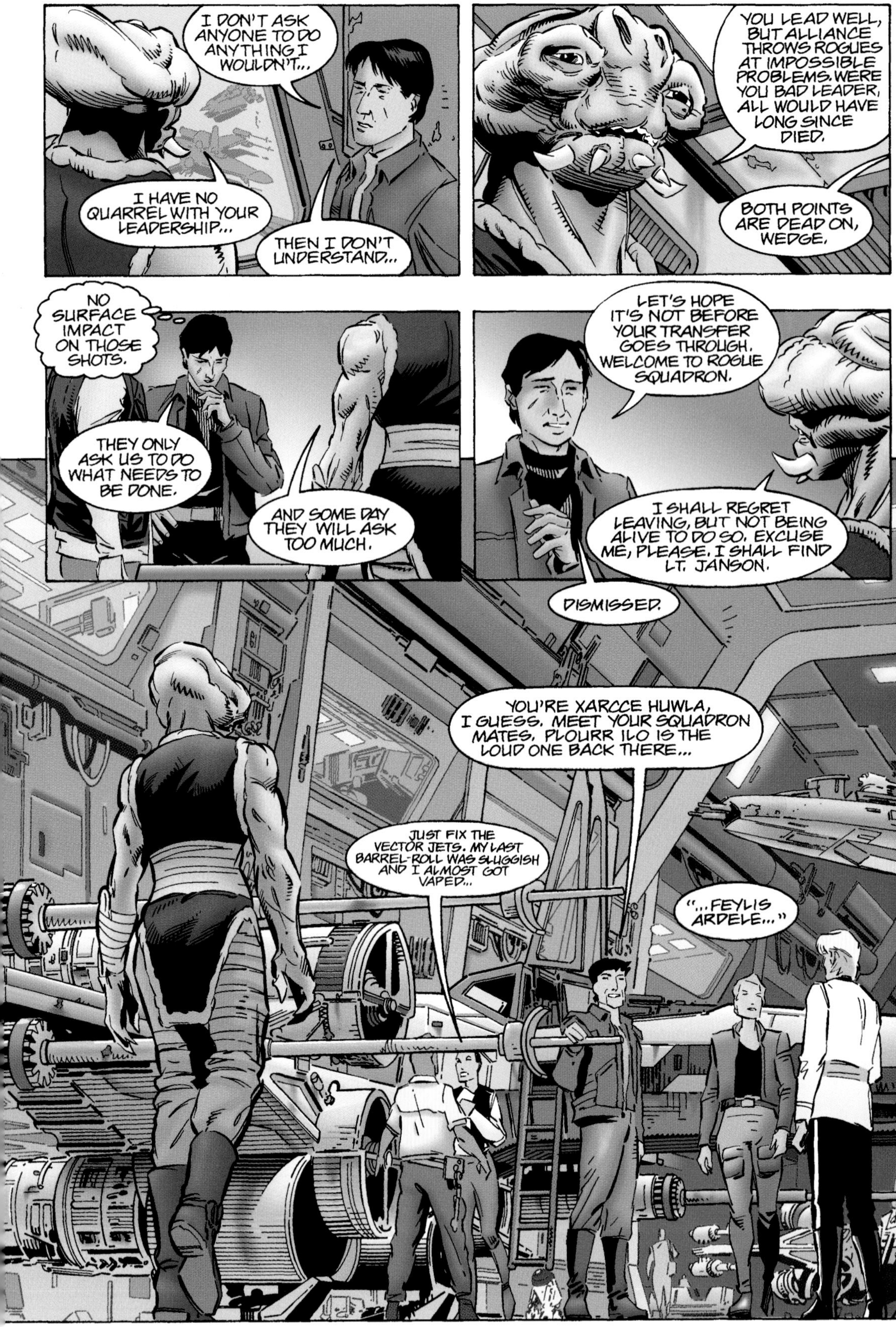
I DON'T ASK ANYONE TO DO ANYTHING I WOULDN'T...
I HAVE NO QUARREL WITH YOUR LEADERSHIP...
THEN I DON'T UNDERSTAND...
YOU LEAD WELL, BUT ALLIANCE THROWS ROGUES AT IMPOSSIBLE PROBLEMS. WERE YOU BAD LEADER, ALL WOULD HAVE LONG SINCE DIED.
BOTH POINTS ARE DEAD ON, WEDGE.
NO SURFACE IMPACT ON THOSE SHOTS.
THEY ONLY ASK US TO DO WHAT NEEDS TO BE DONE.
AND SOME DAY THEY WILL ASK TOO MUCH.
LET'S HOPE IT'S NOT BEFORE YOUR TRANSFER GOES THROUGH. WELCOME TO ROGUE SQUADRON.
I SHALL REGRET LEAVING, BUT NOT BEING ALIVE TO DO SO. EXCUSE ME, PLEASE. I SHALL FIND LT. JANSON.
DISMISSED.
YOU'RE XARCCE HUWLA, I GUESS. MEET YOUR SQUADRON MATES. PLOURR ILO IS THE LOUD ONE BACK THERE...
JUST FIX THE VECTOR JETS. MY LAST BARREL-ROLL WAS SLUGGISH AND I ALMOST GOT VAPED...
"...FEYLIS ARDELE..."

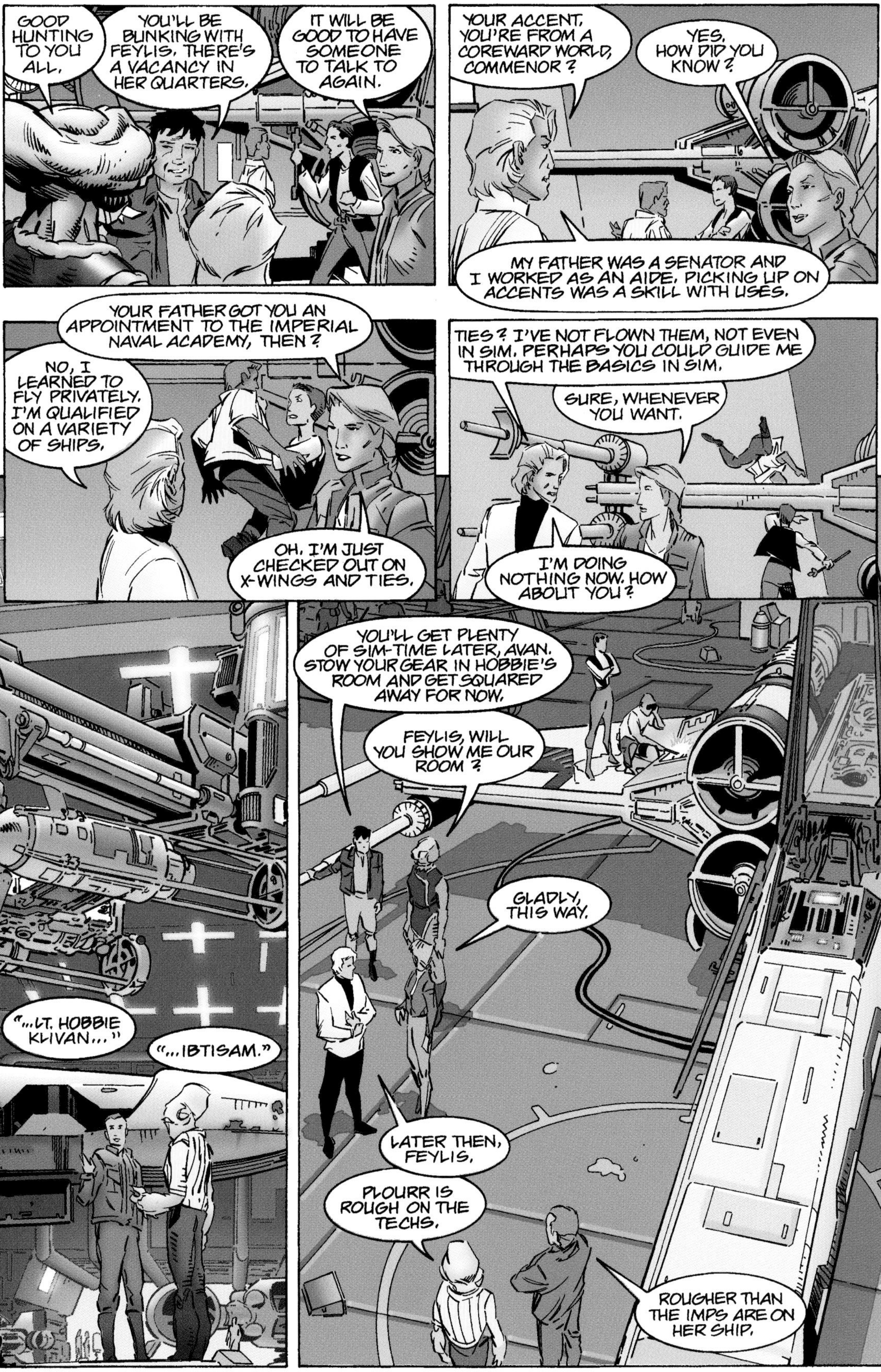
GOOD HUNTING TO YOU ALL.
YOU'LL BE BUNKING WITH FEYLIS. THERE'S A VACANCY IN HER QUARTERS.
IT WILL BE GOOD TO HAVE SOMEONE TO TALK TO AGAIN.
YOUR ACCENT, YOU'RE FROM A COREWARD WORLD, COMMENOR?
YES, HOW DID YOU KNOW?
MY FATHER WAS A SENATOR AND I WORKED AS AN AIDE. PICKING UP ON ACCENTS WAS A SKILL WITH USES.
YOUR FATHER GOT YOU AN APPOINTMENT TO THE IMPERIAL NAVAL ACADEMY, THEN?
NO, I LEARNED TO FLY PRIVATELY. I'M QUALIFIED ON A VARIETY OF SHIPS.
OH. I'M JUST CHECKED OUT ON X-WINGS AND TIES.
TIES? I'VE NOT FLOWN THEM, NOT EVEN IN SIM. PERHAPS YOU COULD GUIDE ME THROUGH THE BASICS IN SIM.
SURE, WHENEVER YOU WANT.
I'M DOING NOTHING NOW. HOW ABOUT YOU?
"...LT. HOBBIE KLIVAN..."
"...IBTISAM."
YOU'LL GET PLENTY OF SIM-TIME LATER, AVAN. STOW YOUR GEAR IN HOBBIE'S ROOM AND GET SQUARED AWAY FOR NOW.
FEYLIS, WILL YOU SHOW ME OUR ROOM?
GLADLY, THIS WAY.
LATER THEN, FEYLIS.
PLOURR IS ROUGH ON THE TECHS.
ROUGHER THAN THE IMPS ARE ON HER SHIP.

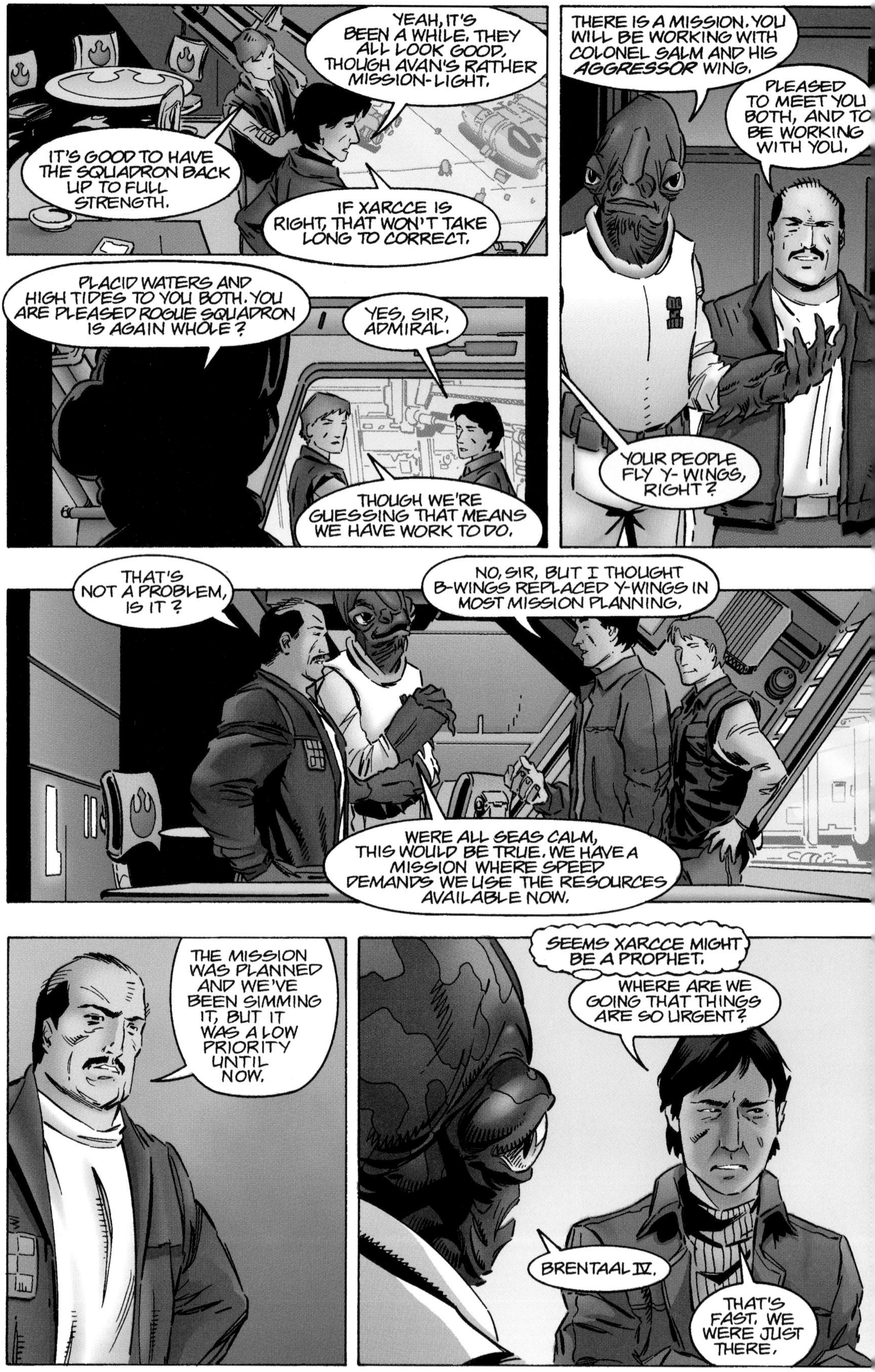

IT'S GOOD TO HAVE THE SQUADRON BACK UP TO FULL STRENGTH.
YEAH, IT'S BEEN A WHILE. THEY ALL LOOK GOOD, THOUGH AVAN'S RATHER MISSION-LIGHT.
IF XARCCE IS RIGHT, THAT WON'T TAKE LONG TO CORRECT.
THERE IS A MISSION. YOU WILL BE WORKING WITH COLONEL SALM AND HIS *AGGRESSOR* WING.
PLEASED TO MEET YOU BOTH, AND TO BE WORKING WITH YOU.
YOUR PEOPLE FLY Y-WINGS, RIGHT?
PLACID WATERS AND HIGH TIDES TO YOU BOTH. YOU ARE PLEASED ROGUE SQUADRON IS AGAIN WHOLE?
YES, SIR, ADMIRAL.
THOUGH WE'RE GUESSING THAT MEANS WE HAVE WORK TO DO.
THAT'S NOT A PROBLEM, IS IT?
NO, SIR, BUT I THOUGHT B-WINGS REPLACED Y-WINGS IN MOST MISSION PLANNING.
WERE ALL SEAS CALM, THIS WOULD BE TRUE. WE HAVE A MISSION WHERE SPEED DEMANDS WE USE THE RESOURCES AVAILABLE NOW.
THE MISSION WAS PLANNED AND WE'VE BEEN SIMMING IT, BUT IT WAS A LOW PRIORITY UNTIL NOW.
SEEMS XARCCE MIGHT BE A PROPHET.
WHERE ARE WE GOING THAT THINGS ARE SO URGENT?
BRENTAAL IV.
THAT'S FAST. WE WERE JUST THERE.

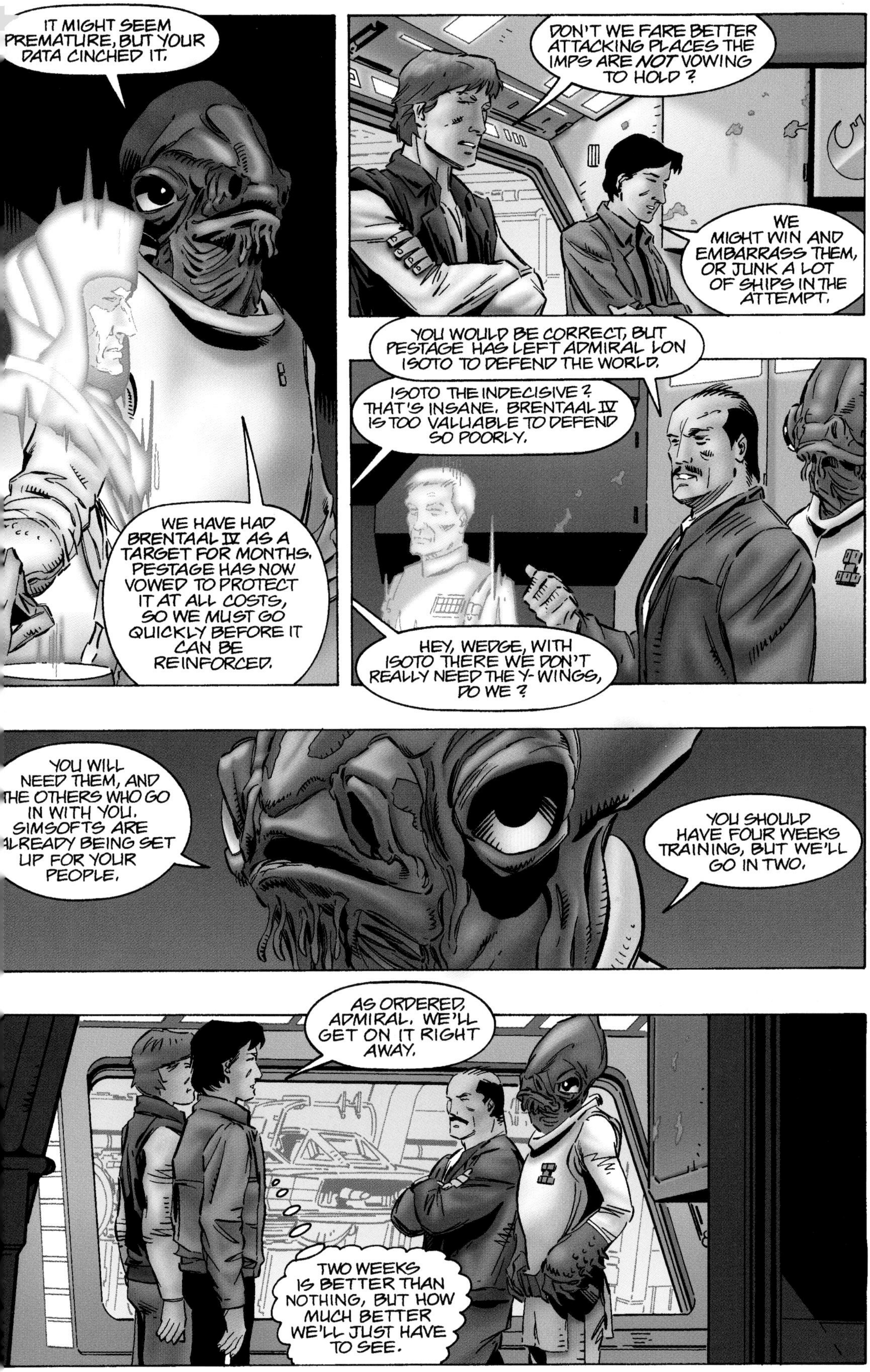
IT MIGHT SEEM PREMATURE, BUT YOUR DATA CINCHED IT.
WE HAVE HAD BRENTAAL IV AS A TARGET FOR MONTHS. PESTAGE HAS NOW VOWED TO PROTECT IT AT ALL COSTS, SO WE MUST GO QUICKLY BEFORE IT CAN BE REINFORCED.
DON'T WE FARE BETTER ATTACKING PLACES THE IMPS ARE *NOT* VOWING TO HOLD?
WE MIGHT WIN AND EMBARRASS THEM, OR JUNK A LOT OF SHIPS IN THE ATTEMPT.
YOU WOULD BE CORRECT, BUT PESTAGE HAS LEFT ADMIRAL LON ISOTO TO DEFEND THE WORLD.
ISOTO THE INDECISIVE? THAT'S INSANE. BRENTAAL IV IS TOO VALUABLE TO DEFEND SO POORLY.
HEY, WEDGE, WITH ISOTO THERE WE DON'T REALLY NEED THE Y-WINGS, DO WE?
YOU WILL NEED THEM, AND THE OTHERS WHO GO IN WITH YOU. SIMSOFTS ARE ALREADY BEING SET UP FOR YOUR PEOPLE.
YOU SHOULD HAVE FOUR WEEKS TRAINING, BUT WE'LL GO IN TWO.
AS ORDERED, ADMIRAL. WE'LL GET ON IT RIGHT AWAY.
TWO WEEKS IS BETTER THAN NOTHING, BUT HOW MUCH BETTER WE'LL JUST HAVE TO SEE.

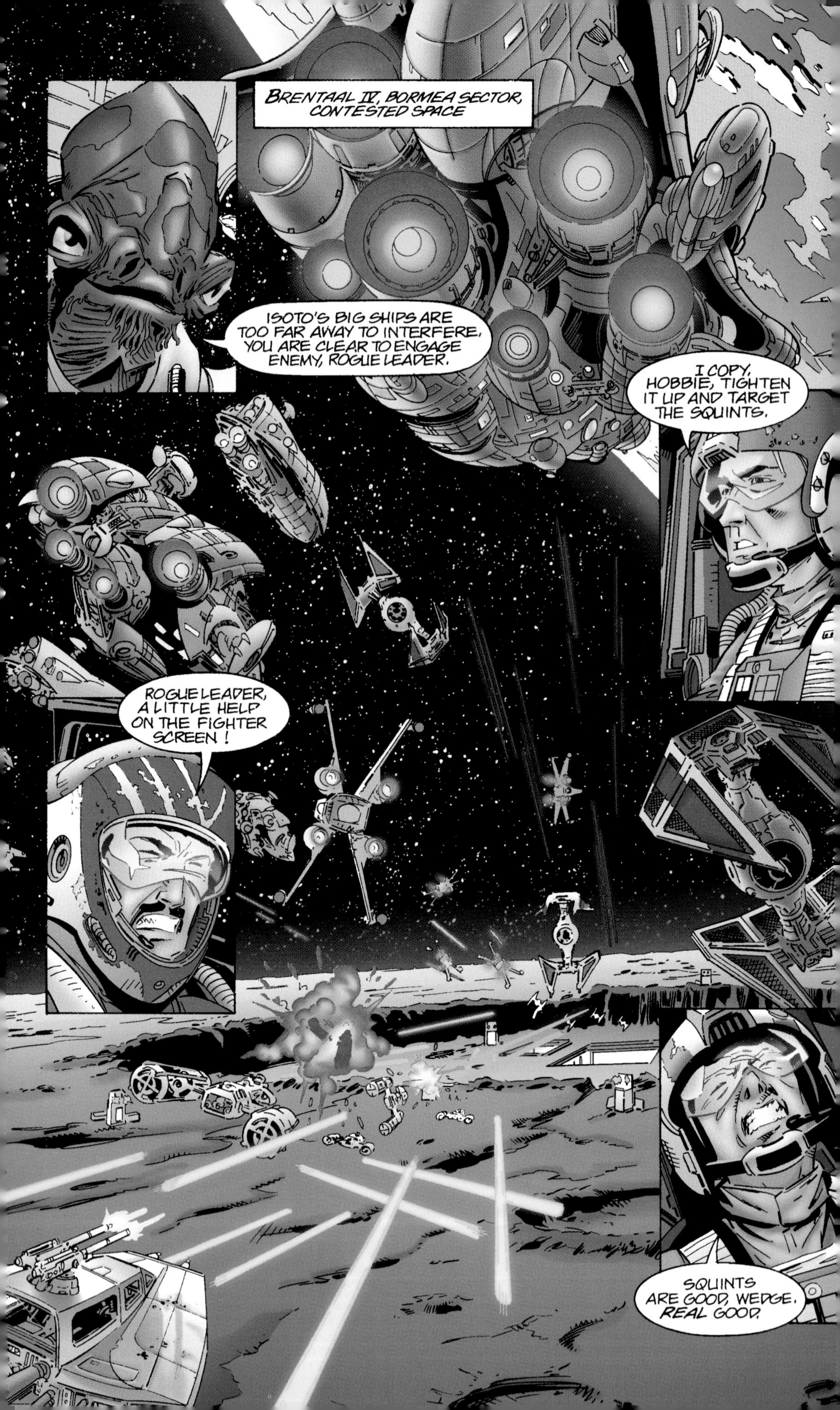
BRENTAAL IV, BORMEA SECTOR, CONTESTED SPACE
ISOTO'S BIG SHIPS ARE TOO FAR AWAY TO INTERFERE. YOU ARE CLEAR TO ENGAGE ENEMY, ROGUE LEADER.
I COPY, HOBBIE, TIGHTEN IT UP AND TARGET THE SQUINTS.
ROGUE LEADER, A LITTLE HELP ON THE FIGHTER SCREEN!
SQUINTS ARE GOOD, WEDGE. REAL GOOD.

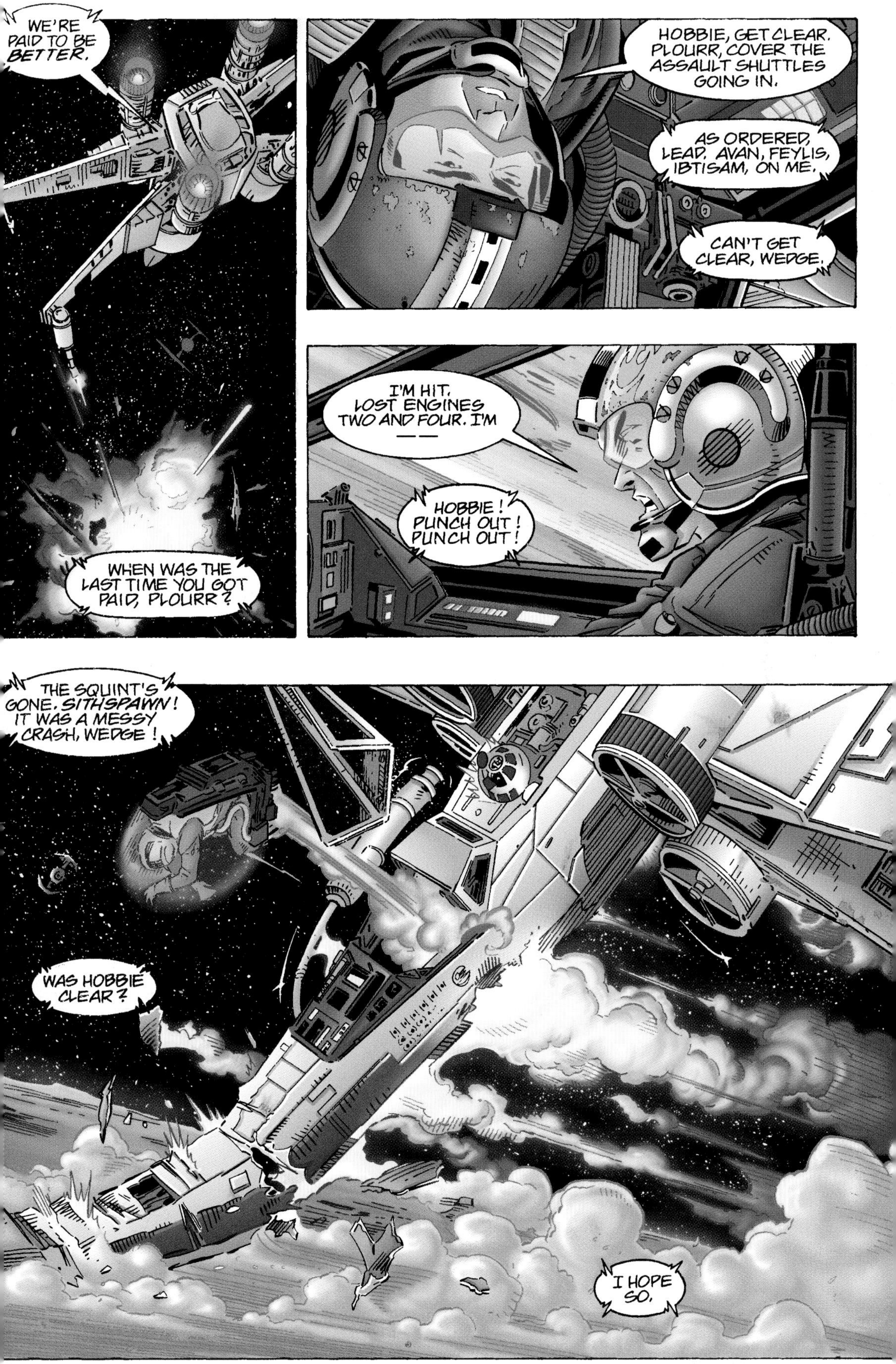
WE'RE PAID TO BE *BETTER*.
WHEN WAS THE LAST TIME YOU GOT PAID, PLOURR?
HOBBIE, GET CLEAR. PLOURR, COVER THE ASSAULT SHUTTLES GOING IN.
AS ORDERED, LEAD. AVAN, FEYLIS, IBTISAM, ON ME.
CAN'T GET CLEAR, WEDGE.
I'M HIT. LOST ENGINES TWO AND FOUR. I'M ——
HOBBIE! PUNCH OUT! PUNCH OUT!
THE SQUINT'S GONE. *SITHSPAWN*! IT WAS A MESSY CRASH, WEDGE!
WAS HOBBIE CLEAR?
I HOPE SO.

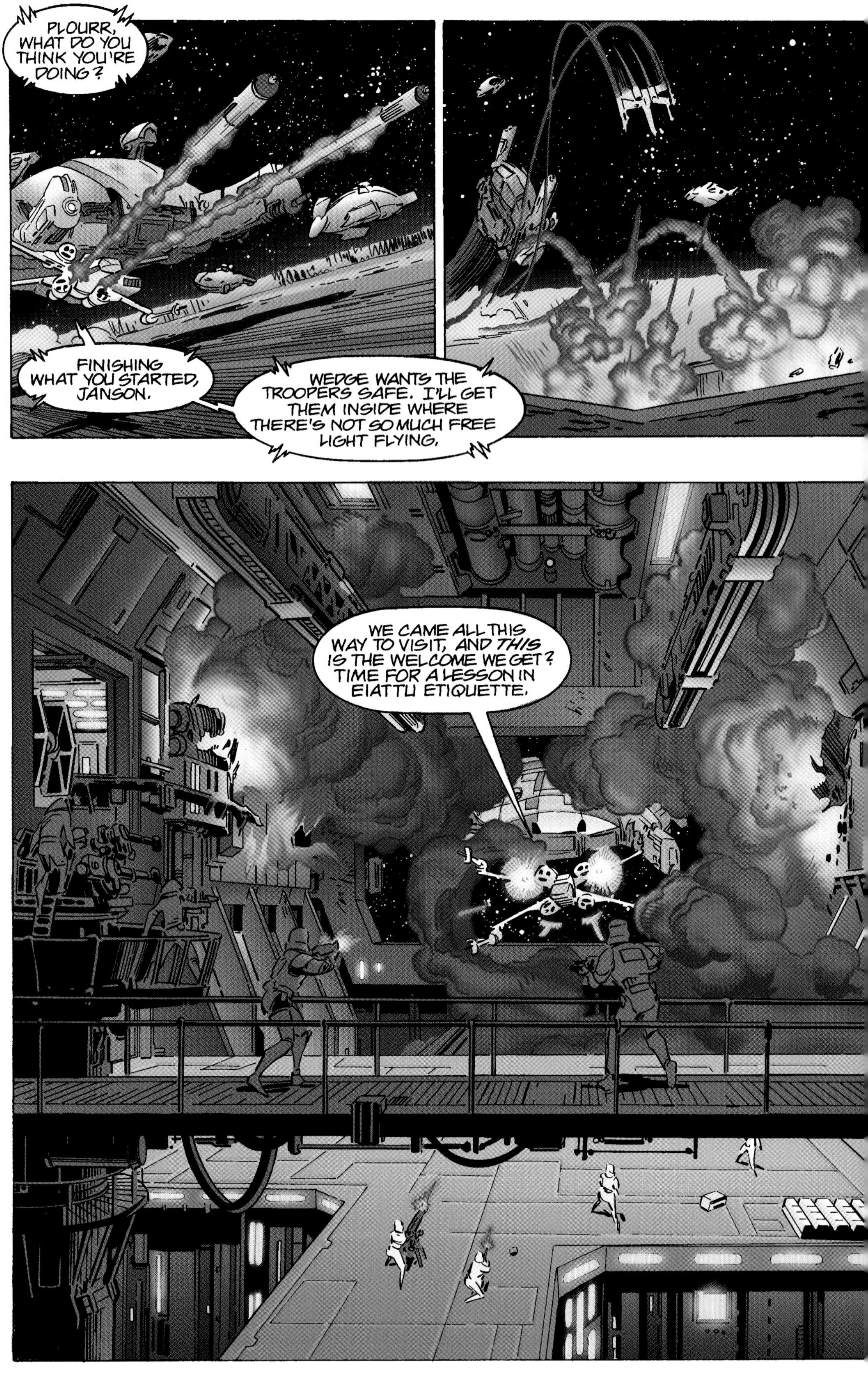
PLOURR, WHAT DO YOU THINK YOU'RE DOING?
FINISHING WHAT YOU STARTED, JANSON.
WEDGE WANTS THE TROOPERS SAFE. I'LL GET THEM INSIDE WHERE THERE'S NOT SO MUCH FREE LIGHT FLYING.
WE CAME ALL THIS WAY TO VISIT, AND *THIS* IS THE WELCOME WE GET? TIME FOR A LESSON IN EIATTU ETIQUETTE.

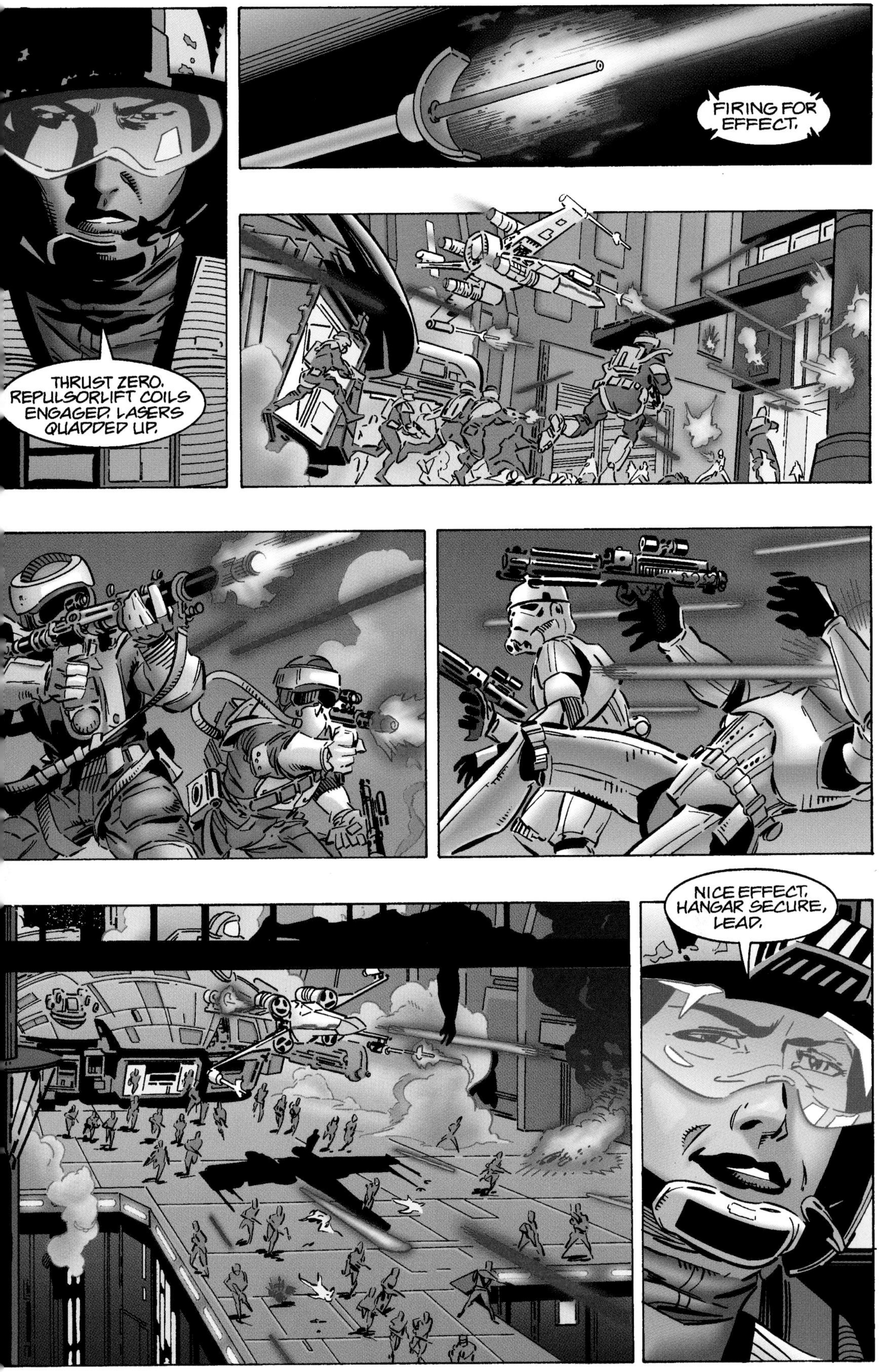
THRUST ZERO. REPULSORLIFT COILS ENGAGED. LASERS QUADDED UP.
FIRING FOR EFFECT.
NICE EFFECT. HANGAR SECURE, LEAD.

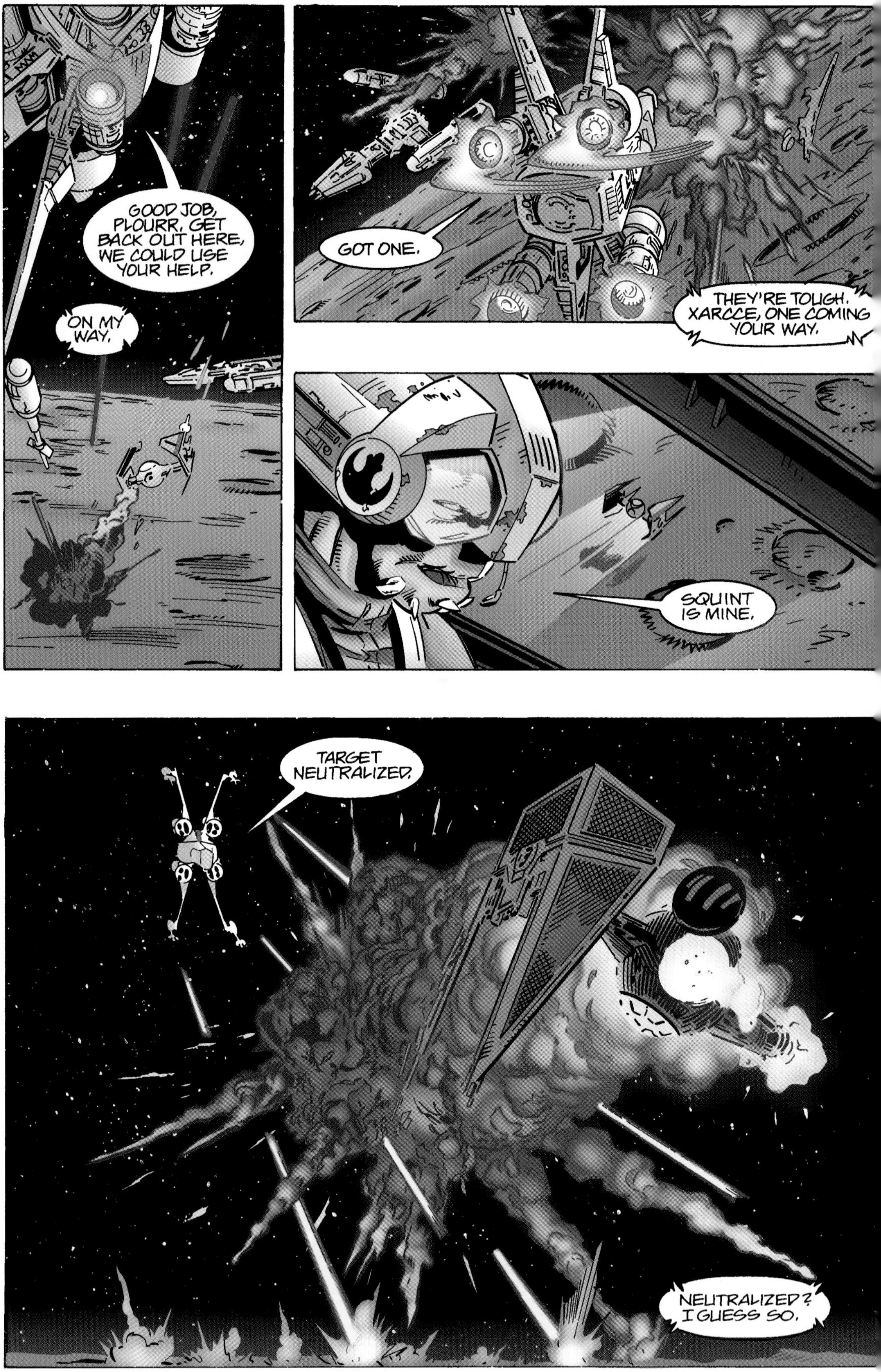
GOOD JOB, PLOURR, GET BACK OUT HERE, WE COULD USE YOUR HELP.
ON MY WAY.
GOT ONE.
THEY'RE TOUGH. XARCCE, ONE COMING YOUR WAY.
SQUINT IS MINE.
TARGET NEUTRALIZED.
NEUTRALIZED? I GUESS SO.

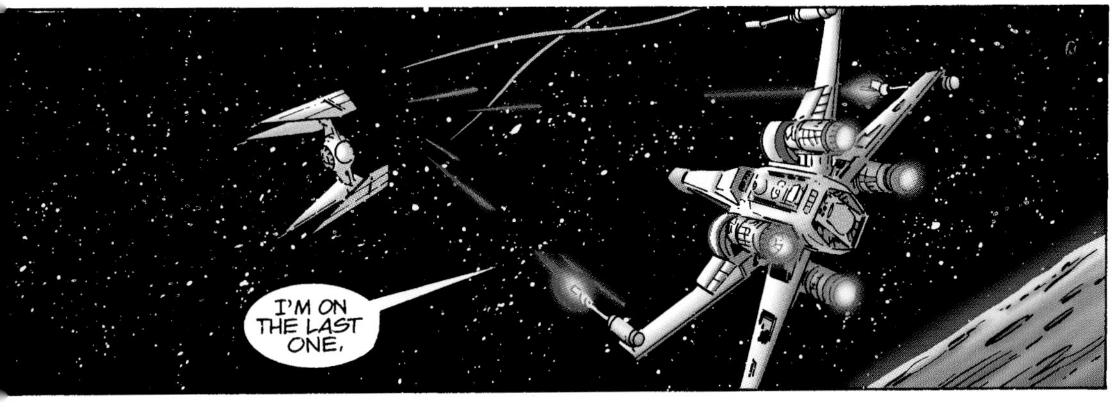
I'M ON THE LAST ONE.
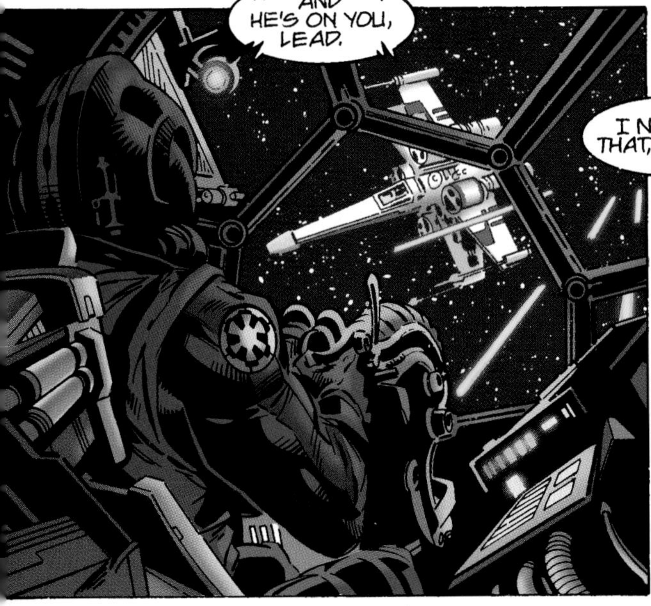
AND HE'S ON YOU, LEAD.
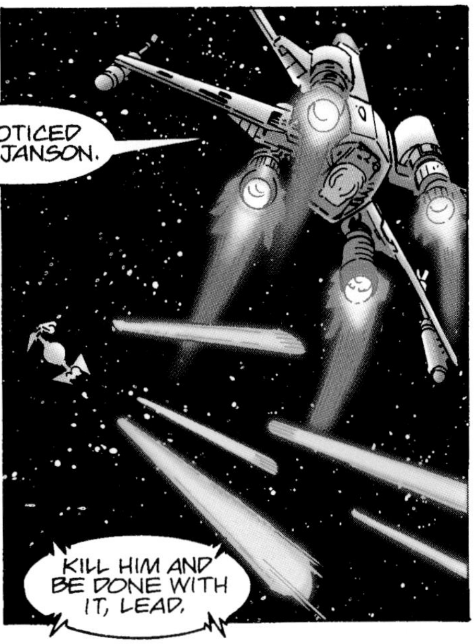
I NOTICED THAT, JANSON.
KILL HIM AND BE DONE WITH IT, LEAD.
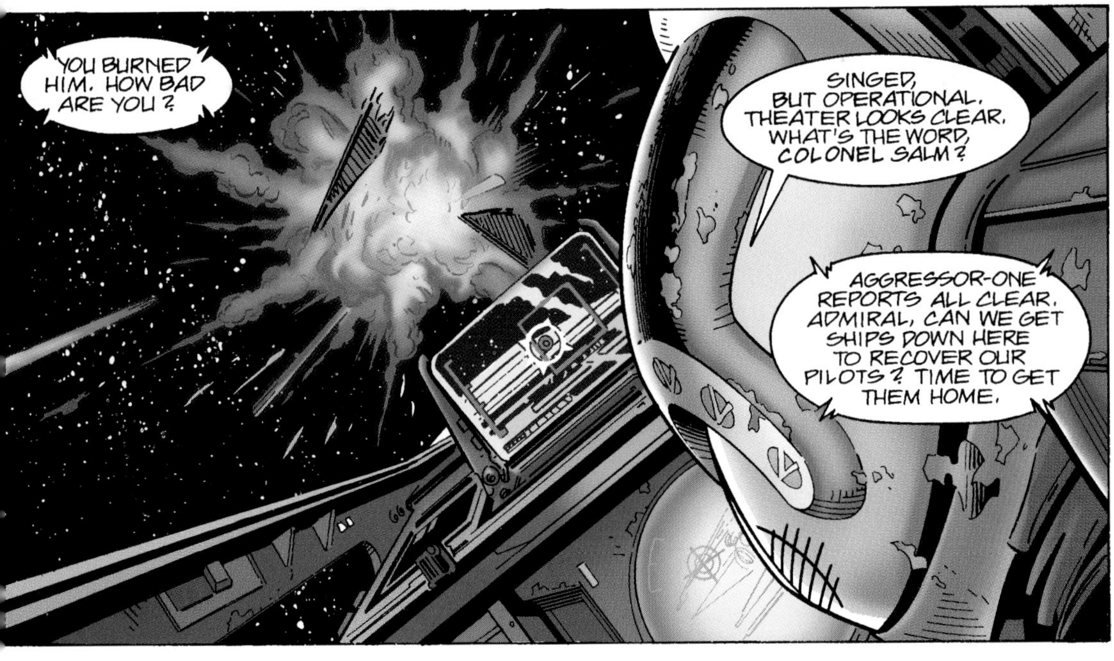
YOU BURNED HIM. HOW BAD ARE YOU?
SINGED, BUT OPERATIONAL. THEATER LOOKS CLEAR. WHAT'S THE WORD, COLONEL SALM?
AGGRESSOR-ONE REPORTS ALL CLEAR. ADMIRAL, CAN WE GET SHIPS DOWN HERE TO RECOVER OUR PILOTS? TIME TO GET THEM HOME.

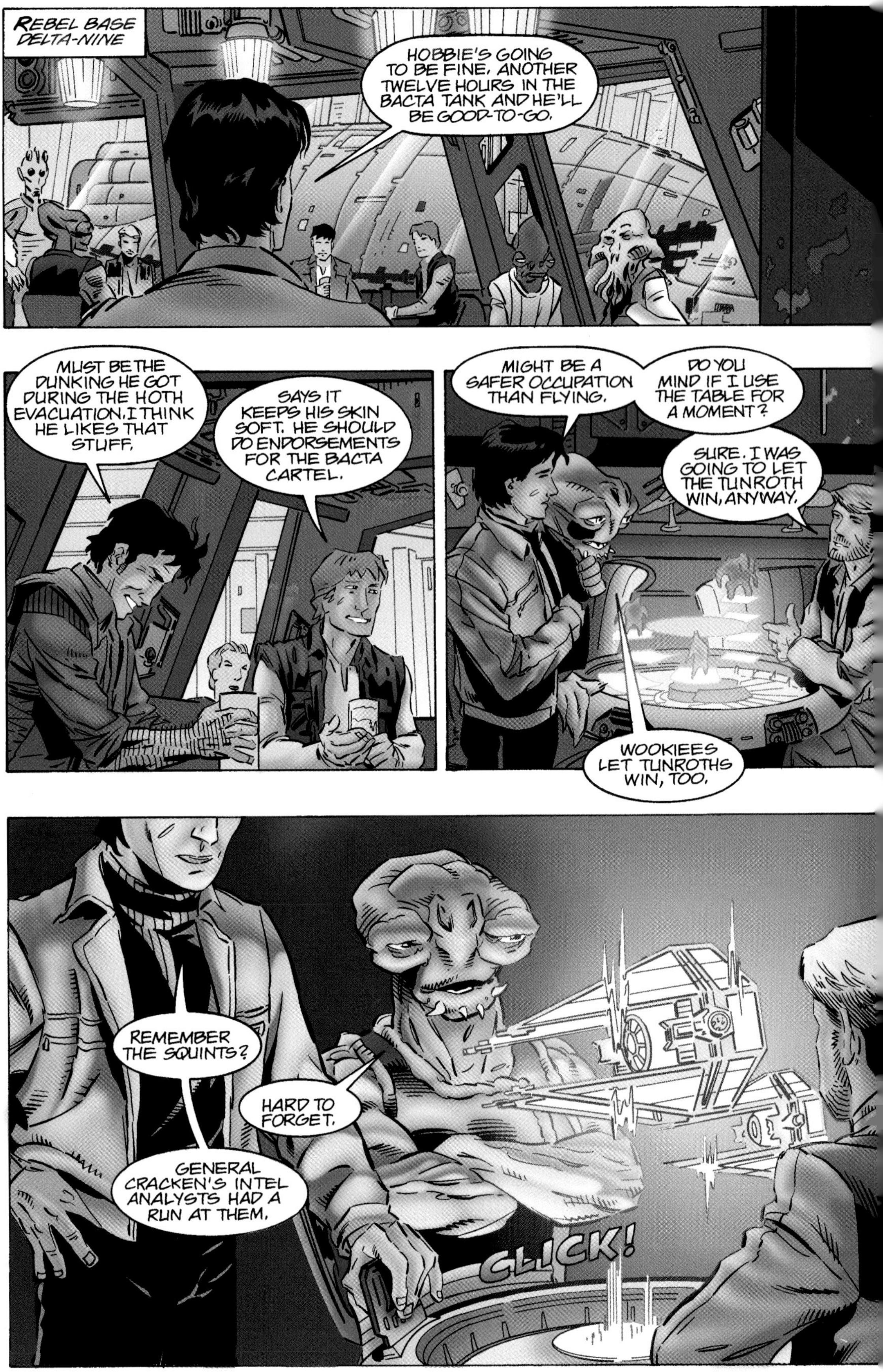
REBEL BASE DELTA-NINE
HOBBIE'S GOING TO BE FINE. ANOTHER TWELVE HOURS IN THE BACTA TANK AND HE'LL BE GOOD-TO-GO.
MUST BE THE DUNKING HE GOT DURING THE HOTH EVACUATION. I THINK HE LIKES THAT STUFF.
SAYS IT KEEPS HIS SKIN SOFT. HE SHOULD DO ENDORSEMENTS FOR THE BACTA CARTEL.
MIGHT BE A SAFER OCCUPATION THAN FLYING.
DO YOU MIND IF I USE THE TABLE FOR A MOMENT?
SURE. I WAS GOING TO LET THE TUNROTH WIN, ANYWAY.
WOOKIEES LET TUNROTHS WIN, TOO.
REMEMBER THE SQUINTS?
HARD TO FORGET.
GENERAL CRACKEN'S INTEL ANALYSTS HAD A RUN AT THEM.
CLICK!

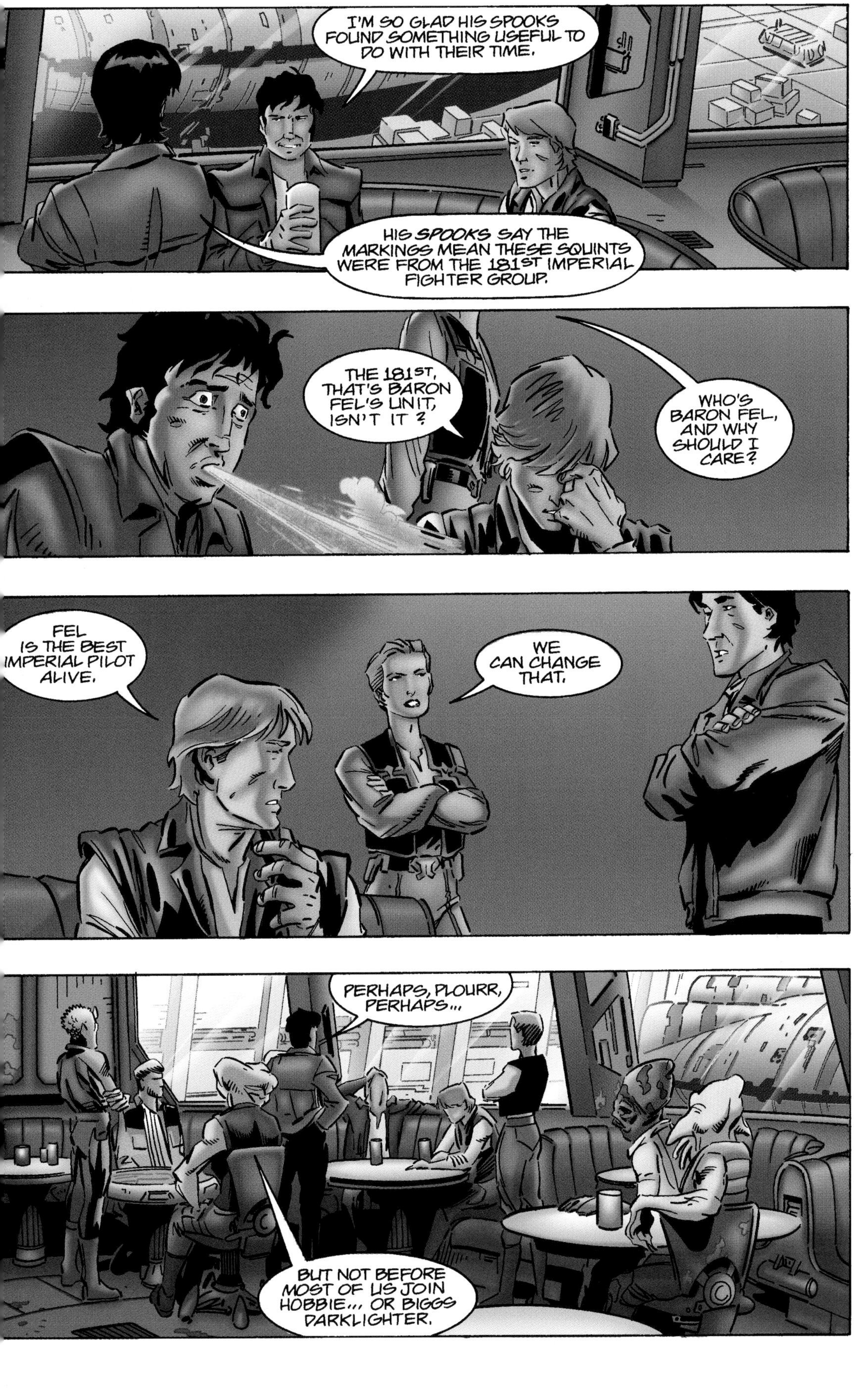
I'M SO GLAD HIS SPOOKS FOUND SOMETHING USEFUL TO DO WITH THEIR TIME.
HIS SPOOKS SAY THE MARKINGS MEAN THESE SQUINTS WERE FROM THE 181ST IMPERIAL FIGHTER GROUP.
THE 181ST, THAT'S BARON FEL'S UNIT, ISN'T IT ?
WHO'S BARON FEL, AND WHY SHOULD I CARE?
FEL IS THE BEST IMPERIAL PILOT ALIVE.
WE CAN CHANGE THAT.
PERHAPS, PLOURR, PERHAPS...
BUT NOT BEFORE MOST OF US JOIN HOBBIE... OR BIGGS DARKLIGHTER.

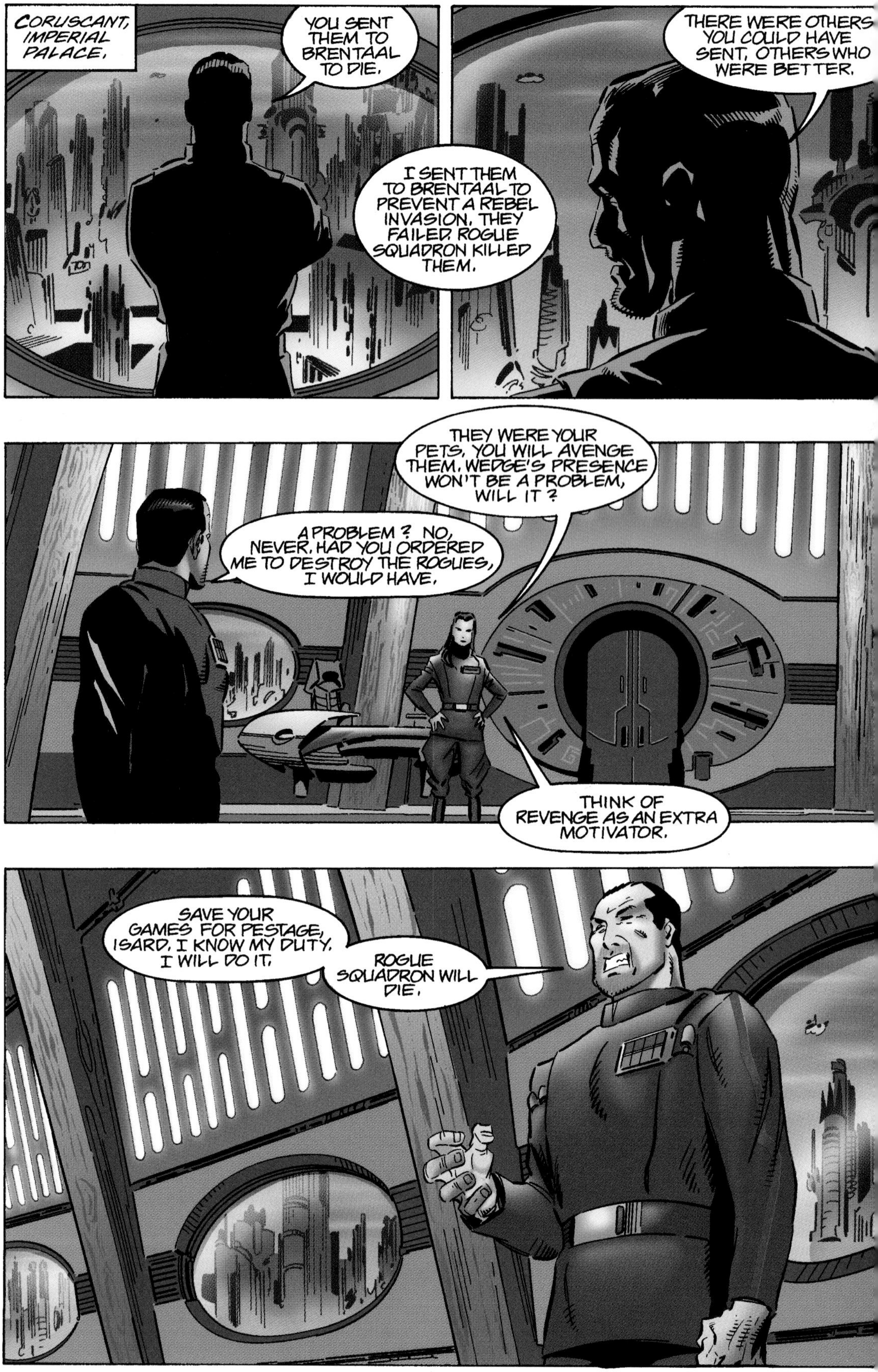
CORUSCANT, IMPERIAL PALACE.
YOU SENT THEM TO BRENTAAL TO DIE.
I SENT THEM TO BRENTAAL TO PREVENT A REBEL INVASION. THEY FAILED. ROGUE SQUADRON KILLED THEM.
THERE WERE OTHERS YOU COULD HAVE SENT, OTHERS WHO WERE BETTER.
THEY WERE YOUR PETS. YOU WILL AVENGE THEM. WEDGE'S PRESENCE WON'T BE A PROBLEM, WILL IT ?
A PROBLEM ? NO, NEVER. HAD YOU ORDERED ME TO DESTROY THE ROGUES, I WOULD HAVE.
THINK OF REVENGE AS AN EXTRA MOTIVATOR.
SAVE YOUR GAMES FOR PESTAGE, ISARD. I KNOW MY DUTY. I WILL DO IT.
ROGUE SQUADRON WILL DIE.

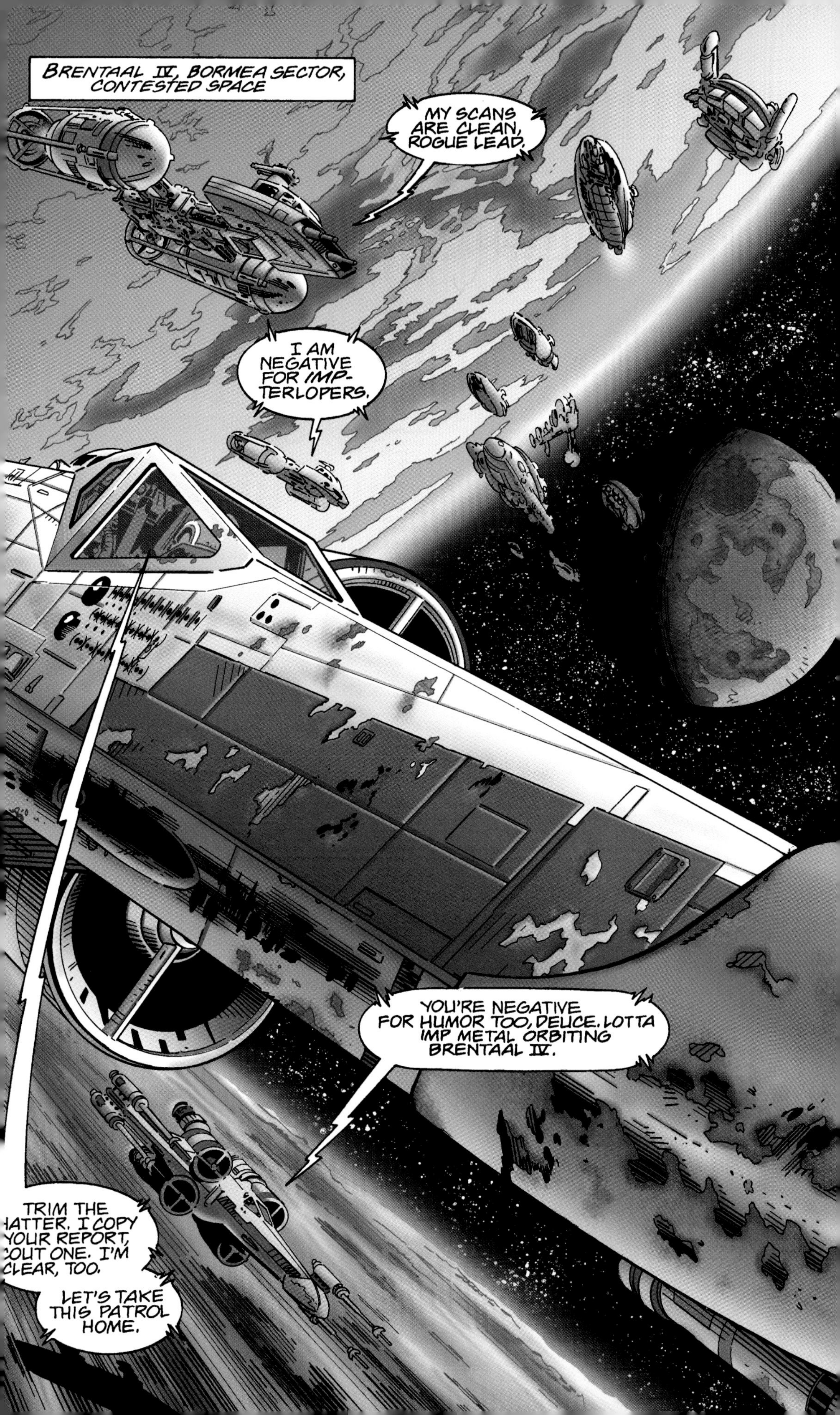
BRENTAAL IV, BORMEA SECTOR, CONTESTED SPACE
MY SCANS ARE CLEAN, ROGUE LEAD.
I AM NEGATIVE FOR IMP-TERLOPERS.
YOU'RE NEGATIVE FOR HUMOR TOO, DEUCE. LOTTA IMP METAL ORBITING BRENTAAL IV.
TRIM THE HATTER. I COPY YOUR REPORT, COUT ONE. I'M CLEAR, TOO.
LET'S TAKE THIS PATROL HOME.

I'M SURPRISED THE IMPS HAVEN'T SCOURED US OFF THIS MOON. THEY'VE NOT EVEN BOTHERED OUR SUPPLY CONVOYS.
THE IMPS FEEL VULNERABLE TO SNUBFIGHTERS, AVAN, SO THEY'LL WAIT FOR TIES TO SCREEN THEM. BESIDES...
...THE IMPS KNOW THAT TO HAVE US ENGAGE IN A CONVENTIONAL FIGHT LEAVES US OPEN TO BEING HURT.
THEY LEARNED HOW STUPID THAT IDEA WAS AT ENDOR, ANTILLES.
WE *DID* GET HURT AT ENDOR, ACE. WEDGE MAY HAVE BLOWN THE DEATH STAR WITH THE *FALCON*'S HELP, BUT OUR FLEET WAS HAMMERED.
YEAH, BUT WE WON.
IF YOU'D BEEN THERE, YOU'D ALSO KNOW WHAT WE LOST.
BOTH SIDES WANT TO USE BRENTAAL TO SHOW ENDOR WAS A FLUKE, AND THAT THEY'VE RECOVERED.
AND BRENTAAL IV IS A KEY TO THE BORMEA SECTOR, WHICH WE WANT SINCE MON MOTHMA'S HOMEWORLD CHANDRILA IS HERE.
AMONG OTHER REASONS.

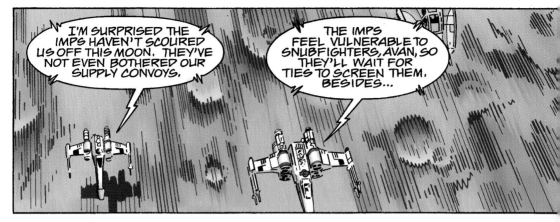

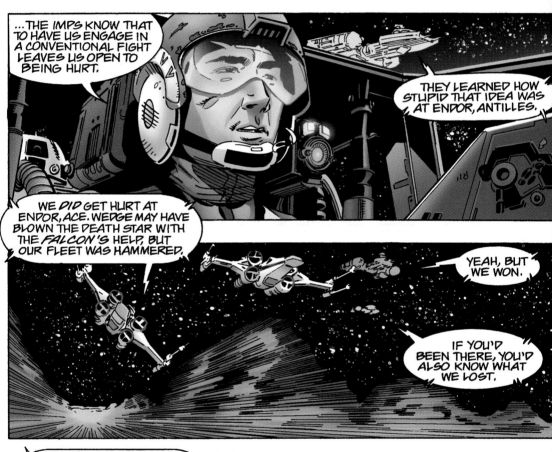

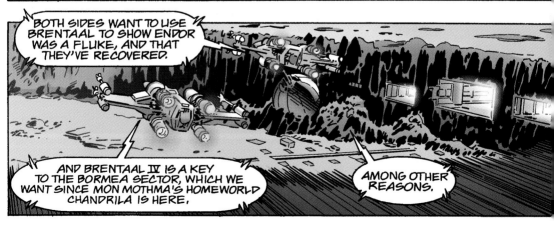

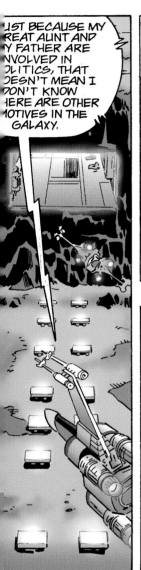

JST BECAUSE MY REAT AUNT AND Y FATHER ARE NVOLVED IN OLITICS, THAT OESN'T MEAN I DON'T KNOW HERE ARE OTHER MOTIVES IN THE GALAXY.

PESTAGE VOWED TO DEFEAT US HERE. IF WE WIN, HE LOOKS WEAK AND MORE PARTS OF THE EMPIRE WILL BREAK OFF.

TRUE, BUT THAT'S POLITICS. DON'T FORGET-- BRENTAAL IS A RICH WORLD, AND THE NEW REPUBLIC COULD USE SOME MONEY.

GOOD POINT. SO DO YOU THINK WE'LL TAKE BRENTAAL?

DID DARTH VADER WEAR BLACK?

ONLY ADMIRALS AND GENERALS CAN ANSWER THAT, AVAN.

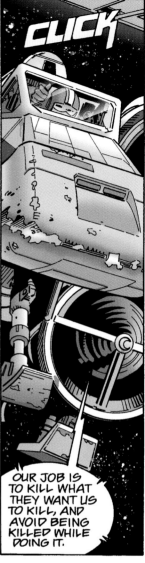

CLICK

OUR JOB IS TO KILL WHAT THEY WANT US TO KILL, AND AVOID BEING KILLED WHILE DOING IT.

YOU MAKE IT OUND SIMPLE AND EASY, ROGUE LEAD.

AT OUR LEVEL, IT *IS* SIMPLE, BUT DON'T EVER THINK IT'S *EASY.* ONLY *EASY* THING WE GET TO DO IS DIE.

WHY IS IT THAT REPORTS FILED AFTER UNEVENTFUL PATROLS TAKE UP AS MUCH MEMORY AS THOSE WHERE SOMETHING HAPPENED?

A QUESTION ONLY CAPTAINS AND COMMANDERS CAN ANSWER, SIR.

SOMEDAY YOU'LL REGRET BEING SO GLIB, FLIGHT-OFFICER BERUSS.

I HOPE SO, SIR. SEE YOU IN THE READY ROOM.

KOYI KOMAD! WHAT ARE *YOU* DOING *HERE*?

REPORTING FOR DUTY, SIR. I'VE BEEN MADE THE SQUADRON'S CHIEF TECH.

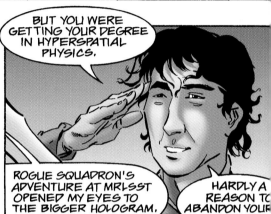

BUT YOU WERE GETTING YOUR DEGREE IN HYPERSPATIAL PHYSICS.

ROGUE SQUADRON'S ADVENTURE AT MRLSST OPENED MY EYES TO THE BIGGER HOLOGRAM.

HARDLY A REASON TO ABANDON YOUR STUDIES.

YES, WELL, RORAX FALKEN WAS DIRECTING MY MASTER'S PROGRAM...

OH, AND HIS DEATH...

RIGHT, BESIDES, THIS BEATS WAITRESSING, SO, I'VE OPTED FOR WORK-STUDY.

MOST OF THE T-65s IN THE UNIT ARE IN PRETTY GOOD SHAPE. I CAN EVEN FIX PLOURR'S PROBLEM.

HER ATTITUDE?

I'M GOOD WITH A HYDROSPANNER, BUT NOT *THAT* GOOD.

I DUNNO... ONE GOOD WHACK AND...

GETTING HER VECTO JETS ALIGNED MIGHT CALM HER DOWN A BIT. I'LL GET ON IT RIGHT AWAY.

THAT'LL BE SOMETHING. THANKS, KOYI. GLAD TO HAVE YOU HERE.

GLAD TO BE HERE, CAPTAIN, GLAD TO BE DOING MORE THAN THEORIZING.

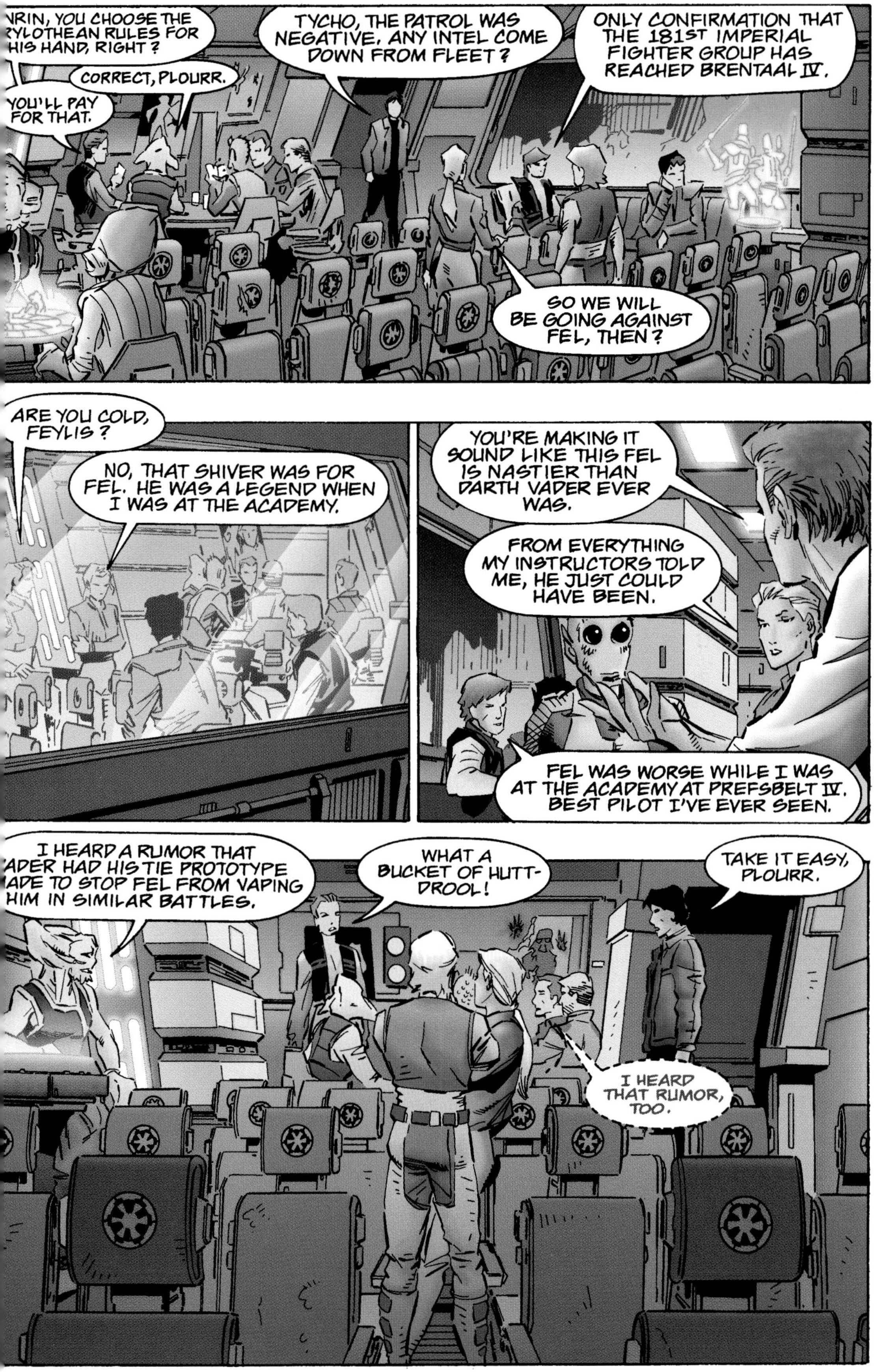
NRIN, YOU CHOOSE THE RYLOTHEAN RULES FOR THIS HAND, RIGHT?
CORRECT, PLOURR.
YOU'LL PAY FOR THAT.
TYCHO, THE PATROL WAS NEGATIVE. ANY INTEL COME DOWN FROM FLEET?
ONLY CONFIRMATION THAT THE 181ST IMPERIAL FIGHTER GROUP HAS REACHED BRENTAAL IV.
SO WE WILL BE GOING AGAINST FEL, THEN?
ARE YOU COLD, FEYLIS?
NO, THAT SHIVER WAS FOR FEL. HE WAS A LEGEND WHEN I WAS AT THE ACADEMY.
YOU'RE MAKING IT SOUND LIKE THIS FEL IS NASTIER THAN DARTH VADER EVER WAS.
FROM EVERYTHING MY INSTRUCTORS TOLD ME, HE JUST COULD HAVE BEEN.
FEL WAS WORSE WHILE I WAS AT THE ACADEMY AT PREFSBELT IV. BEST PILOT I'VE EVER SEEN.
I HEARD A RUMOR THAT ADER HAD HIS TIE PROTOTYPE ADE TO STOP FEL FROM VAPING HIM IN SIMILAR BATTLES.
WHAT A BUCKET OF HUTT-DROOL!
TAKE IT EASY, PLOURR.
I HEARD THAT RUMOR, TOO.

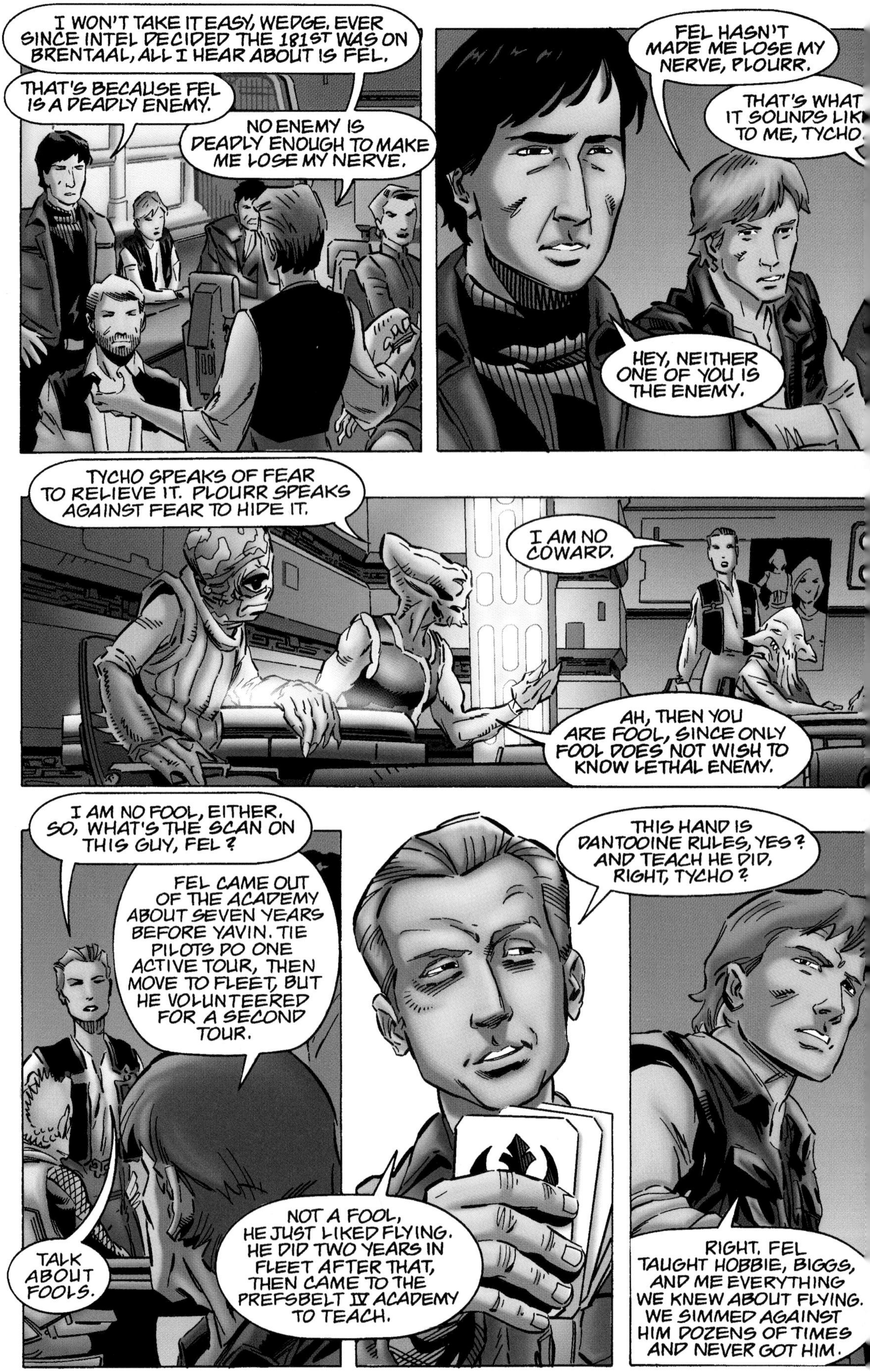
I WON'T TAKE IT EASY, WEDGE. EVER SINCE INTEL DECIDED THE 181ST WAS ON BRENTAAL, ALL I HEAR ABOUT IS FEL.
THAT'S BECAUSE FEL IS A DEADLY ENEMY.
NO ENEMY IS DEADLY ENOUGH TO MAKE ME LOSE MY NERVE.
FEL HASN'T MADE ME LOSE MY NERVE, PLOURR.
THAT'S WHAT IT SOUNDS LIK TO ME, TYCHO.
HEY, NEITHER ONE OF YOU IS THE ENEMY.
TYCHO SPEAKS OF FEAR TO RELIEVE IT. PLOURR SPEAKS AGAINST FEAR TO HIDE IT.
I AM NO COWARD.
AH, THEN YOU ARE FOOL, SINCE ONLY FOOL DOES NOT WISH TO KNOW LETHAL ENEMY.
I AM NO FOOL, EITHER. SO, WHAT'S THE SCAN ON THIS GUY, FEL?
FEL CAME OUT OF THE ACADEMY ABOUT SEVEN YEARS BEFORE YAVIN. TIE PILOTS DO ONE ACTIVE TOUR, THEN MOVE TO FLEET, BUT HE VOLUNTEERED FOR A SECOND TOUR.
TALK ABOUT FOOLS.
NOT A FOOL, HE JUST LIKED FLYING. HE DID TWO YEARS IN FLEET AFTER THAT, THEN CAME TO THE PREFSBELT IV ACADEMY TO TEACH.
THIS HAND IS DANTOOINE RULES, YES? AND TEACH HE DID, RIGHT, TYCHO?
RIGHT. FEL TAUGHT HOBBIE, BIGGS, AND ME EVERYTHING WE KNEW ABOUT FLYING. WE SIMMED AGAINST HIM DOZENS OF TIMES AND NEVER GOT HIM.

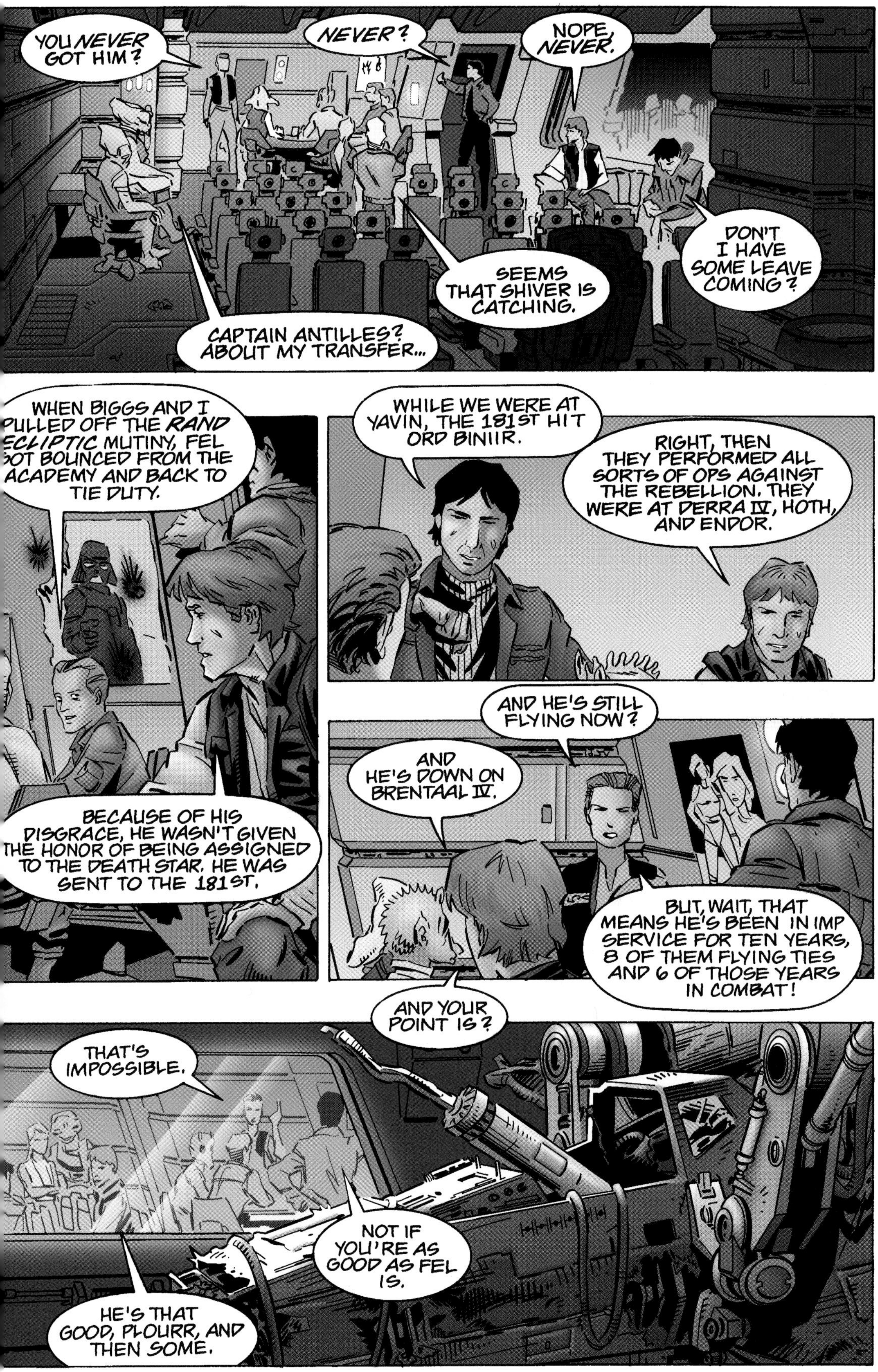
YOU NEVER GOT HIM?
NEVER?
NOPE, NEVER.
CAPTAIN ANTILLES? ABOUT MY TRANSFER...
SEEMS THAT SHIVER IS CATCHING.
DON'T I HAVE SOME LEAVE COMING?
WHEN BIGGS AND I PULLED OFF THE RAND ECLIPTIC MUTINY, FEL GOT BOUNCED FROM THE ACADEMY AND BACK TO TIE DUTY.
BECAUSE OF HIS DISGRACE, HE WASN'T GIVEN THE HONOR OF BEING ASSIGNED TO THE DEATH STAR. HE WAS SENT TO THE 181ST.
WHILE WE WERE AT YAVIN, THE 181ST HIT ORD BINIIR.
RIGHT, THEN THEY PERFORMED ALL SORTS OF OPS AGAINST THE REBELLION. THEY WERE AT DERRA IV, HOTH, AND ENDOR.
AND HE'S STILL FLYING NOW?
AND HE'S DOWN ON BRENTAAL IV.
BUT, WAIT, THAT MEANS HE'S BEEN IN IMP SERVICE FOR TEN YEARS, 8 OF THEM FLYING TIES AND 6 OF THOSE YEARS IN COMBAT!
AND YOUR POINT IS?
THAT'S IMPOSSIBLE.
NOT IF YOU'RE AS GOOD AS FEL IS.
HE'S THAT GOOD, PLOURR, AND THEN SOME.

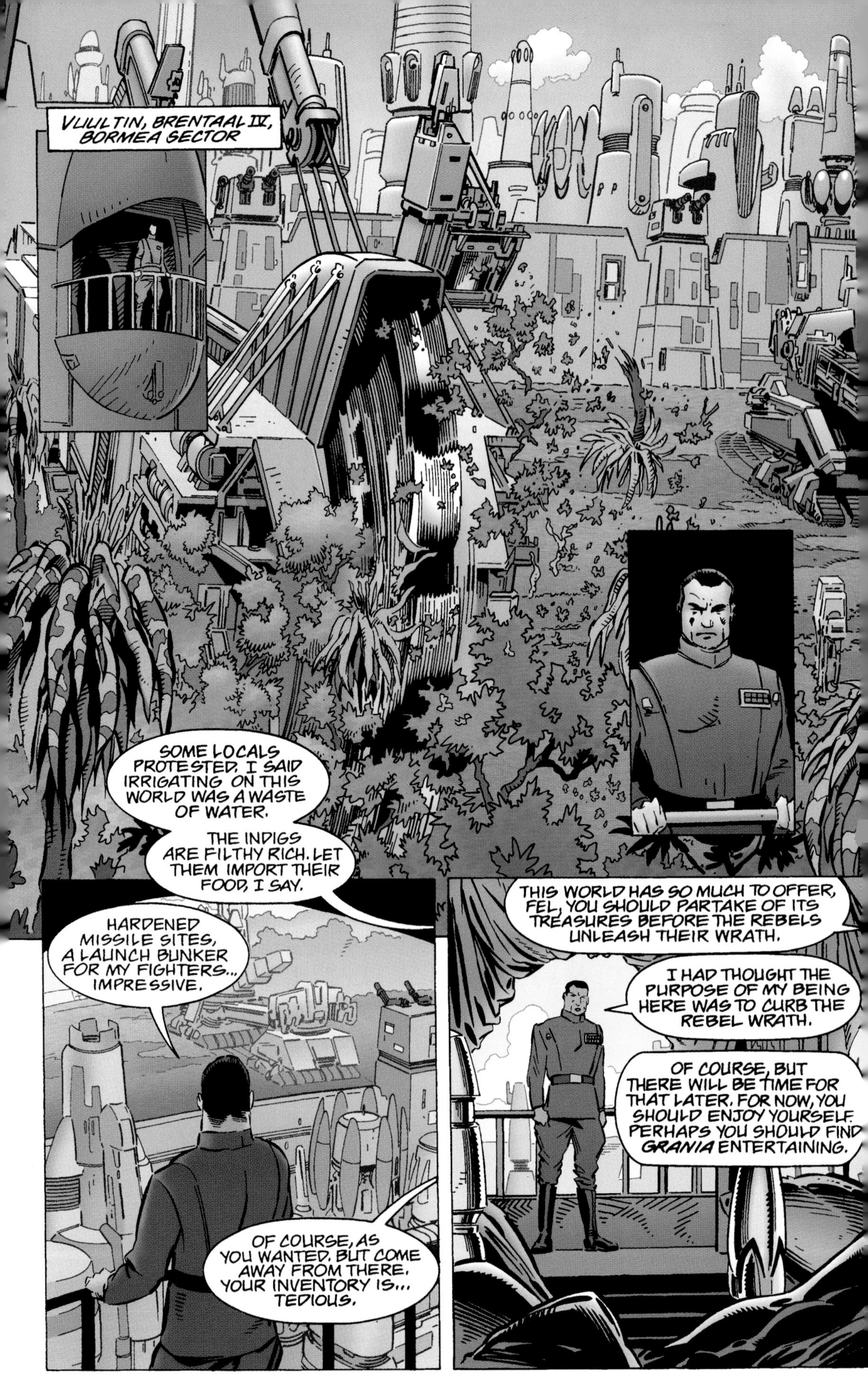
VUULTIN, BRENTAAL IV, BORMEA SECTOR
SOME LOCALS PROTESTED. I SAID IRRIGATING ON THIS WORLD WAS A WASTE OF WATER.
THE INDIGS ARE FILTHY RICH. LET THEM IMPORT THEIR FOOD, I SAY.
HARDENED MISSILE SITES, A LAUNCH BUNKER FOR MY FIGHTERS... IMPRESSIVE.
OF COURSE, AS YOU WANTED. BUT COME AWAY FROM THERE. YOUR INVENTORY IS... TEDIOUS.
THIS WORLD HAS SO MUCH TO OFFER, FEL. YOU SHOULD PARTAKE OF ITS TREASURES BEFORE THE REBELS UNLEASH THEIR WRATH.
I HAD THOUGHT THE PURPOSE OF MY BEING HERE WAS TO CURB THE REBEL WRATH.
OF COURSE, BUT THERE WILL BE TIME FOR THAT LATER. FOR NOW, YOU SHOULD ENJOY YOURSELF. PERHAPS YOU SHOULD FIND GRANIA ENTERTAINING.

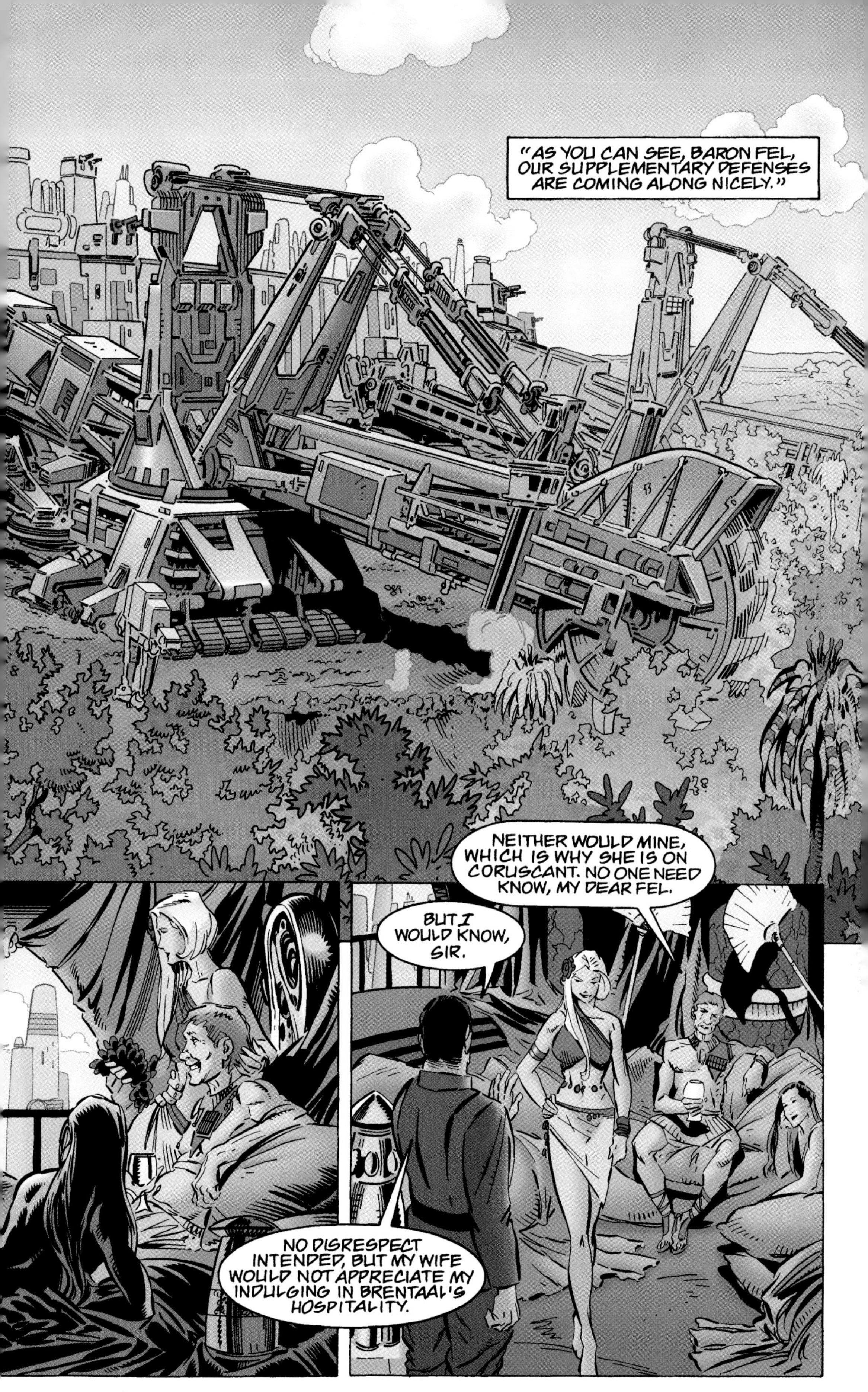
"AS YOU CAN SEE, BARON FEL, OUR SUPPLEMENTARY DEFENSES ARE COMING ALONG NICELY."
NO DISRESPECT INTENDED, BUT MY WIFE WOULD NOT APPRECIATE MY INDULGING IN BRENTAAL'S HOSPITALITY.
NEITHER WOULD MINE, WHICH IS WHY SHE IS ON CORUSCANT. NO ONE NEED KNOW, MY DEAR FEL.
BUT I WOULD KNOW, SIR.

TAKE HEART, GRANIA. I SHALL BE YOUR CONSOLATION PRIZE.

MY LORD IS MOST KIND.

YOU HEAR THAT, FEL? YOU DISAPPOINT HER AND SHE IS GRATIFIED IN HAVING ME. WONDERFUL PEOPLE, TRULY WONDERFUL.

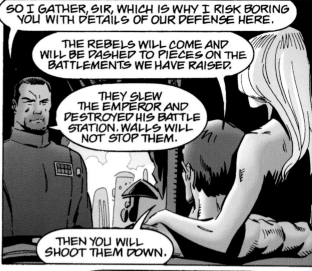

SO I GATHER, SIR, WHICH IS WHY I RISK BORING YOU WITH DETAILS OF OUR DEFENSE HERE.

THE REBELS WILL COME AND WILL BE DASHED TO PIECES ON THE BATTLEMENTS WE HAVE RAISED.

THEY SLEW THE EMPEROR AND DESTROYED HIS BATTLE STATION. WALLS WILL NOT STOP THEM.

THEN YOU WILL SHOOT THEM DOWN.

WE WILL, SIR, BUT OVER WHICH CITY?

THEY WILL COME TO VUULTIN, OF COURSE.

STRATEGICALLY, VUULTIN IS WORTHLESS.

BUT I AM HERE.

VALID POINT, BUT ORADIN, TO THE WEST, HAS THE SPACEPORT FACILITIES THEY NEED TO BRING TROOPS DOWN. WHILE WE MIGHT HOPE THEY WOULD STRIKE HERE, I SUSPECT THAT WILL BE THEIR TARGET.

IF YOU WISH TO SEND SOME OF YOUR UNIT THERE, PLEASE DO, BUT YOU WILL LEAVE ME A FLIGHT OR TWO IN CASE YOU ARE WRONG.

I'M NOT WRONG.

BUT YOU ARE UNDER MY COMMAND. DO WHAT YOU MUST DO. FEAR NOT, I SHALL FORGIVE YOU LATER.

INDEED, SIR, YOU ARE MOST KIND. GOOD DAY TO YOU.

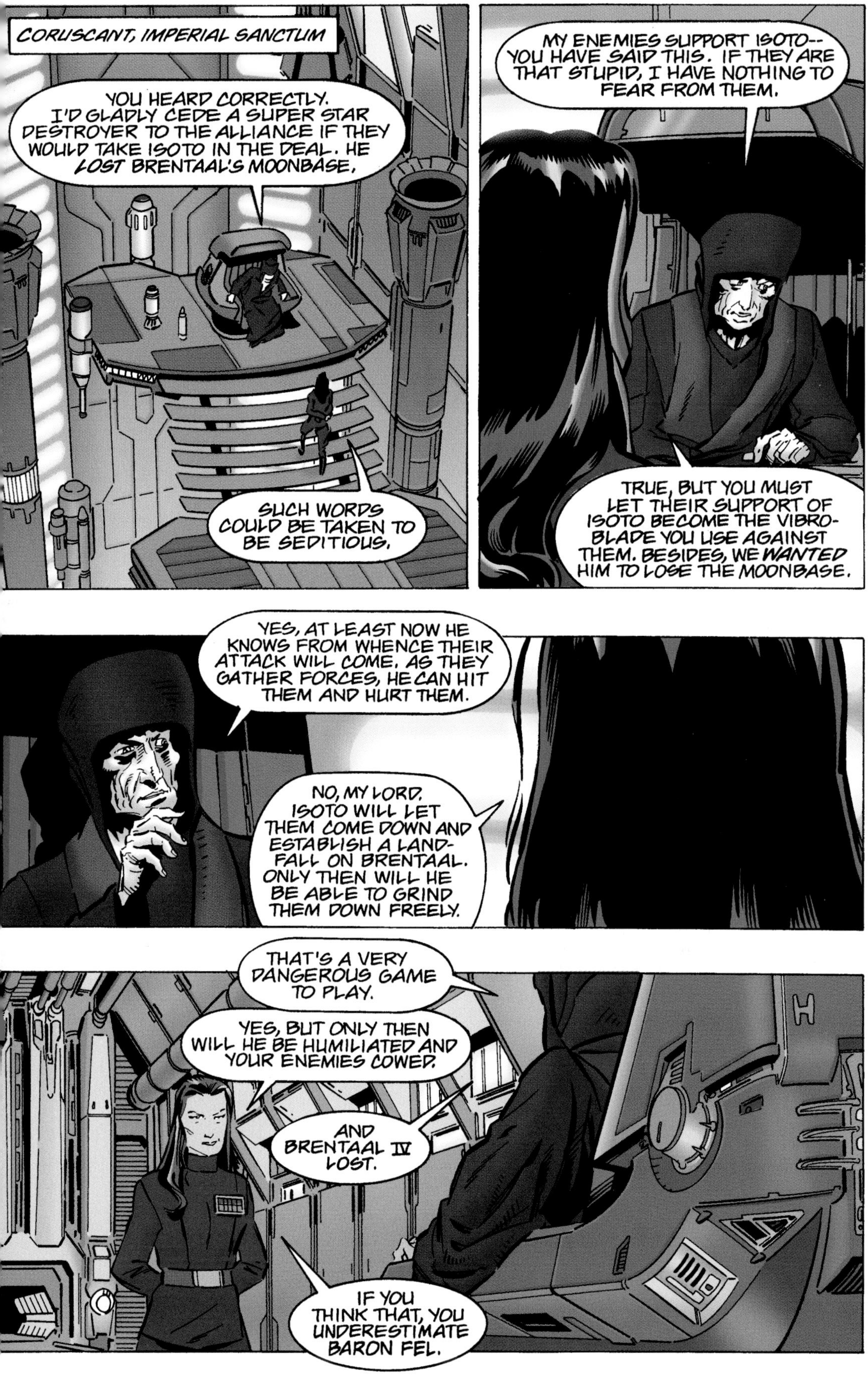
CORUSCANT, IMPERIAL SANCTUM
YOU HEARD CORRECTLY. I'D GLADLY CEDE A SUPER STAR DESTROYER TO THE ALLIANCE IF THEY WOULD TAKE ISOTO IN THE DEAL. HE LOST BRENTAAL'S MOONBASE.
SUCH WORDS COULD BE TAKEN TO BE SEDITIOUS.
MY ENEMIES SUPPORT ISOTO-- YOU HAVE SAID THIS. IF THEY ARE THAT STUPID, I HAVE NOTHING TO FEAR FROM THEM.
TRUE, BUT YOU MUST LET THEIR SUPPORT OF ISOTO BECOME THE VIBRO-BLADE YOU USE AGAINST THEM. BESIDES, WE WANTED HIM TO LOSE THE MOONBASE.
YES, AT LEAST NOW HE KNOWS FROM WHENCE THEIR ATTACK WILL COME. AS THEY GATHER FORCES, HE CAN HIT THEM AND HURT THEM.
NO, MY LORD. ISOTO WILL LET THEM COME DOWN AND ESTABLISH A LAND-FALL ON BRENTAAL. ONLY THEN WILL HE BE ABLE TO GRIND THEM DOWN FREELY.
THAT'S A VERY DANGEROUS GAME TO PLAY.
YES, BUT ONLY THEN WILL HE BE HUMILIATED AND YOUR ENEMIES COWED.
AND BRENTAAL IV LOST.
IF YOU THINK THAT, YOU UNDERESTIMATE BARON FEL.

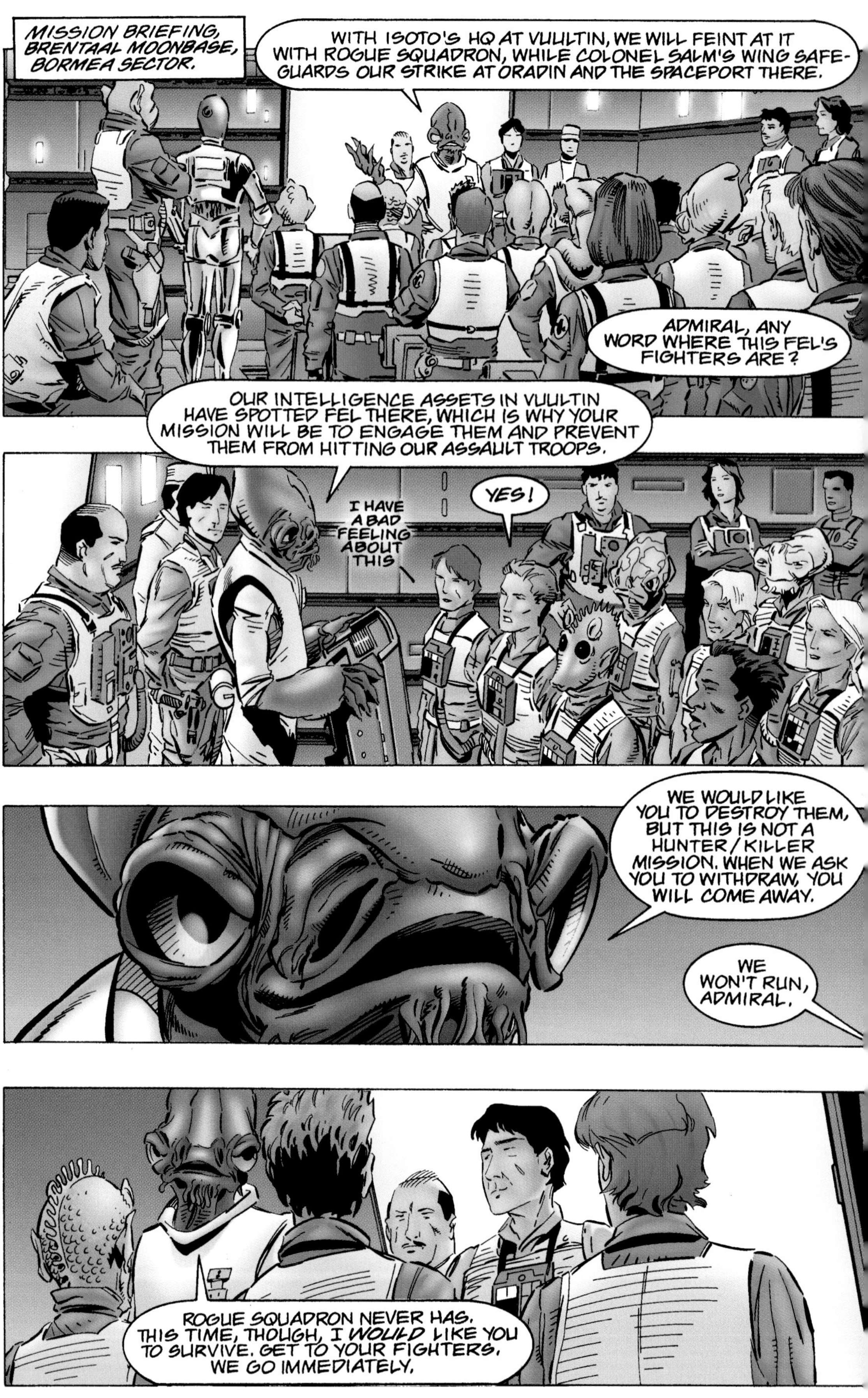
MISSION BRIEFING, BRENTAAL MOONBASE, BORMEA SECTOR.
WITH ISOTO'S HQ AT VUULTIN, WE WILL FEINT AT IT WITH ROGUE SQUADRON, WHILE COLONEL SALM'S WING SAFE-GUARDS OUR STRIKE AT ORADIN AND THE SPACEPORT THERE.
ADMIRAL, ANY WORD WHERE THIS FEL'S FIGHTERS ARE?
OUR INTELLIGENCE ASSETS IN VUULTIN HAVE SPOTTED FEL THERE, WHICH IS WHY YOUR MISSION WILL BE TO ENGAGE THEM AND PREVENT THEM FROM HITTING OUR ASSAULT TROOPS.
I HAVE A BAD FEELING ABOUT THIS
YES!
WE WOULD LIKE YOU TO DESTROY THEM, BUT THIS IS NOT A HUNTER/KILLER MISSION. WHEN WE ASK YOU TO WITHDRAW, YOU WILL COME AWAY.
WE WON'T RUN, ADMIRAL.
ROGUE SQUADRON NEVER HAS. THIS TIME, THOUGH, I *WOULD* LIKE YOU TO SURVIVE. GET TO YOUR FIGHTERS. WE GO IMMEDIATELY.

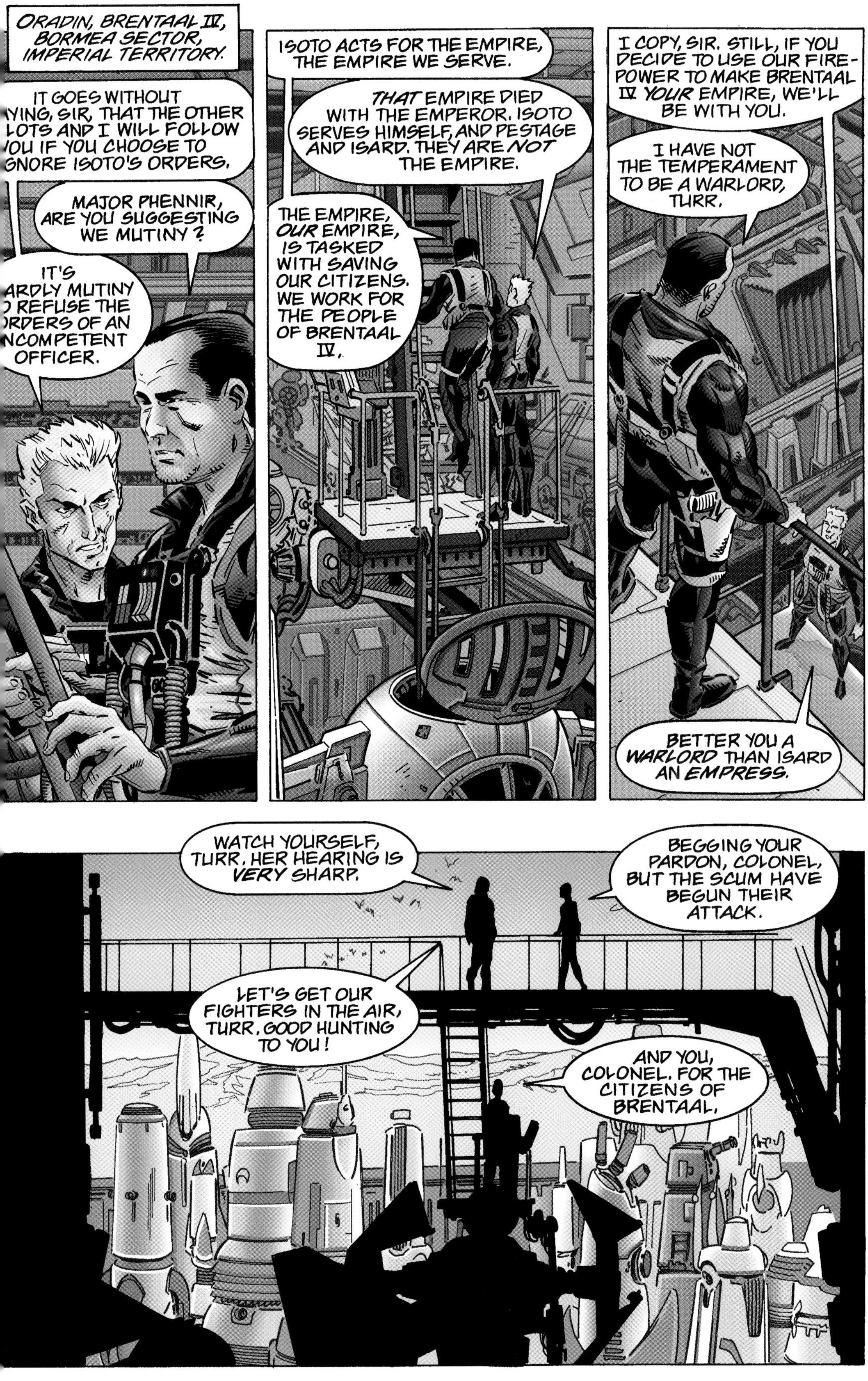

ORADIN, BRENTAAL IV, BORMEA SECTOR, IMPERIAL TERRITORY.
IT GOES WITHOUT YING, SIR, THAT THE OTHER LOTS AND I WILL FOLLOW OU IF YOU CHOOSE TO GNORE ISOTO'S ORDERS.
MAJOR PHENNIR, ARE YOU SUGGESTING WE MUTINY?
IT'S ARDLY MUTINY REFUSE THE RDERS OF AN NCOMPETENT OFFICER.
ISOTO ACTS FOR THE EMPIRE, THE EMPIRE WE SERVE.
THAT EMPIRE DIED WITH THE EMPEROR. ISOTO SERVES HIMSELF, AND PESTAGE AND ISARD. THEY ARE NOT THE EMPIRE.
THE EMPIRE, OUR EMPIRE, IS TASKED WITH SAVING OUR CITIZENS. WE WORK FOR THE PEOPLE OF BRENTAAL IV.
I COPY, SIR. STILL, IF YOU DECIDE TO USE OUR FIRE-POWER TO MAKE BRENTAAL IV YOUR EMPIRE, WE'LL BE WITH YOU.
I HAVE NOT THE TEMPERAMENT TO BE A WARLORD, TURR.
BETTER YOU A WARLORD THAN ISARD AN EMPRESS.
WATCH YOURSELF, TURR. HER HEARING IS VERY SHARP.
BEGGING YOUR PARDON, COLONEL, BUT THE SCUM HAVE BEGUN THEIR ATTACK.
LET'S GET OUR FIGHTERS IN THE AIR, TURR. GOOD HUNTING TO YOU!
AND YOU, COLONEL. FOR THE CITIZENS OF BRENTAAL.

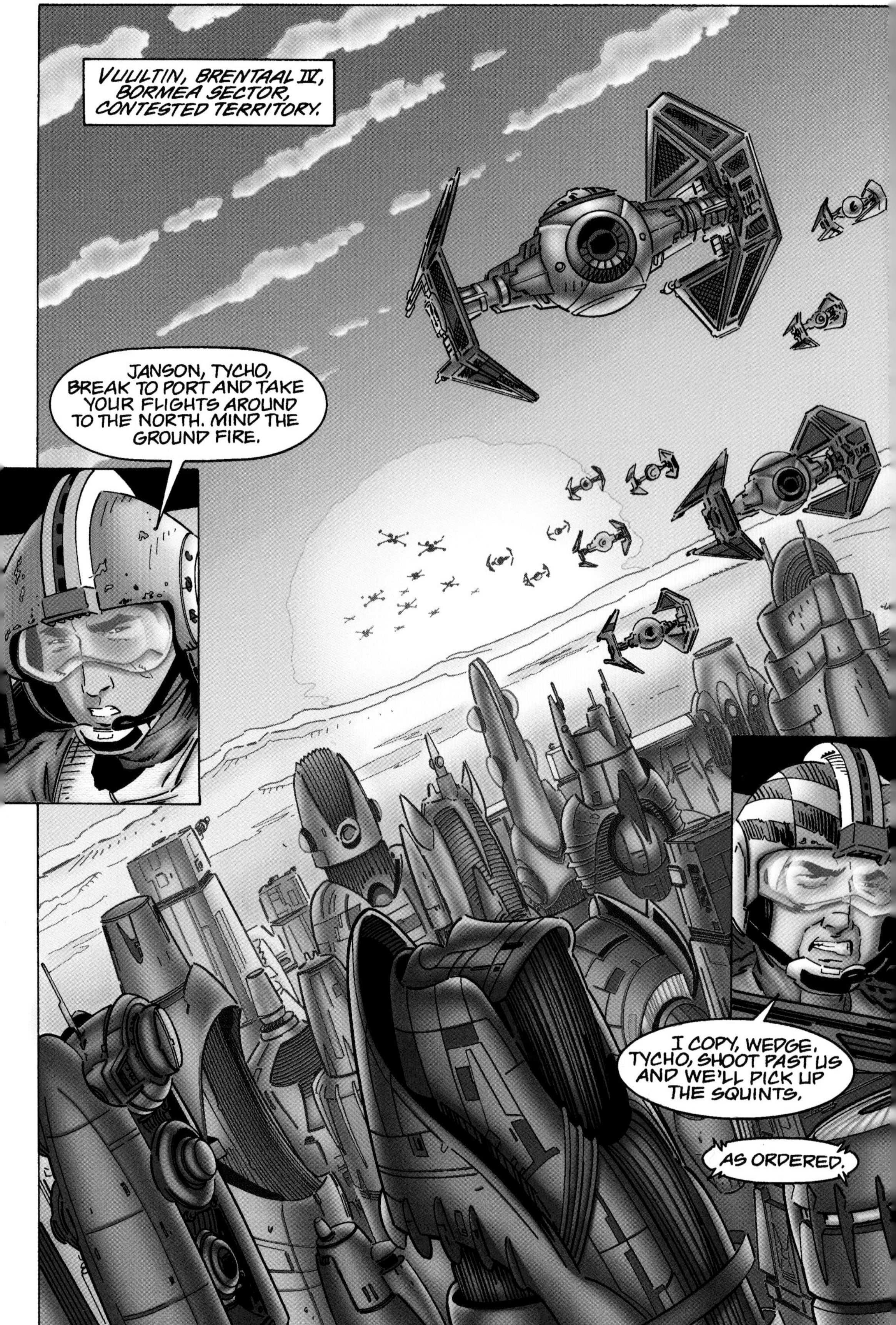
VUULTIN, BRENTAAL IV, BORMEA SECTOR, CONTESTED TERRITORY.
JANSON, TYCHO, BREAK TO PORT AND TAKE YOUR FLIGHTS AROUND TO THE NORTH. MIND THE GROUND FIRE.
I COPY, WEDGE. TYCHO, SHOOT PAST US AND WE'LL PICK UP THE SQUINTS.
AS ORDERED.

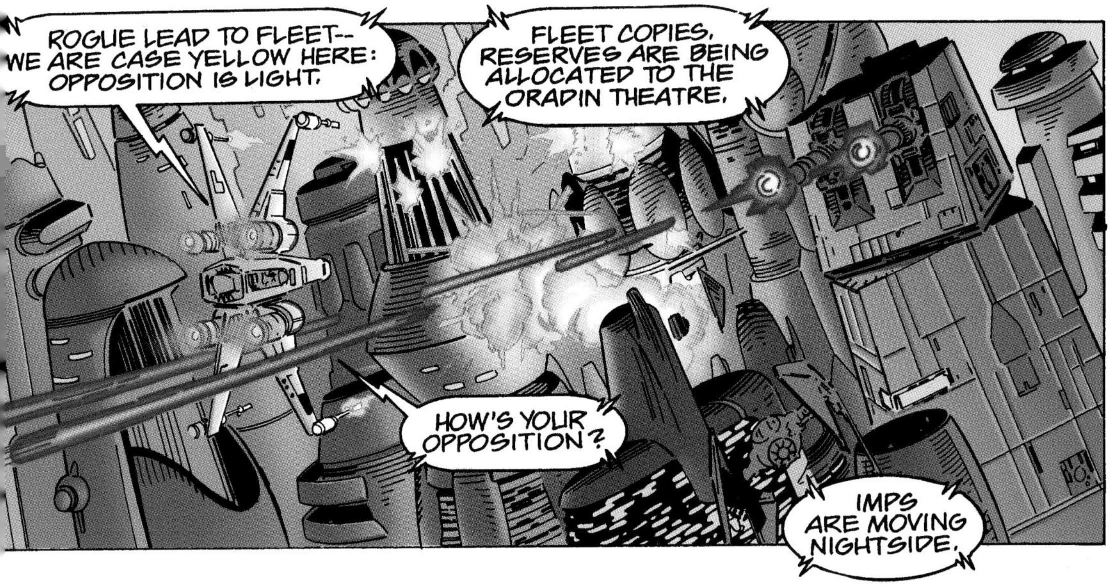
ROGUE LEAD TO FLEET-- WE ARE CASE YELLOW HERE: OPPOSITION IS LIGHT.
FLEET COPIES. RESERVES ARE BEING ALLOCATED TO THE ORADIN THEATRE.
HOW'S YOUR OPPOSITION?
IMPS ARE MOVING NIGHTSIDE.
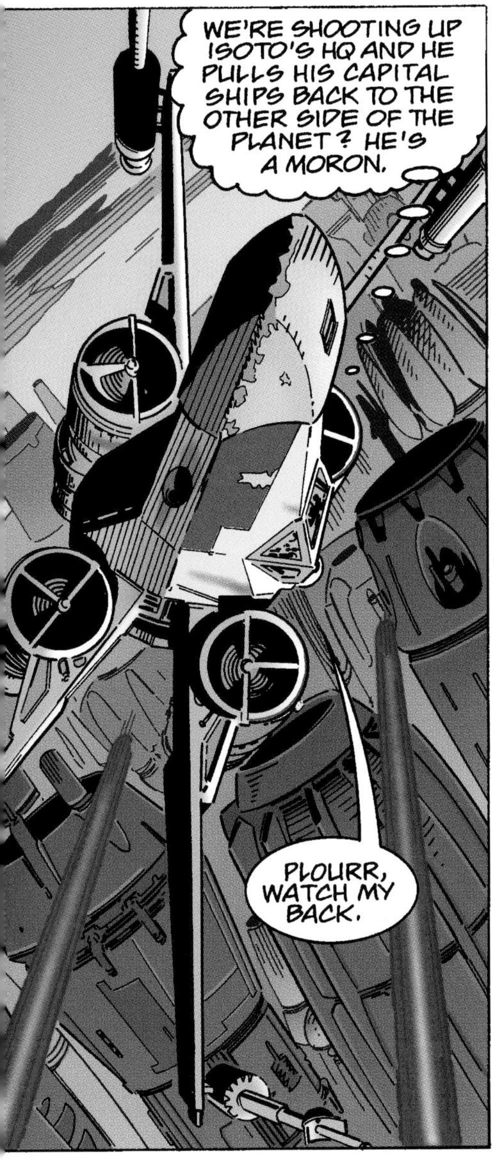
WE'RE SHOOTING UP ISOTO'S HQ AND HE PULLS HIS CAPITAL SHIPS BACK TO THE OTHER SIDE OF THE PLANET? HE'S A MORON.
PLOURR, WATCH MY BACK.
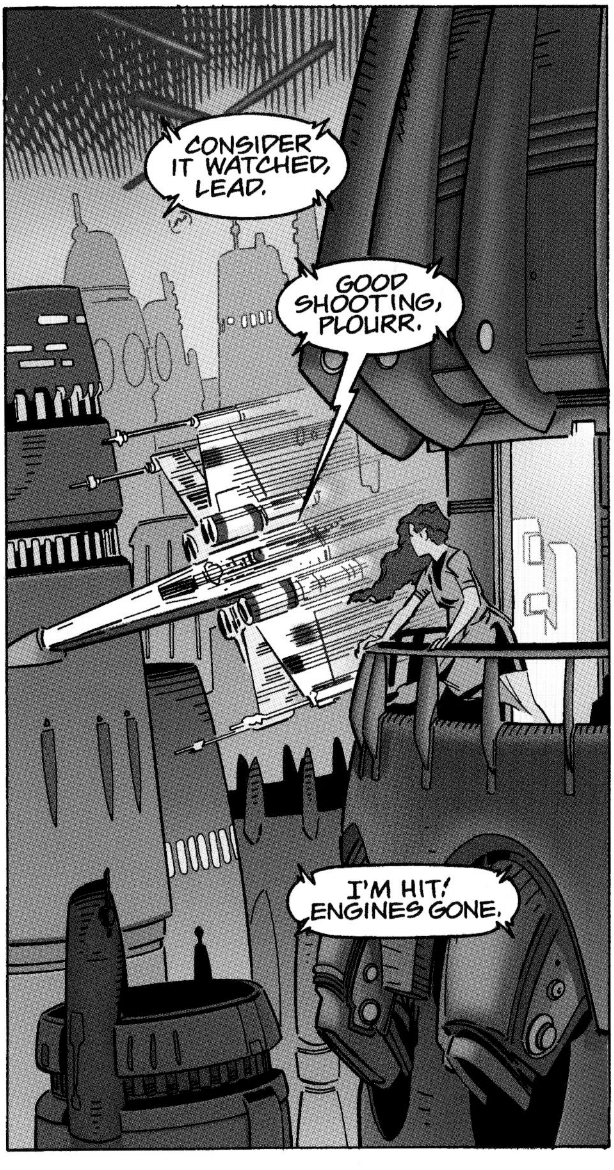
CONSIDER IT WATCHED, LEAD.
GOOD SHOOTING, PLOURR.
I'M HIT! ENGINES GONE.

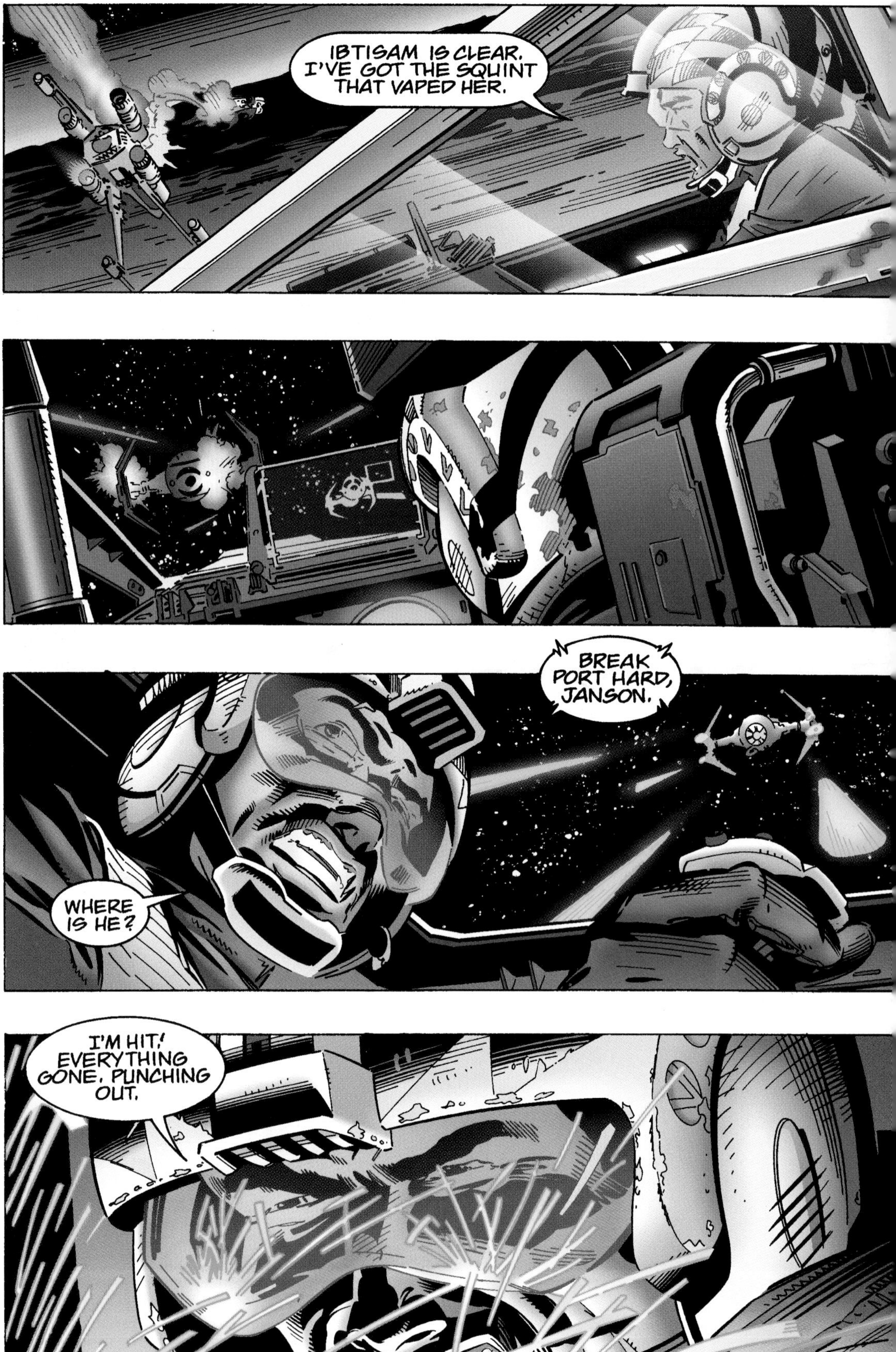
IBTISAM IS CLEAR. I'VE GOT THE SQUINT THAT VAPED HER.
BREAK PORT HARD, JANSON.
WHERE IS HE?
I'M HIT! EVERYTHING GONE, PUNCHING OUT.

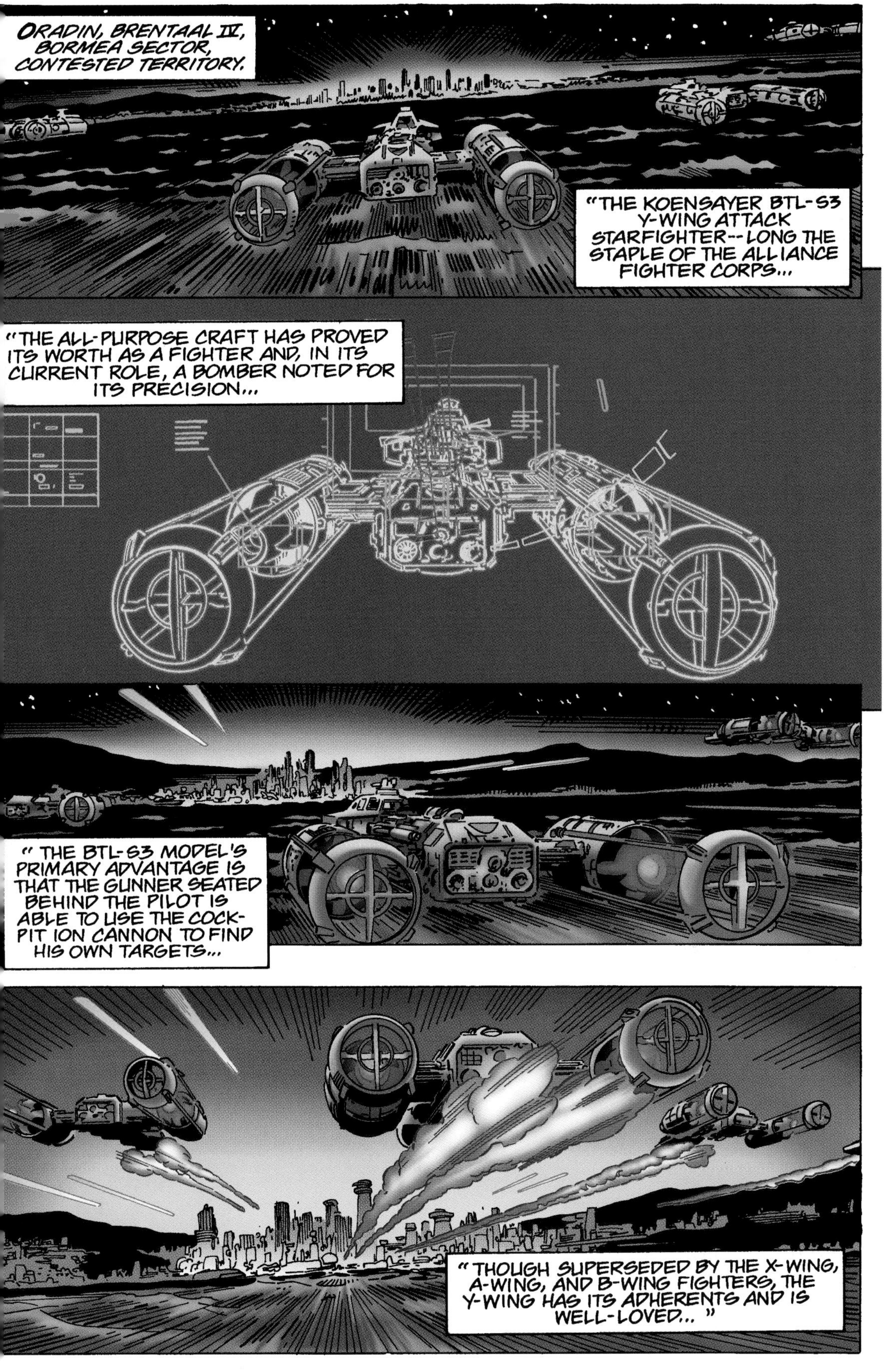
ORADIN, BRENTAAL IV, BORMEA SECTOR, CONTESTED TERRITORY.
"THE KOENSAYER BTL-S3 Y-WING ATTACK STARFIGHTER--LONG THE STAPLE OF THE ALLIANCE FIGHTER CORPS...
"THE ALL-PURPOSE CRAFT HAS PROVED ITS WORTH AS A FIGHTER AND, IN ITS CURRENT ROLE, A BOMBER NOTED FOR ITS PRECISION...
"THE BTL-S3 MODEL'S PRIMARY ADVANTAGE IS THAT THE GUNNER SEATED BEHIND THE PILOT IS ABLE TO USE THE COCK-PIT ION CANNON TO FIND HIS OWN TARGETS...
"THOUGH SUPERSEDED BY THE X-WING, A-WING, AND B-WING FIGHTERS, THE Y-WING HAS ITS ADHERENTS AND IS WELL-LOVED..."

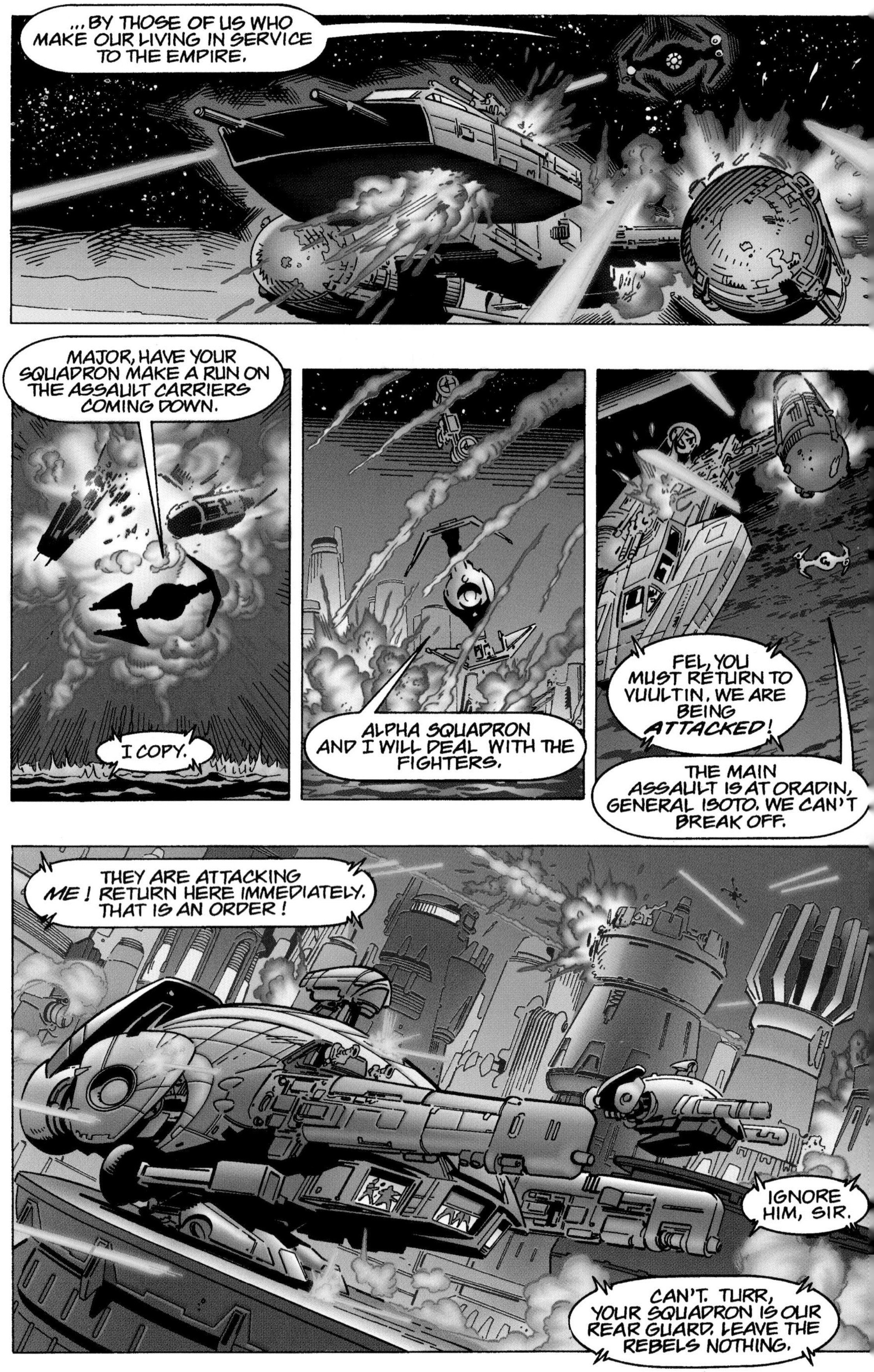
...BY THOSE OF US WHO MAKE OUR LIVING IN SERVICE TO THE EMPIRE.
MAJOR, HAVE YOUR SQUADRON MAKE A RUN ON THE ASSAULT CARRIERS COMING DOWN.
I COPY.
ALPHA SQUADRON AND I WILL DEAL WITH THE FIGHTERS.
FEL, YOU MUST RETURN TO VUULTIN. WE ARE BEING *ATTACKED*!
THE MAIN ASSAULT IS AT ORADIN, GENERAL ISOTO. WE CAN'T BREAK OFF.
THEY ARE ATTACKING *ME*! RETURN HERE IMMEDIATELY. THAT IS AN ORDER!
IGNORE HIM, SIR.
CAN'T. TURR, YOUR SQUADRON IS OUR REAR GUARD. LEAVE THE REBELS NOTHING.

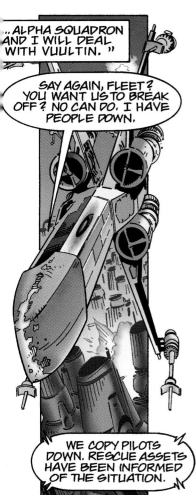

"..ALPHA SQUADRON AND I WILL DEAL WITH VUULTIN."

SAY AGAIN, FLEET? YOU WANT US TO BREAK OFF? NO CAN DO. I HAVE PEOPLE DOWN.

WE COPY PILOTS DOWN. RESCUE ASSETS HAVE BEEN INFORMED OF THE SITUATION.

THE AREA IS HOSTILE, FLEET.

WE ARE AWARE OF THE SITUATION, ROGUE LEAD. YOUR RECALL IS ORDERED NOW!

C'MON, IB; NRIN WOULD BE SKIPPING HIS WAY TO COVER.

⸮GROAN⸮

ROGUES, BACK TO THE INDEPENDENCE. NOW!

BUT WE HAVE PILOTS ON THE GROUND.

DON'T WORRY, NRIN. SOMEONE WILL FIND THEM. WE TAKE CARE OF OUR OWN.

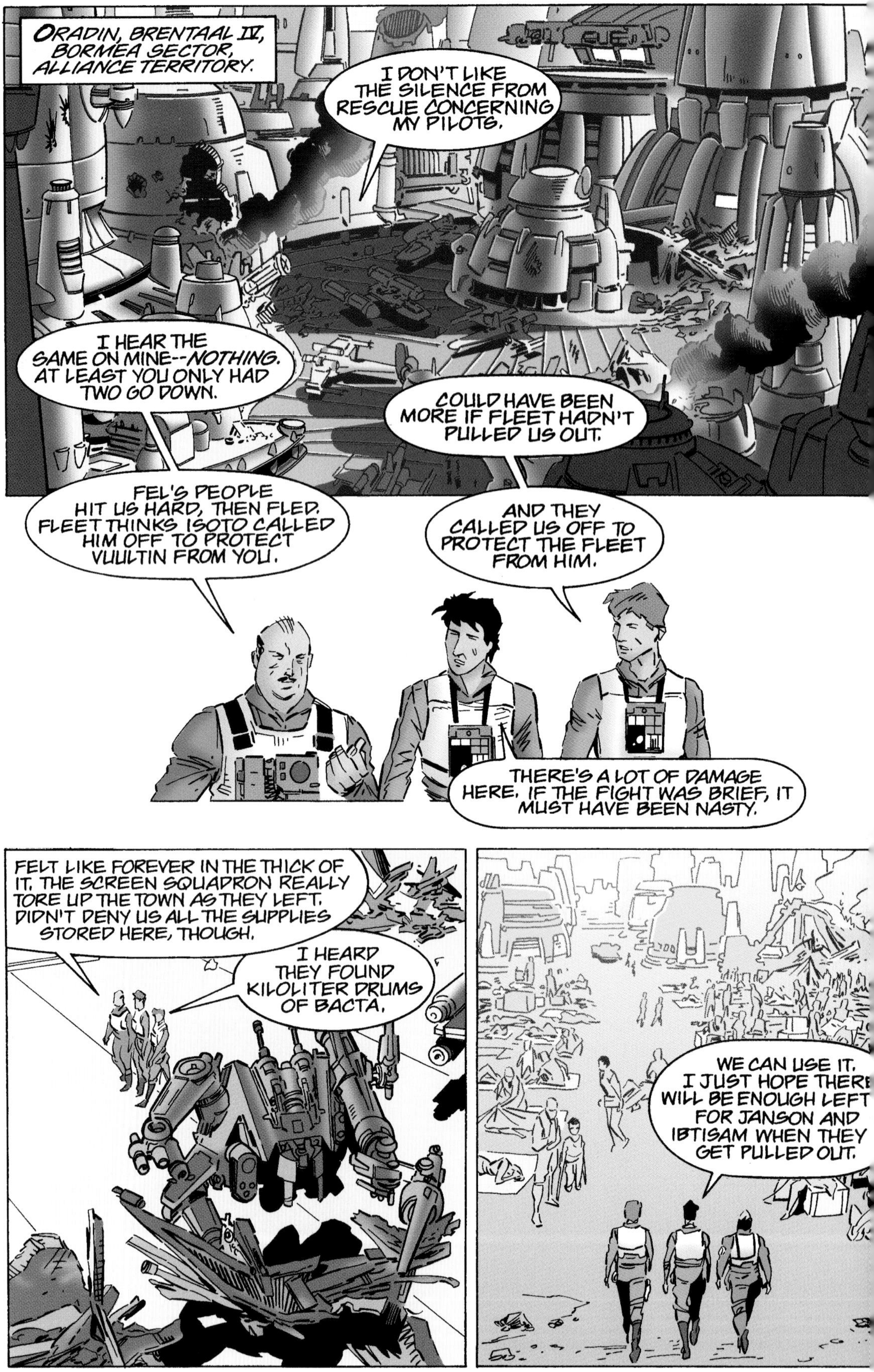
ORADIN, BRENTAAL IV, BORMEA SECTOR, ALLIANCE TERRITORY.
I DON'T LIKE THE SILENCE FROM RESCUE CONCERNING MY PILOTS.
I HEAR THE SAME ON MINE--*NOTHING.* AT LEAST YOU ONLY HAD TWO GO DOWN.
COULD HAVE BEEN MORE IF FLEET HADN'T PULLED US OUT.
FEL'S PEOPLE HIT US HARD, THEN FLED. FLEET THINKS ISOTO CALLED HIM OFF TO PROTECT VUULTIN FROM YOU.
AND THEY CALLED US OFF TO PROTECT THE FLEET FROM HIM.
THERE'S A LOT OF DAMAGE HERE. IF THE FIGHT WAS BRIEF, IT MUST HAVE BEEN NASTY.
FELT LIKE FOREVER IN THE THICK OF IT. THE SCREEN SQUADRON REALLY TORE UP THE TOWN AS THEY LEFT. DIDN'T DENY US ALL THE SUPPLIES STORED HERE, THOUGH.
I HEARD THEY FOUND KILOLITER DRUMS OF BACTA.
WE CAN USE IT. I JUST HOPE THERE WILL BE ENOUGH LEFT FOR JANSON AND IBTISAM WHEN THEY GET PULLED OUT.

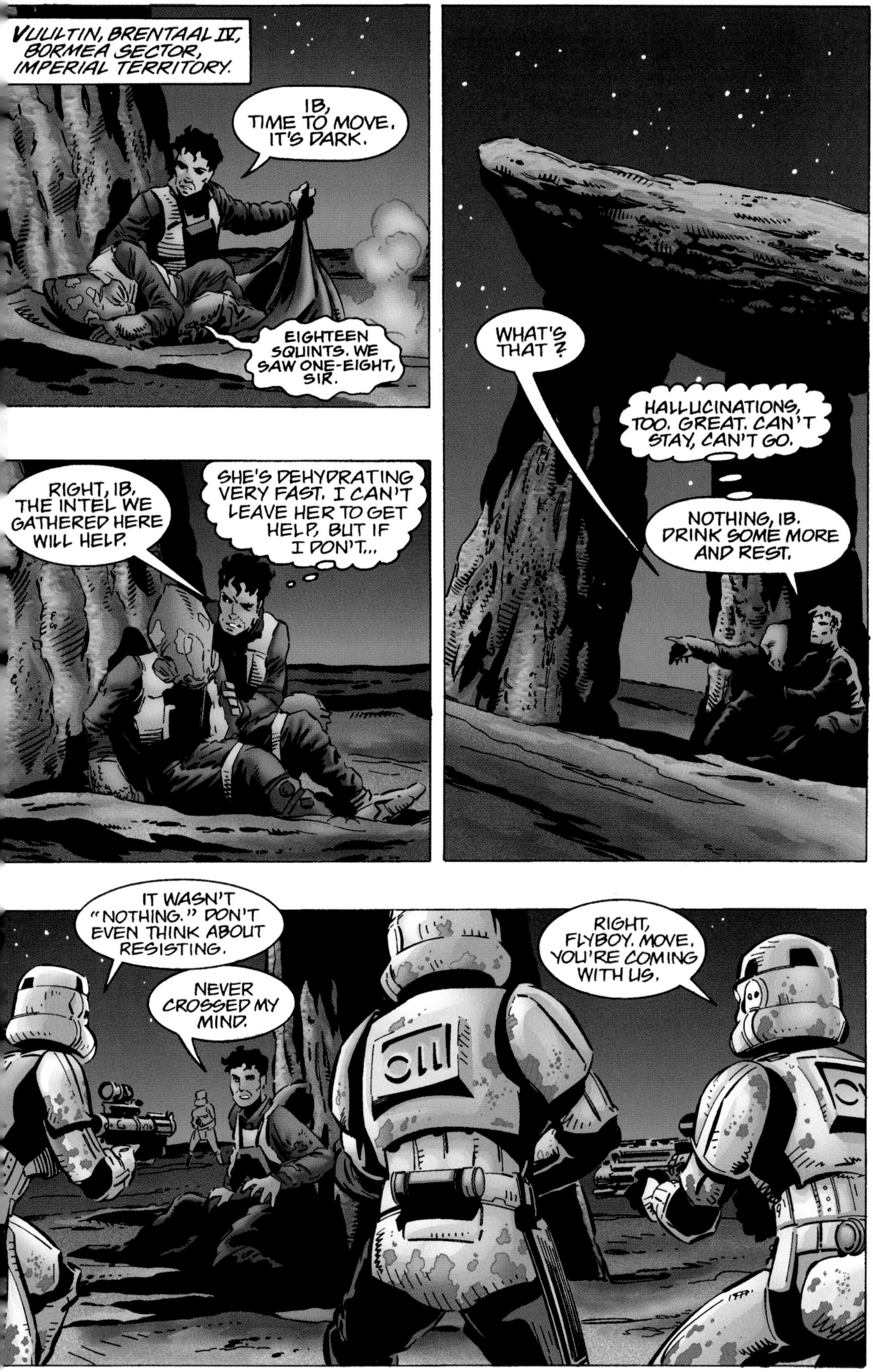
VUULTIN, BRENTAAL IV, BORMEA SECTOR, IMPERIAL TERRITORY.
IB, TIME TO MOVE. IT'S DARK.
EIGHTEEN SQUINTS. WE SAW ONE-EIGHT, SIR.
RIGHT, IB, THE INTEL WE GATHERED HERE WILL HELP.
SHE'S DEHYDRATING VERY FAST. I CAN'T LEAVE HER TO GET HELP, BUT IF I DON'T...
WHAT'S THAT ?
HALLUCINATIONS, TOO. GREAT. CAN'T STAY, CAN'T GO.
NOTHING, IB. DRINK SOME MORE AND REST.
IT WASN'T "NOTHING." DON'T EVEN THINK ABOUT RESISTING.
NEVER CROSSED MY MIND.
RIGHT, FLYBOY. MOVE. YOU'RE COMING WITH US.

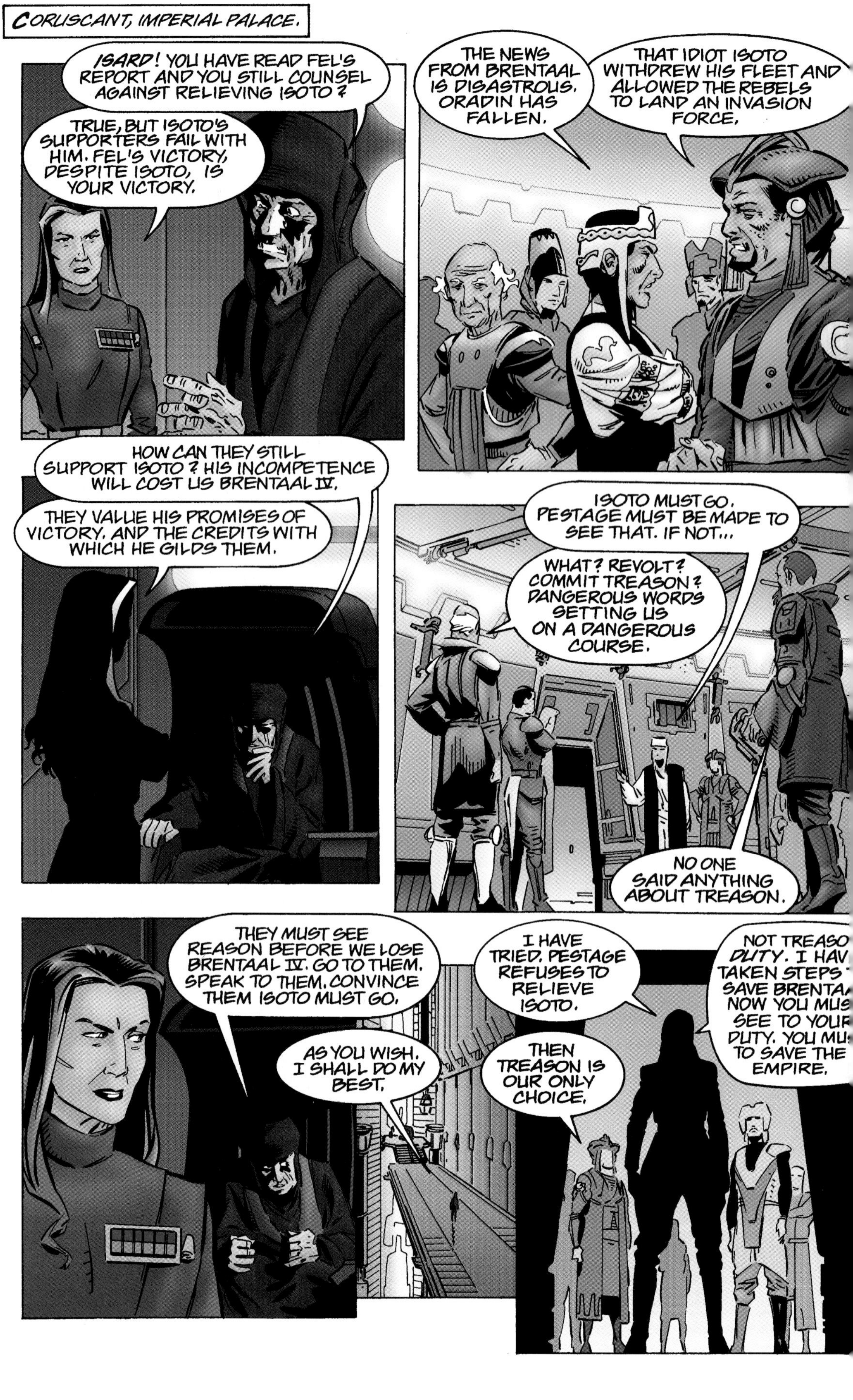
CORUSCANT, IMPERIAL PALACE.
ISARD! YOU HAVE READ FEL'S REPORT AND YOU STILL COUNSEL AGAINST RELIEVING ISOTO?
TRUE, BUT ISOTO'S SUPPORTERS FAIL WITH HIM. FEL'S VICTORY, DESPITE ISOTO, IS YOUR VICTORY.
THE NEWS FROM BRENTAAL IS DISASTROUS. ORADIN HAS FALLEN.
THAT IDIOT ISOTO WITHDREW HIS FLEET AND ALLOWED THE REBELS TO LAND AN INVASION FORCE.
HOW CAN THEY STILL SUPPORT ISOTO? HIS INCOMPETENCE WILL COST US BRENTAAL IV.
THEY VALUE HIS PROMISES OF VICTORY, AND THE CREDITS WITH WHICH HE GILDS THEM.
ISOTO MUST GO. PESTAGE MUST BE MADE TO SEE THAT. IF NOT...
WHAT? REVOLT? COMMIT TREASON? DANGEROUS WORDS SETTING US ON A DANGEROUS COURSE.
NO ONE SAID ANYTHING ABOUT TREASON.
THEY MUST SEE REASON BEFORE WE LOSE BRENTAAL IV. GO TO THEM. SPEAK TO THEM. CONVINCE THEM ISOTO MUST GO.
AS YOU WISH. I SHALL DO MY BEST.
I HAVE TRIED. PESTAGE REFUSES TO RELIEVE ISOTO.
THEN TREASON IS OUR ONLY CHOICE.
NOT TREASO DUTY. I HAV TAKEN STEPS SAVE BRENTA NOW YOU MUS SEE TO YOUR DUTY. YOU MU TO SAVE THE EMPIRE.

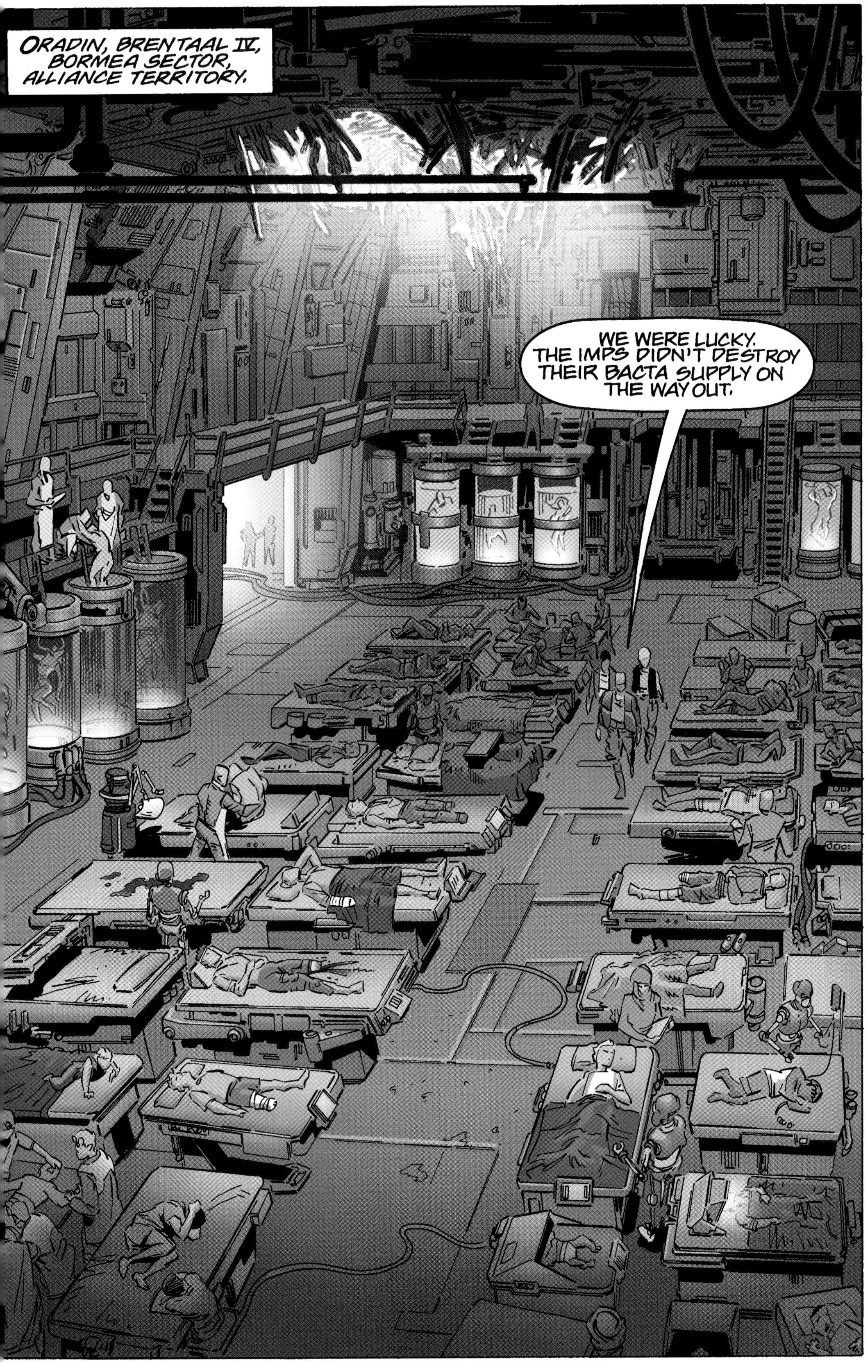
ORADIN, BRENTAAL IV, BORMEA SECTOR, ALLIANCE TERRITORY.
WE WERE LUCKY. THE IMPS DIDN'T DESTROY THEIR BACTA SUPPLY ON THE WAY OUT.

BUT WITH THIS MANY CASUALTIES, CAN IT BE ENOUGH?

WE'RE USING NORMAL TRIAGE RULES-- THOSE WHO CAN BE HELPED ARE BEING HELPED.

WHERE DID ALL THE CHILDREN COME FROM?

AN ASSAULT SHUTTLE WENT DOWN AND HIT A SCHOOL. MOST OF THE CASUALTIES HERE ARE FROM THAT SITE.

OTHERS, LIKE LT. CAYR HERE, WERE IN MY WING AND GOT SHOT DOWN. HOW ARE YOU DOING, TEL SIJ?

CAN'T COMPLAIN, COLONEL, SIR.

WE HEARD THE BATTLING HERE WAS PRETTY NASTY.

YOU SAW WORSE AT ENDOR, SIR. I'M NEW, SO THIS WAS BAD ENOUGH.

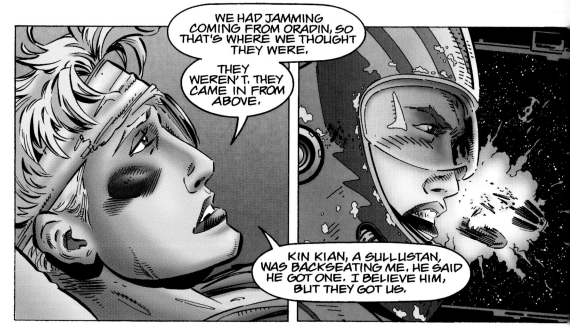

WE HAD JAMMING COMING FROM ORADIN, SO THAT'S WHERE WE THOUGHT THEY WERE.

THEY WEREN'T. THEY CAME IN FROM ABOVE.

KIN KIAN, A SULLUSTAN, WAS BACKSEATING ME. HE SAID HE GOT ONE. I BELIEVE HIM, BUT THEY GOT US.

SEVEN IS HIT, GOING DOWN.

" HITTING THE WATER HURT ME MORE THAN THE IMPS. STOVE IN PART OF THE COCKPIT, TOOK MY LEG, MY EYE AND BUSTED SOME RIBS.

" I GOT OUT OF THERE AND MADE IT TO THE SURFACE. AND SHORE, SOMEHOW.

" I HOPE KIN MADE IT OUT. HAVEN'T HEARD. I GUESS HE DIDN'T. "

DROIDS SAY THEY CAN FIX ME. I'LL BE BACK FLYING WITH YOU IN NO TIME, SIR.

CAREFUL, LT. TALK LIKE THAT AND CAPTAIN ANTILLES WILL CLAIM YOU AS A ROGUE. REST NOW. YOU'VE EARNED IT.

GUTSY PEOPLE FLYING WITH YOU, COLONEL.

THEY'RE ALL FIGHTERS, AND SHE'LL FLY AGAIN. WATCH. NONE OF US WILL EVER FORGET ORADIN...

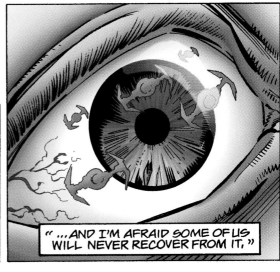

" ...AND I'M AFRAID SOME OF US WILL NEVER RECOVER FROM IT. "

VUULTIN, BRENTAAL IV, BORMEA SECTOR, IMPERIAL TERRITORY.

THEY WILL NEVER RECOVER FROM THE DRUBBING YOU ADMINISTERED TO THEM.

YOUR VICTORY HAS SHOWN THAT RABBLE THAT OUR MIGHT IS AN OUTGROWTH OF OUR MORAL SUPERIORITY. YOU SHOULD BE PROUD AND YOU WILL BE REWARDED.

ALL OF YOU ARE HEROES, OF COURSE, BUT ONE OF YOU IS MORE. SINGLEHANDEDLY, HE BROUGHT DOWN AN ASSAULT SHUTTLE, MAJOR TURR PHENNIR, STEP FORWARD.

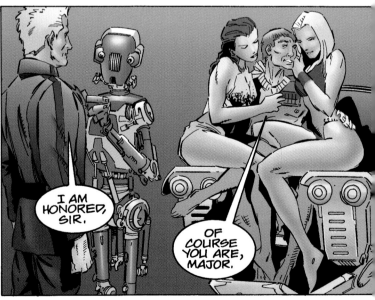

TO YOU, SIR, GOES THE FIRST EVER VUULTIN STARBURST. I DESIGNED IT MYSELF TO REWARD YOUR VALOR.

I AM HONORED, SIR.

OF COURSE YOU ARE, MAJOR.

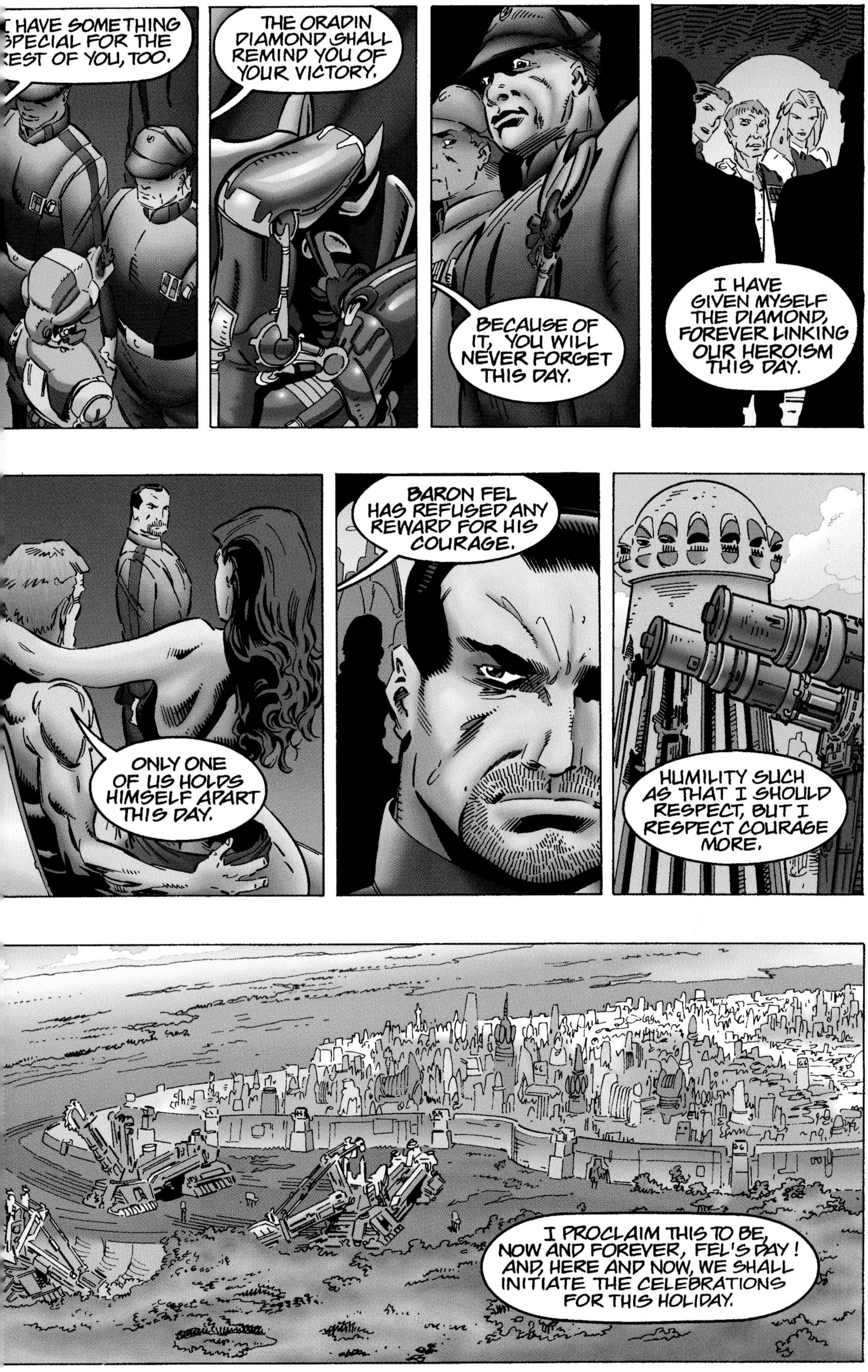
I HAVE SOMETHING SPECIAL FOR THE REST OF YOU, TOO.
THE ORADIN DIAMOND SHALL REMIND YOU OF YOUR VICTORY.
BECAUSE OF IT, YOU WILL NEVER FORGET THIS DAY.
I HAVE GIVEN MYSELF THE DIAMOND, FOREVER LINKING OUR HEROISM THIS DAY.
ONLY ONE OF US HOLDS HIMSELF APART THIS DAY.
BARON FEL HAS REFUSED ANY REWARD FOR HIS COURAGE.
HUMILITY SUCH AS THAT I SHOULD RESPECT, BUT I RESPECT COURAGE MORE.
I PROCLAIM THIS TO BE, NOW AND FOREVER, FEL'S DAY! AND, HERE AND NOW, WE SHALL INITIATE THE CELEBRATIONS FOR THIS HOLIDAY.

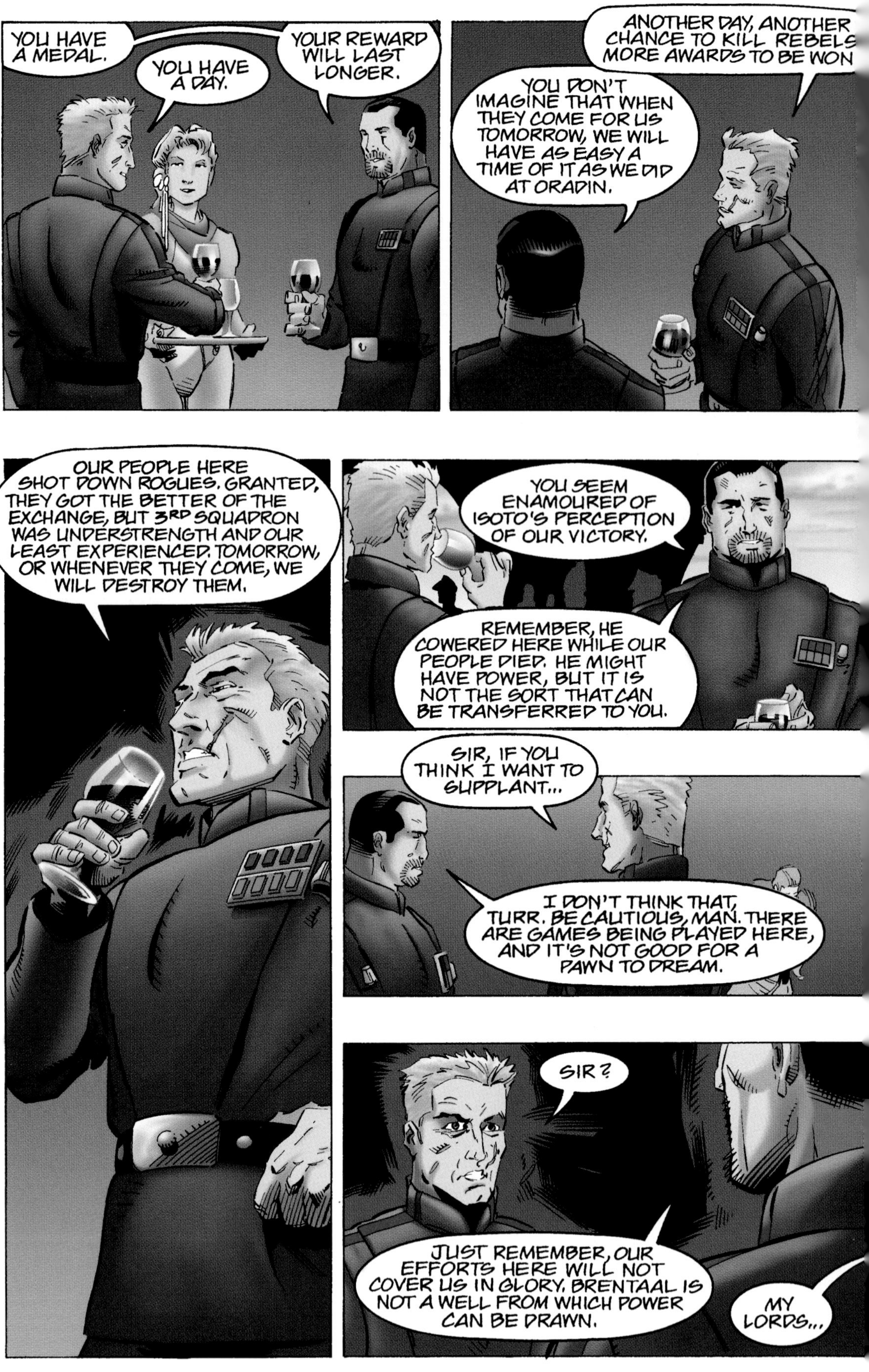
YOU HAVE A MEDAL.
YOU HAVE A DAY.
YOUR REWARD WILL LAST LONGER.
ANOTHER DAY, ANOTHER CHANCE TO KILL REBELS MORE AWARDS TO BE WON
YOU DON'T IMAGINE THAT WHEN THEY COME FOR US TOMORROW, WE WILL HAVE AS EASY A TIME OF IT AS WE DID AT ORADIN.
OUR PEOPLE HERE SHOT DOWN ROGUES. GRANTED, THEY GOT THE BETTER OF THE EXCHANGE, BUT 3RD SQUADRON WAS UNDERSTRENGTH AND OUR LEAST EXPERIENCED. TOMORROW, OR WHENEVER THEY COME, WE WILL DESTROY THEM.
YOU SEEM ENAMOURED OF ISOTO'S PERCEPTION OF OUR VICTORY.
REMEMBER, HE COWERED HERE WHILE OUR PEOPLE DIED. HE MIGHT HAVE POWER, BUT IT IS NOT THE SORT THAT CAN BE TRANSFERRED TO YOU.
SIR, IF YOU THINK I WANT TO SUPPLANT...
I DON'T THINK THAT, TURR. BE CAUTIOUS, MAN. THERE ARE GAMES BEING PLAYED HERE, AND IT'S NOT GOOD FOR A PAWN TO DREAM.
SIR?
JUST REMEMBER, OUR EFFORTS HERE WILL NOT COVER US IN GLORY. BRENTAAL IS NOT A WELL FROM WHICH POWER CAN BE DRAWN.
MY LORDS...

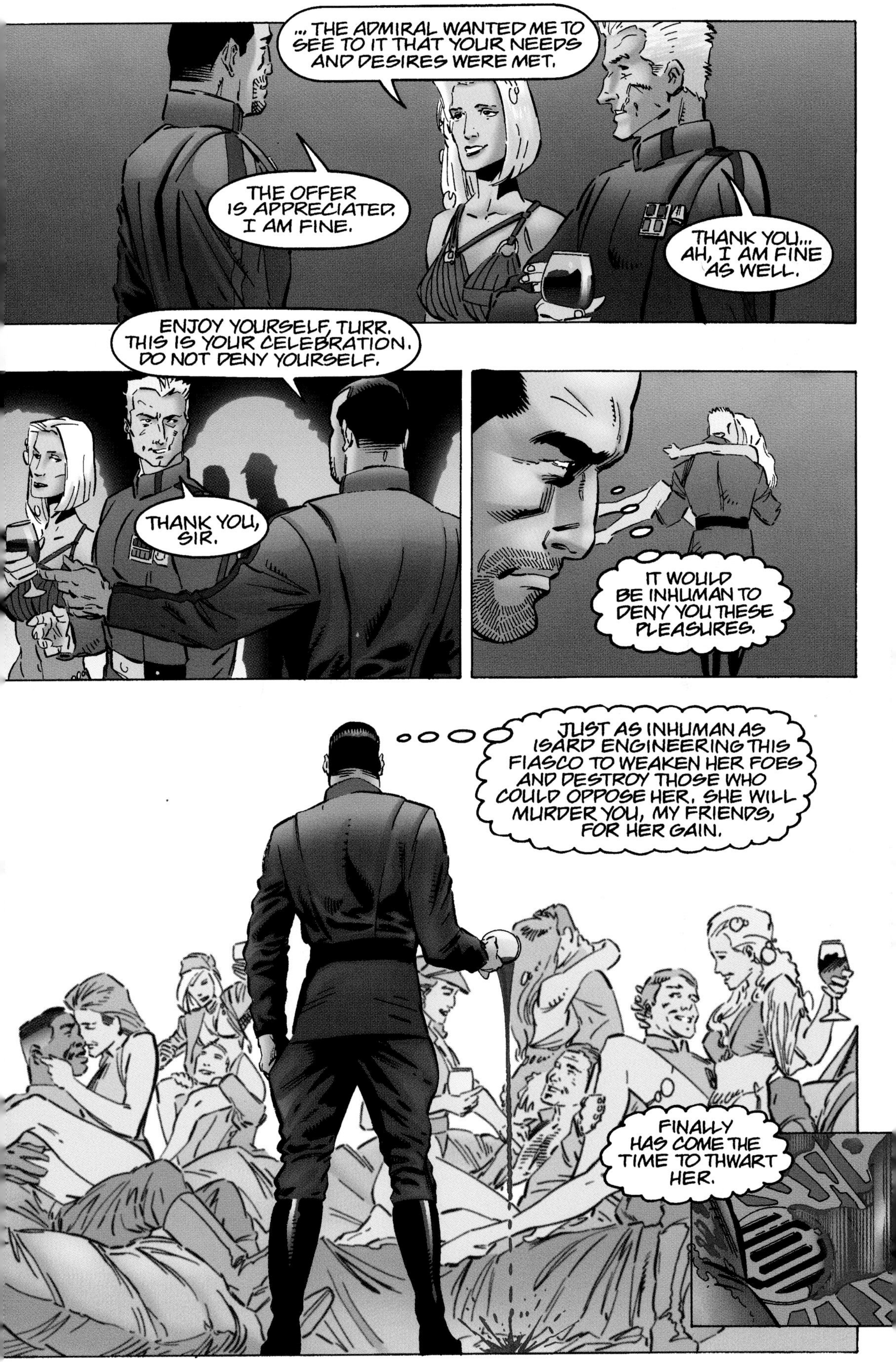
...THE ADMIRAL WANTED ME TO SEE TO IT THAT YOUR NEEDS AND DESIRES WERE MET.
THE OFFER IS APPRECIATED. I AM FINE.
THANK YOU... AH, I AM FINE AS WELL.
ENJOY YOURSELF, TURR. THIS IS YOUR CELEBRATION. DO NOT DENY YOURSELF.
THANK YOU, SIR.
IT WOULD BE INHUMAN TO DENY YOU THESE PLEASURES.
JUST AS INHUMAN AS ISARD ENGINEERING THIS FIASCO TO WEAKEN HER FOES AND DESTROY THOSE WHO COULD OPPOSE HER. SHE WILL MURDER YOU, MY FRIENDS, FOR HER GAIN.
FINALLY HAS COME THE TIME TO THWART HER.

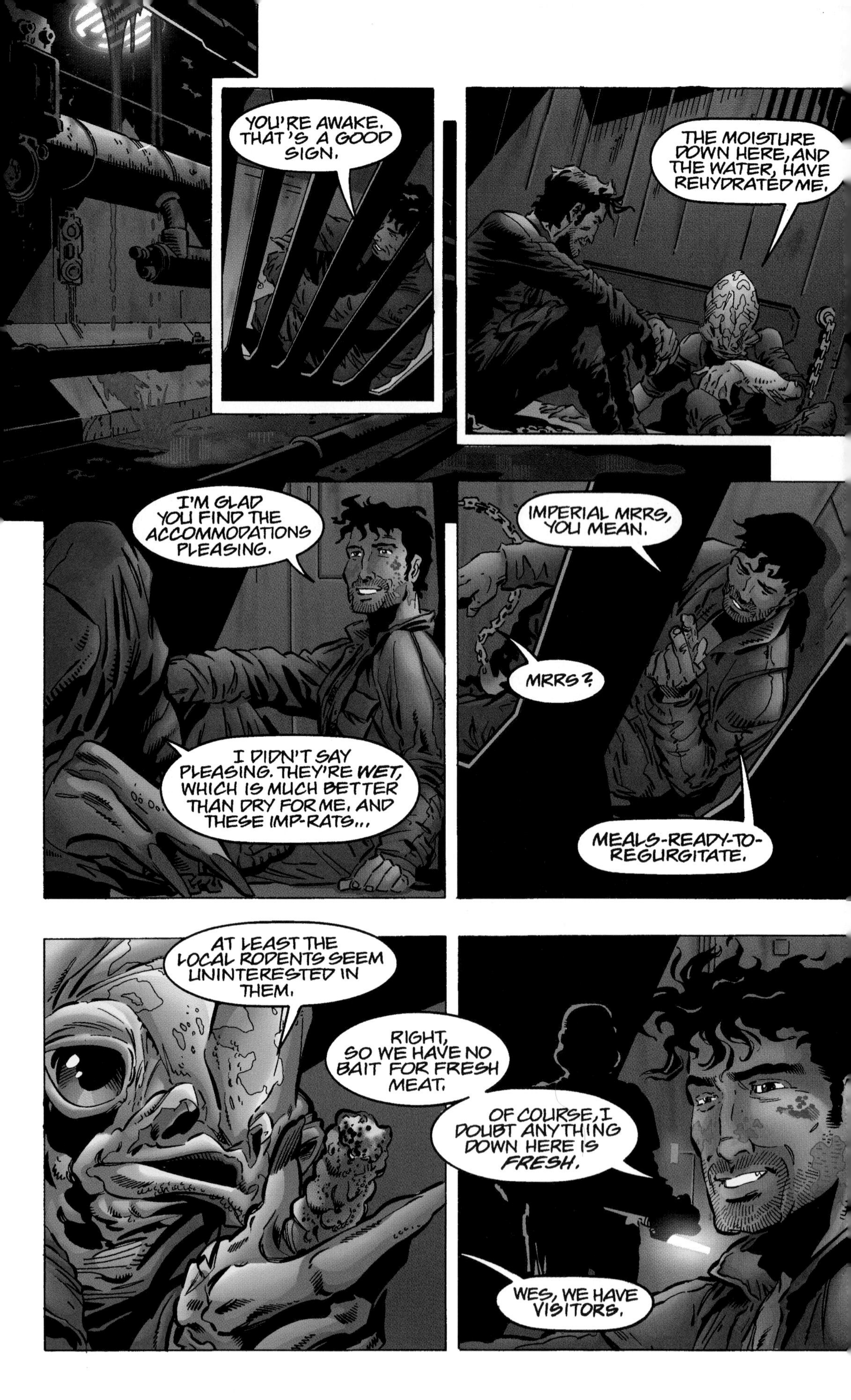
YOU'RE AWAKE. THAT'S A GOOD SIGN.
THE MOISTURE DOWN HERE, AND THE WATER, HAVE REHYDRATED ME.
I'M GLAD YOU FIND THE ACCOMMODATIONS PLEASING.
I DIDN'T SAY PLEASING. THEY'RE *WET*, WHICH IS MUCH BETTER THAN DRY FOR ME. AND THESE IMP-RATS...
IMPERIAL MRRS, YOU MEAN.
MRRS?
MEALS-READY-TO-REGURGITATE.
AT LEAST THE LOCAL RODENTS SEEM UNINTERESTED IN THEM.
RIGHT, SO WE HAVE NO BAIT FOR FRESH MEAT.
OF COURSE, I DOUBT ANYTHING DOWN HERE IS *FRESH*.
WES, WE HAVE VISITORS.

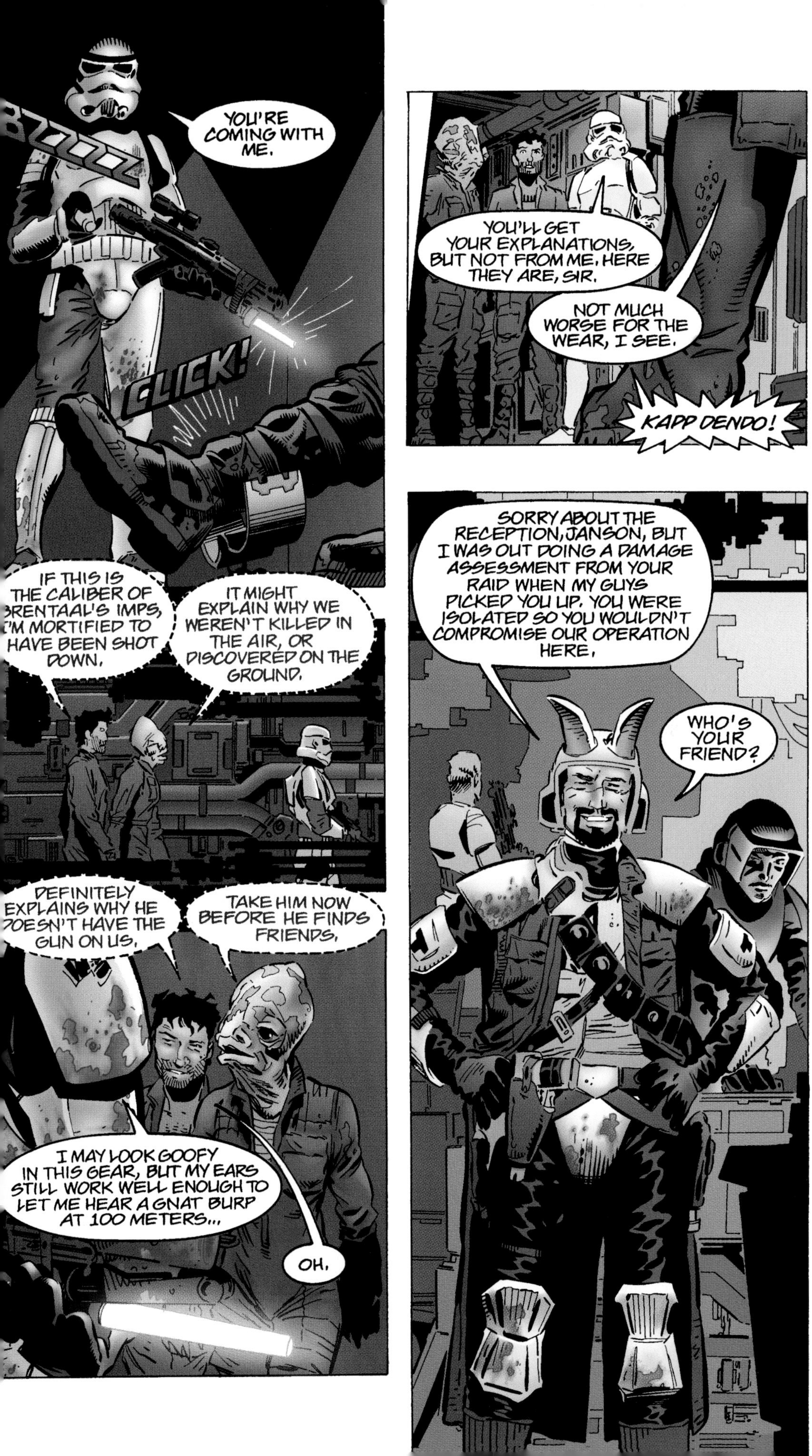
YOU'RE COMING WITH ME.
CLICK!
IF THIS IS THE CALIBER OF BRENTAAL'S IMPS, I'M MORTIFIED TO HAVE BEEN SHOT DOWN.
IT MIGHT EXPLAIN WHY WE WEREN'T KILLED IN THE AIR, OR DISCOVERED ON THE GROUND.
DEFINITELY EXPLAINS WHY HE DOESN'T HAVE THE GUN ON US.
TAKE HIM NOW BEFORE HE FINDS FRIENDS.
I MAY LOOK GOOFY IN THIS GEAR, BUT MY EARS STILL WORK WELL ENOUGH TO LET ME HEAR A GNAT BURP AT 100 METERS...
OH.
YOU'LL GET YOUR EXPLANATIONS, BUT NOT FROM ME. HERE THEY ARE, SIR.
NOT MUCH WORSE FOR THE WEAR, I SEE.
KAPP DENDO!
SORRY ABOUT THE RECEPTION, JANSON, BUT I WAS OUT DOING A DAMAGE ASSESSMENT FROM YOUR RAID WHEN MY GUYS PICKED YOU UP. YOU WERE ISOLATED SO YOU WOULDN'T COMPROMISE OUR OPERATION HERE.
WHO'S YOUR FRIEND?

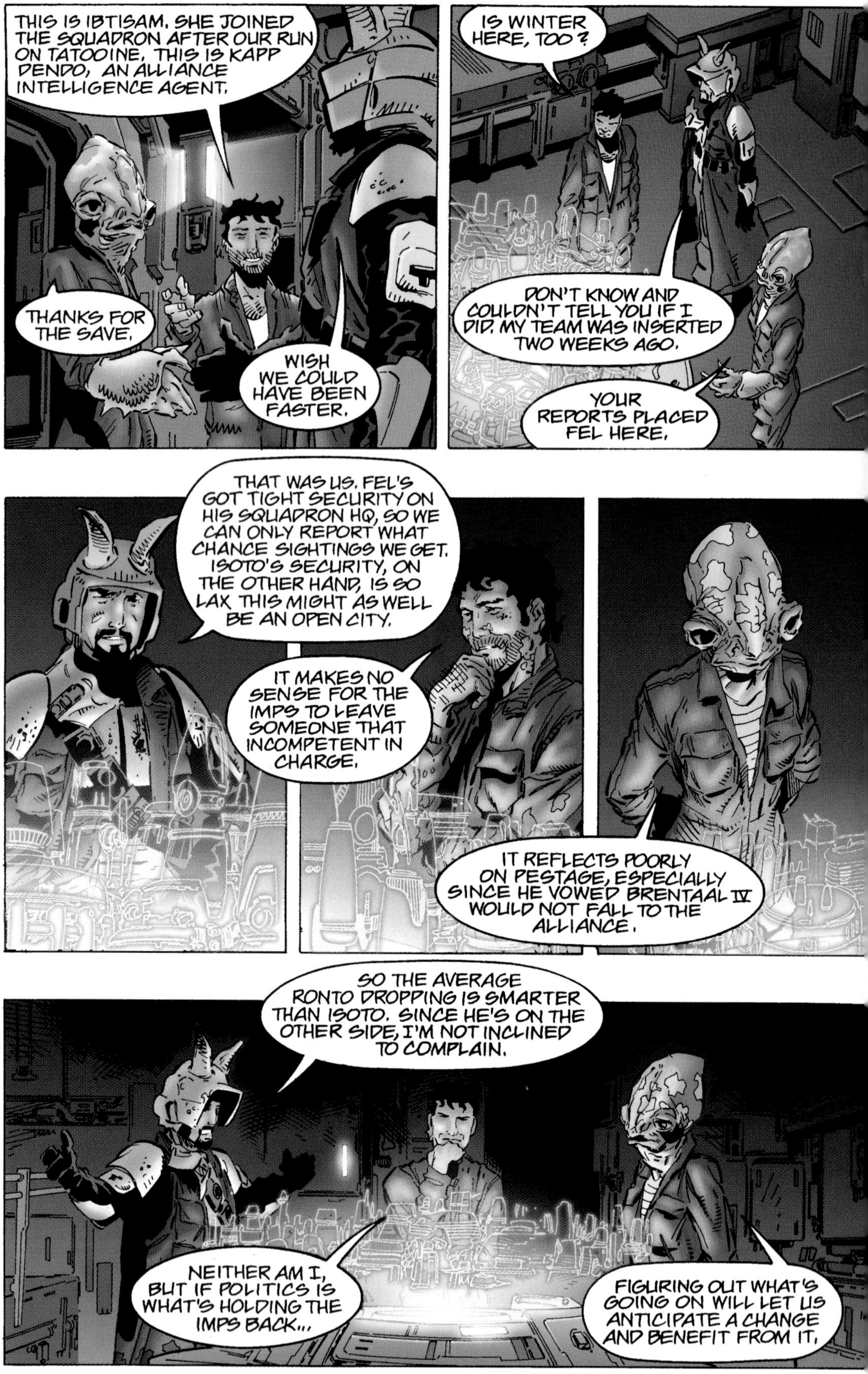
THIS IS IBTISAM. SHE JOINED THE SQUADRON AFTER OUR RUN ON TATOOINE. THIS IS KAPP DENDO, AN ALLIANCE INTELLIGENCE AGENT.
THANKS FOR THE SAVE.
WISH WE COULD HAVE BEEN FASTER.
IS WINTER HERE, TOO?
DON'T KNOW AND COULDN'T TELL YOU IF I DID. MY TEAM WAS INSERTED TWO WEEKS AGO.
YOUR REPORTS PLACED FEL HERE.
THAT WAS US. FEL'S GOT TIGHT SECURITY ON HIS SQUADRON HQ, SO WE CAN ONLY REPORT WHAT CHANCE SIGHTINGS WE GET. ISOTO'S SECURITY, ON THE OTHER HAND, IS SO LAX THIS MIGHT AS WELL BE AN OPEN CITY.
IT MAKES NO SENSE FOR THE IMPS TO LEAVE SOMEONE THAT INCOMPETENT IN CHARGE.
IT REFLECTS POORLY ON PESTAGE, ESPECIALLY SINCE HE VOWED BRENTAAL IV WOULD NOT FALL TO THE ALLIANCE.
SO THE AVERAGE RONTO DROPPING IS SMARTER THAN ISOTO. SINCE HE'S ON THE OTHER SIDE, I'M NOT INCLINED TO COMPLAIN.
NEITHER AM I, BUT IF POLITICS IS WHAT'S HOLDING THE IMPS BACK...
FIGURING OUT WHAT'S GOING ON WILL LET US ANTICIPATE A CHANGE AND BENEFIT FROM IT.

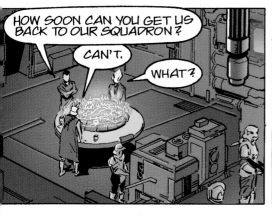

HOW SOON CAN YOU GET US BACK TO OUR SQUADRON?

CAN'T.

WHAT?

I CAN'T SPARE THE PEOPLE TO GET YOU TO ORADIN. YOU DON'T HAVE FIGHTERS TO FLY, SO YOU CAN'T HELP THEM ANYWAY. FINALLY, YOU'LL BE MORE USE TO THE ALLIANCE HERE THAN IN THE AIR.

OH, YEAH?

FOLLOW ME AND I'LL SHOW YOU WHAT WE'RE UP AGAINST. WE HAVE TWO MISSIONS TOMORROW. THE SECOND IS TO GET ISOTO ALIVE IF WE CAN.

I HAVE A DEMOLITION JOB AND I RECALL YOU'RE PRETTY GOOD IN A FIREFIGHT. IS SHE?

SHE SMOKED IRRUKIINE ON MALREV 4.

IRRUKIINE?

THINK GUNDARKS, BUT MEANER.

NICE TO HAVE YOU WITH US, IBTISAM.

THE MISSION, DENDO?

OH, YEAH, ISOTO HAD THAT BEAST FITTED WITH E-WEBS FOR ANTI-FIGHTER PURPOSES. WE'RE GOING TO BLOW IT UP.

BIG TARGET, HARD TO MISS.

TRUE ENOUGH, DARLING, ESPECIALLY BECAUSE WE'LL BE INSIDE IT WHEN WE STRIKE.

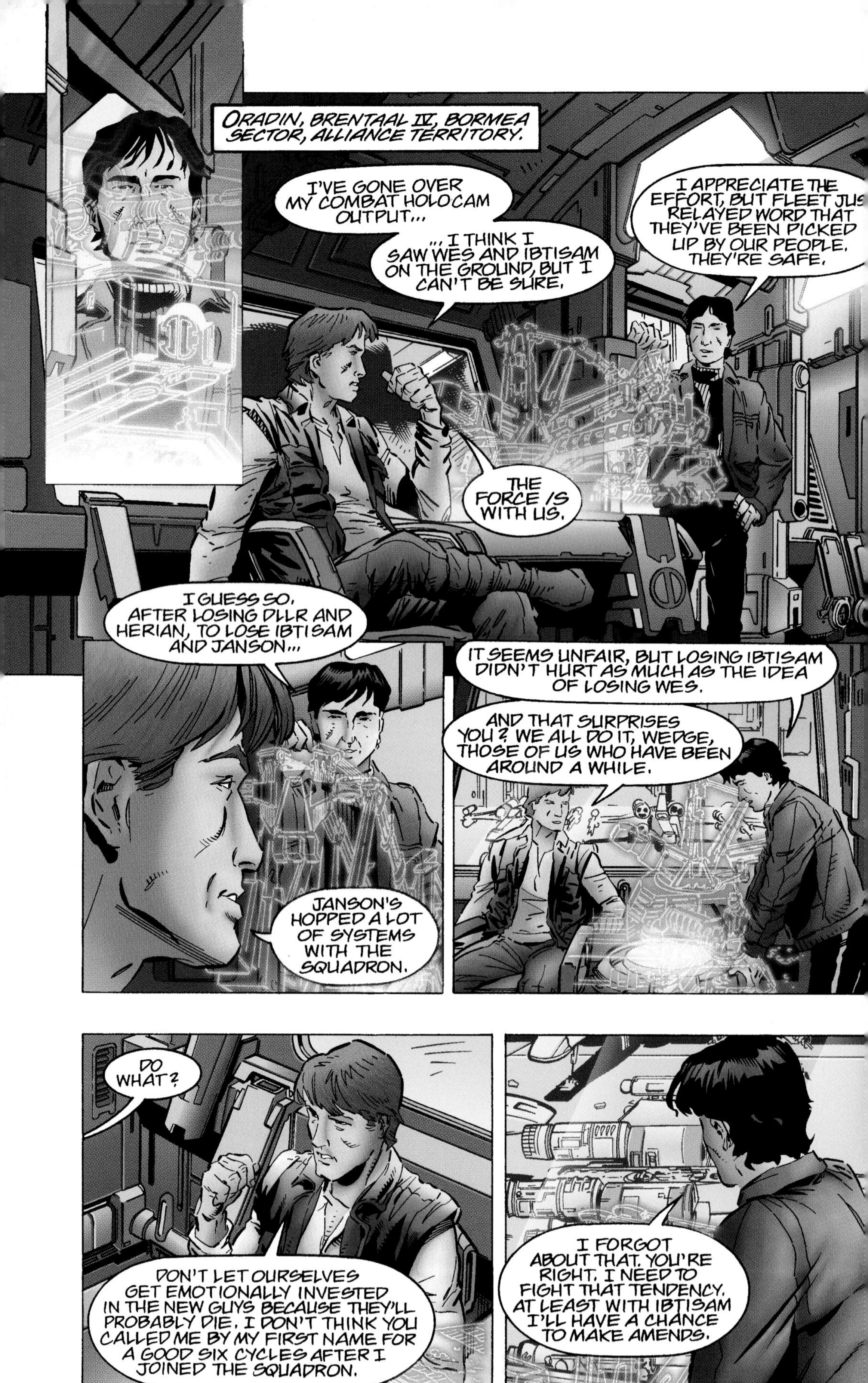
ORADIN, BRENTAAL IV, BORMEA SECTOR, ALLIANCE TERRITORY.
I'VE GONE OVER MY COMBAT HOLOCAM OUTPUT...
...I THINK I SAW WES AND IBTISAM ON THE GROUND, BUT I CAN'T BE SURE.
I APPRECIATE THE EFFORT, BUT FLEET JUS RELAYED WORD THAT THEY'VE BEEN PICKED UP BY OUR PEOPLE. THEY'RE SAFE.
THE FORCE IS WITH US.
I GUESS SO. AFTER LOSING DLLR AND HERIAN, TO LOSE IBTISAM AND JANSON...
JANSON'S HOPPED A LOT OF SYSTEMS WITH THE SQUADRON.
IT SEEMS UNFAIR, BUT LOSING IBTISAM DIDN'T HURT AS MUCH AS THE IDEA OF LOSING WES.
AND THAT SURPRISES YOU? WE ALL DO IT, WEDGE, THOSE OF US WHO HAVE BEEN AROUND A WHILE.
DO WHAT?
DON'T LET OURSELVES GET EMOTIONALLY INVESTED IN THE NEW GUYS BECAUSE THEY'LL PROBABLY DIE. I DON'T THINK YOU CALLED ME BY MY FIRST NAME FOR A GOOD SIX CYCLES AFTER I JOINED THE SQUADRON.
I FORGOT ABOUT THAT. YOU'RE RIGHT. I NEED TO FIGHT THAT TENDENCY. AT LEAST WITH IBTISAM I'LL HAVE A CHANCE TO MAKE AMENDS.

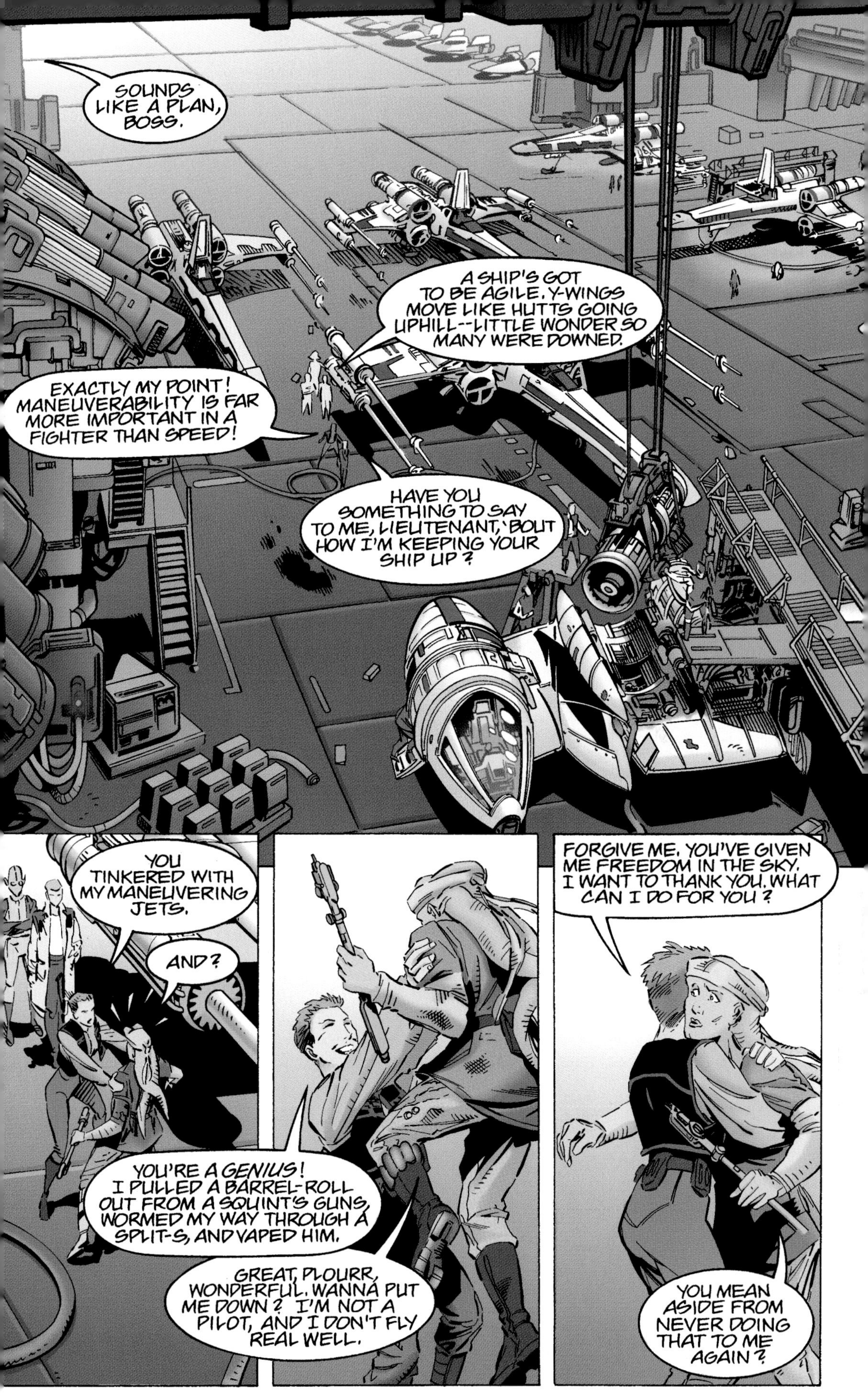
SOUNDS LIKE A PLAN, BOSS.
A SHIP'S GOT TO BE AGILE. Y-WINGS MOVE LIKE HUTTS GOING UPHILL--LITTLE WONDER SO MANY WERE DOWNED.
EXACTLY MY POINT! MANEUVERABILITY IS FAR MORE IMPORTANT IN A FIGHTER THAN SPEED!
HAVE YOU SOMETHING TO SAY TO ME, LIEUTENANT, 'BOUT HOW I'M KEEPING YOUR SHIP UP?
YOU TINKERED WITH MY MANEUVERING JETS.
AND?
YOU'RE A GENIUS! I PULLED A BARREL-ROLL OUT FROM A SQUINT'S GUNS, WORMED MY WAY THROUGH A SPLIT-S, AND VAPED HIM.
GREAT, PLOURR, WONDERFUL. WANNA PUT ME DOWN? I'M NOT A PILOT, AND I DON'T FLY REAL WELL.
FORGIVE ME. YOU'VE GIVEN ME FREEDOM IN THE SKY. I WANT TO THANK YOU. WHAT CAN I DO FOR YOU?
YOU MEAN ASIDE FROM NEVER DOING THAT TO ME AGAIN?

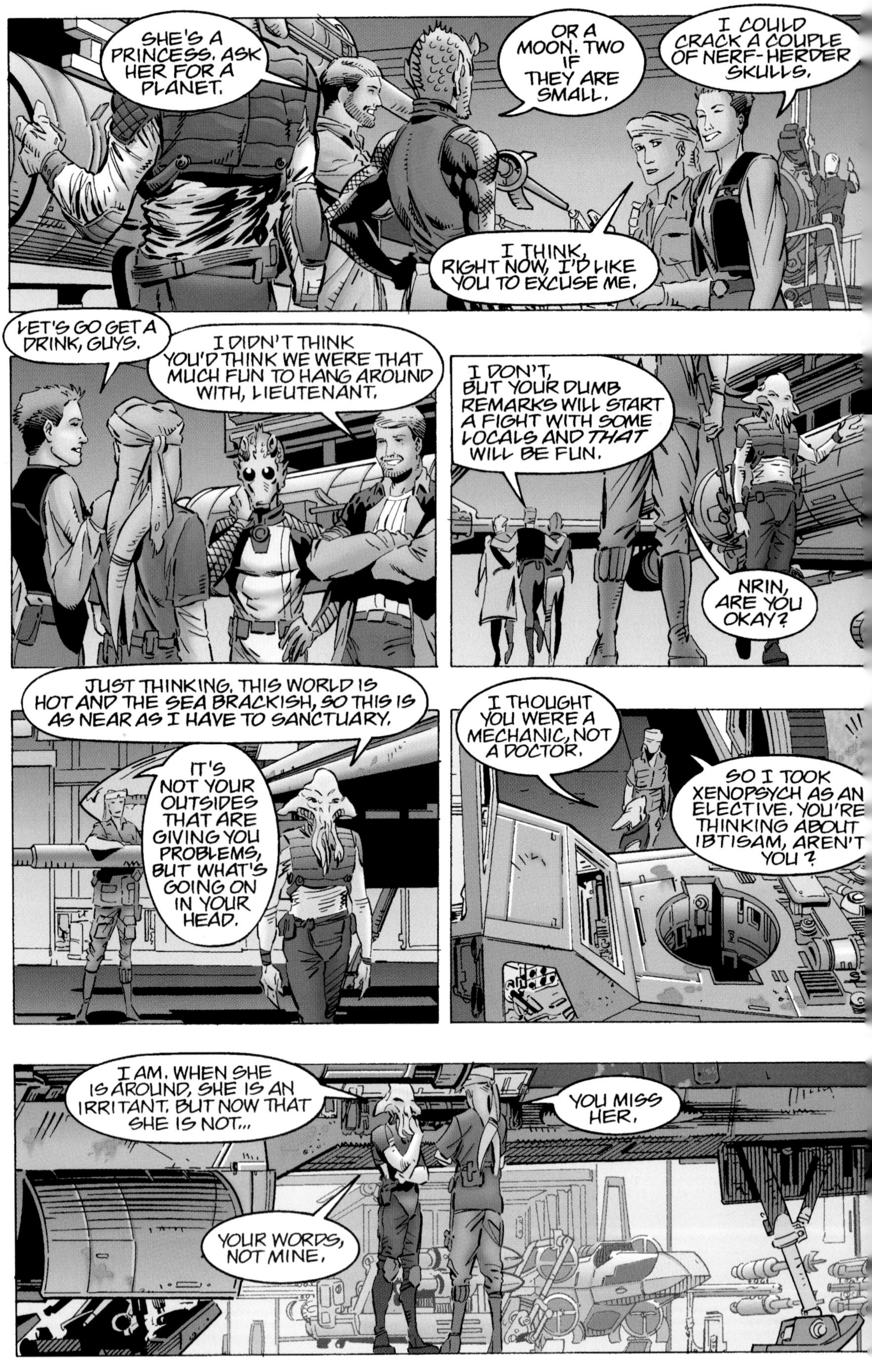
SHE'S A PRINCESS. ASK HER FOR A PLANET.
OR A MOON. TWO IF THEY ARE SMALL.
I COULD CRACK A COUPLE OF NERF-HERDER SKULLS.
I THINK, RIGHT NOW, I'D LIKE YOU TO EXCUSE ME.
LET'S GO GET A DRINK, GUYS.
I DIDN'T THINK YOU'D THINK WE WERE THAT MUCH FUN TO HANG AROUND WITH, LIEUTENANT.
I DON'T, BUT YOUR DUMB REMARKS WILL START A FIGHT WITH SOME LOCALS AND THAT WILL BE FUN.
NRIN, ARE YOU OKAY?
JUST THINKING. THIS WORLD IS HOT AND THE SEA BRACKISH, SO THIS IS AS NEAR AS I HAVE TO SANCTUARY.
IT'S NOT YOUR OUTSIDES THAT ARE GIVING YOU PROBLEMS, BUT WHAT'S GOING ON IN YOUR HEAD.
I THOUGHT YOU WERE A MECHANIC, NOT A DOCTOR.
SO I TOOK XENOPSYCH AS AN ELECTIVE. YOU'RE THINKING ABOUT IBTISAM, AREN'T YOU?
I AM. WHEN SHE IS AROUND, SHE IS AN IRRITANT, BUT NOW THAT SHE IS NOT...
YOU MISS HER.
YOUR WORDS, NOT MINE.

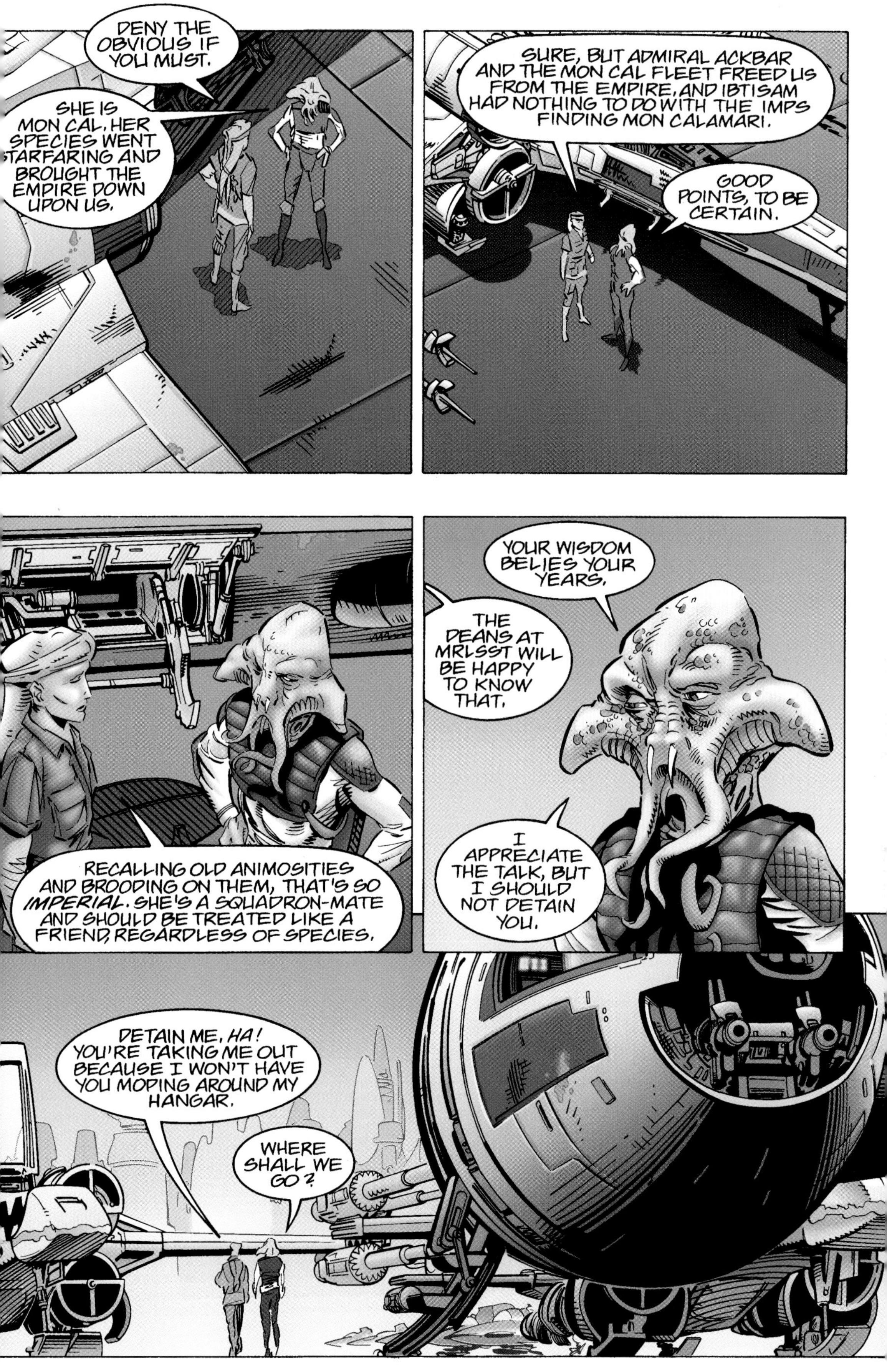
DENY THE OBVIOUS IF YOU MUST.
SHE IS MON CAL. HER SPECIES WENT STARFARING AND BROUGHT THE EMPIRE DOWN UPON US.
SURE, BUT ADMIRAL ACKBAR AND THE MON CAL FLEET FREED US FROM THE EMPIRE, AND IBTISAM HAD NOTHING TO DO WITH THE IMPS FINDING MON CALAMARI.
GOOD POINTS, TO BE CERTAIN.
RECALLING OLD ANIMOSITIES AND BROODING ON THEM, THAT'S SO *IMPERIAL*. SHE'S A SQUADRON-MATE AND SHOULD BE TREATED LIKE A FRIEND, REGARDLESS OF SPECIES.
YOUR WISDOM BELIES YOUR YEARS.
THE DEANS AT MRLSST WILL BE HAPPY TO KNOW THAT.
I APPRECIATE THE TALK, BUT I SHOULD NOT DETAIN YOU.
DETAIN ME, *HA*! YOU'RE TAKING ME OUT BECAUSE I WON'T HAVE YOU MOPING AROUND MY HANGAR.
WHERE SHALL WE GO?

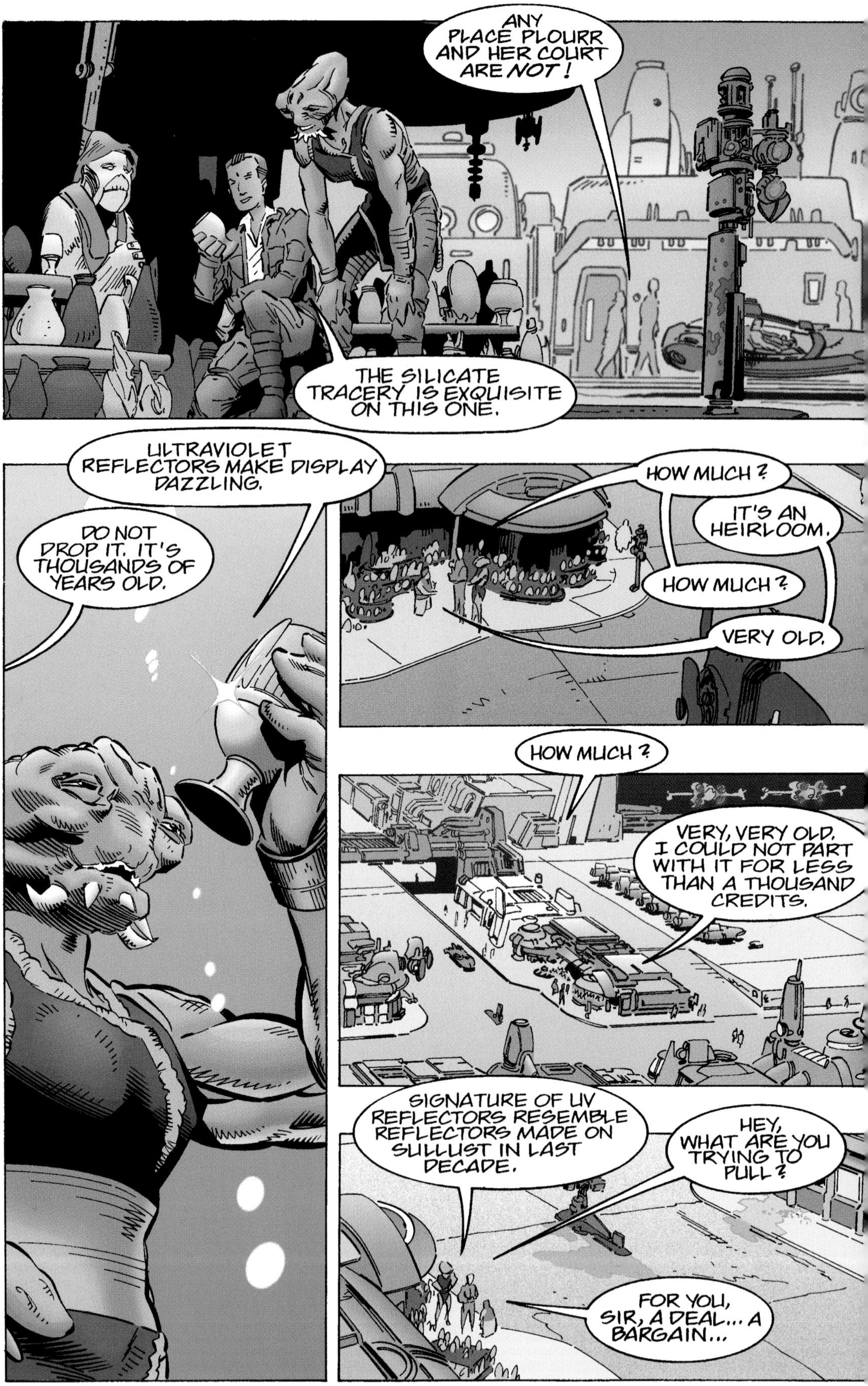
ANY PLACE PLOURR AND HER COURT ARE *NOT*!
THE SILICATE TRACERY IS EXQUISITE ON THIS ONE.
ULTRAVIOLET REFLECTORS MAKE DISPLAY DAZZLING.
DO NOT DROP IT. IT'S THOUSANDS OF YEARS OLD.
HOW MUCH?
IT'S AN HEIRLOOM.
HOW MUCH?
VERY OLD.
HOW MUCH?
VERY, VERY OLD. I COULD NOT PART WITH IT FOR LESS THAN A THOUSAND CREDITS.
SIGNATURE OF UV REFLECTORS RESEMBLE REFLECTORS MADE ON SULLUST IN LAST DECADE.
HEY, WHAT ARE YOU TRYING TO PULL?
FOR YOU, SIR, A DEAL... A BARGAIN...

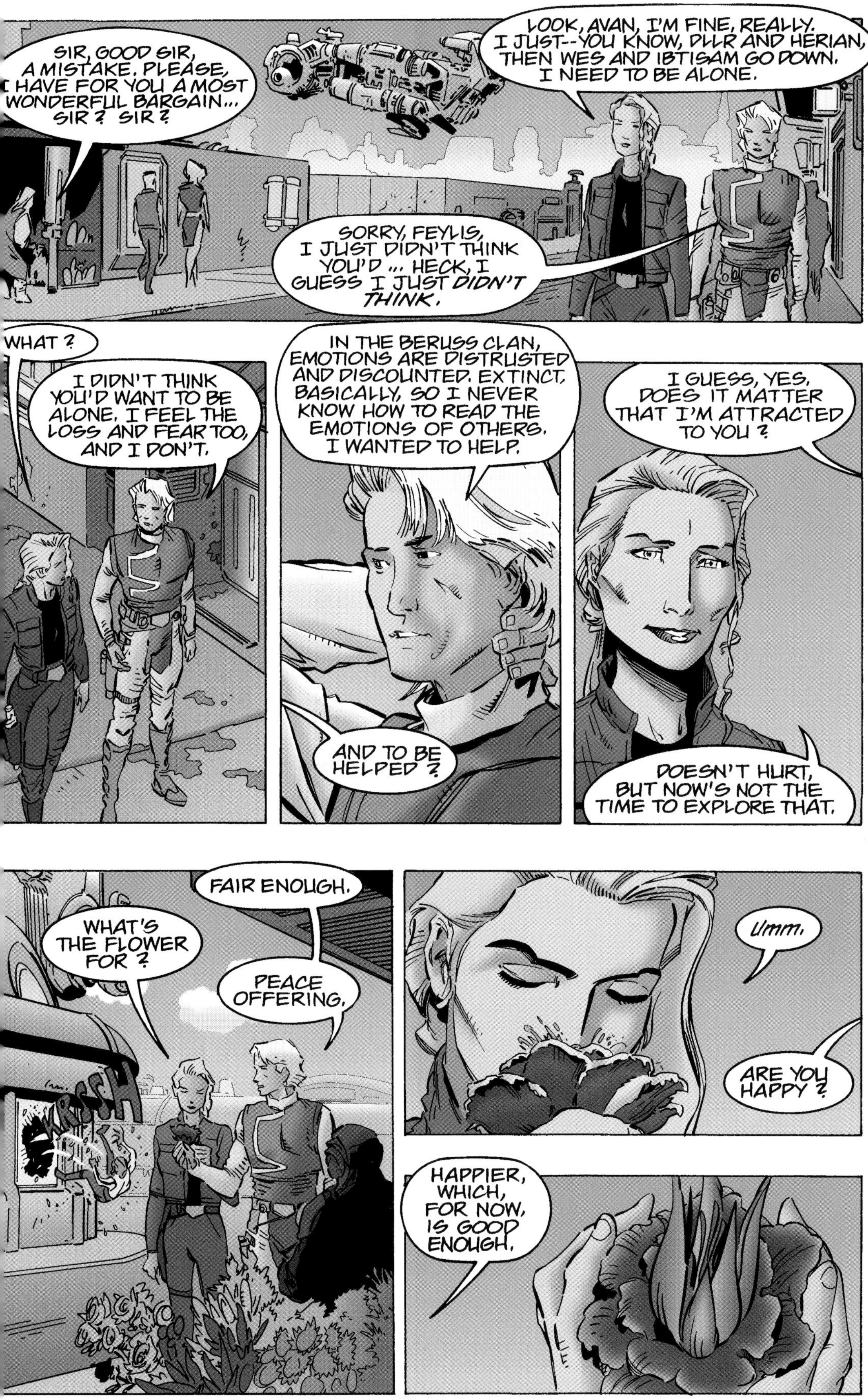
SIR, GOOD SIR, A MISTAKE. PLEASE, I HAVE FOR YOU A MOST WONDERFUL BARGAIN... SIR? SIR?
LOOK, AVAN, I'M FINE, REALLY. I JUST--YOU KNOW, DLLR AND HERIAN, THEN WES AND IBTISAM GO DOWN. I NEED TO BE ALONE.
SORRY, FEYLIS, I JUST DIDN'T THINK YOU'D ... HECK, I GUESS I JUST *DIDN'T THINK*.
WHAT?
I DIDN'T THINK YOU'D WANT TO BE ALONE. I FEEL THE LOSS AND FEAR TOO, AND I DON'T.
IN THE BERUSS CLAN, EMOTIONS ARE DISTRUSTED AND DISCOUNTED. EXTINCT, BASICALLY, SO I NEVER KNOW HOW TO READ THE EMOTIONS OF OTHERS. I WANTED TO HELP.
AND TO BE HELPED?
I GUESS, YES. DOES IT MATTER THAT I'M ATTRACTED TO YOU?
DOESN'T HURT, BUT NOW'S NOT THE TIME TO EXPLORE THAT.
WHAT'S THE FLOWER FOR?
FAIR ENOUGH.
PEACE OFFERING.
KRASH
Umm.
ARE YOU HAPPY?
HAPPIER, WHICH, FOR NOW, IS GOOD ENOUGH.

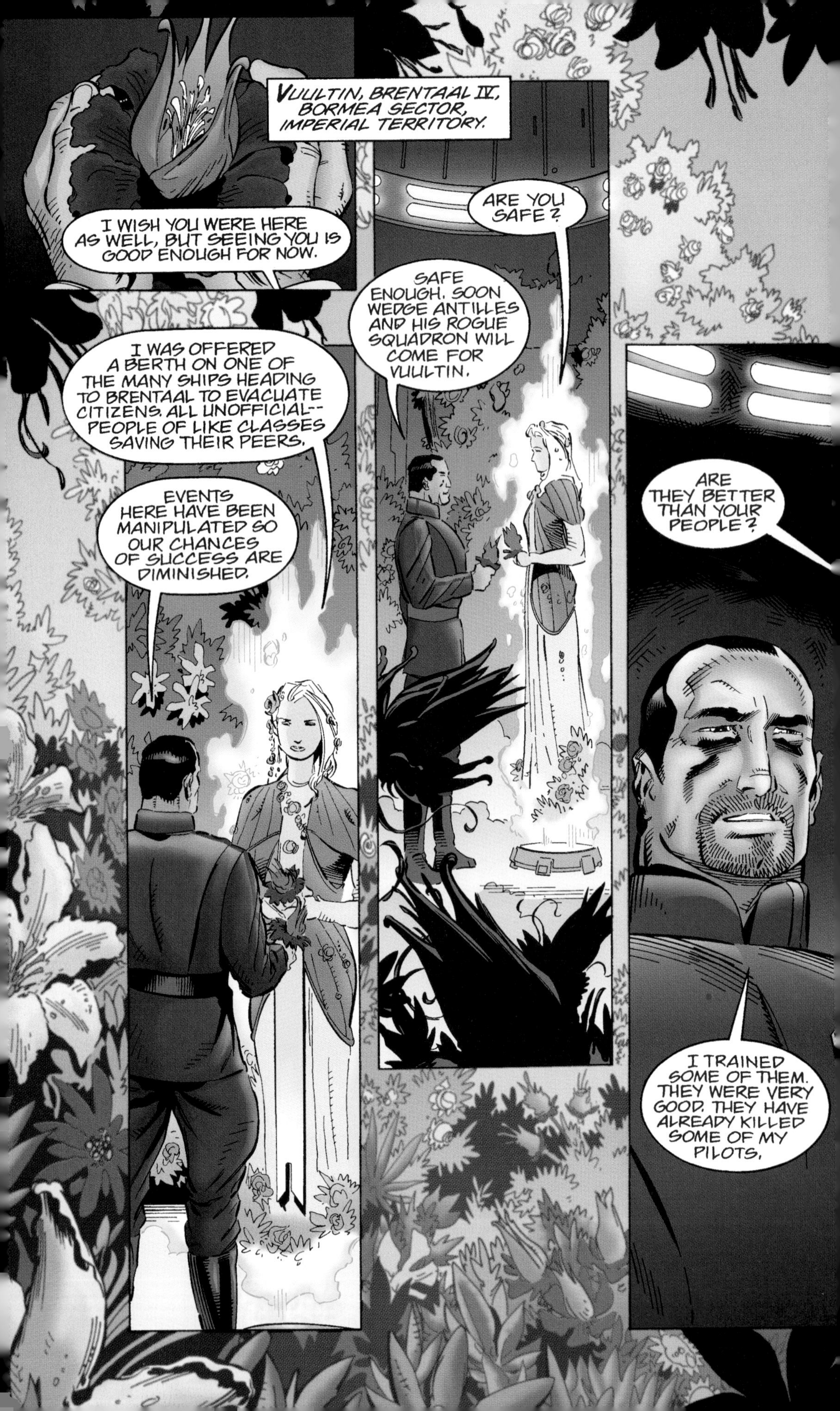
I WISH YOU WERE HERE AS WELL, BUT SEEING YOU IS GOOD ENOUGH FOR NOW.
VUULTIN, BRENTAAL IV, BORMEA SECTOR, IMPERIAL TERRITORY.
ARE YOU SAFE?
SAFE ENOUGH. SOON WEDGE ANTILLES AND HIS ROGUE SQUADRON WILL COME FOR VUULTIN.
I WAS OFFERED A BERTH ON ONE OF THE MANY SHIPS HEADING TO BRENTAAL TO EVACUATE CITIZENS. ALL UNOFFICIAL-- PEOPLE OF LIKE CLASSES SAVING THEIR PEERS.
EVENTS HERE HAVE BEEN MANIPULATED SO OUR CHANCES OF SUCCESS ARE DIMINISHED.
ARE THEY BETTER THAN YOUR PEOPLE?
I TRAINED SOME OF THEM. THEY WERE VERY GOOD. THEY HAVE ALREADY KILLED SOME OF MY PILOTS.

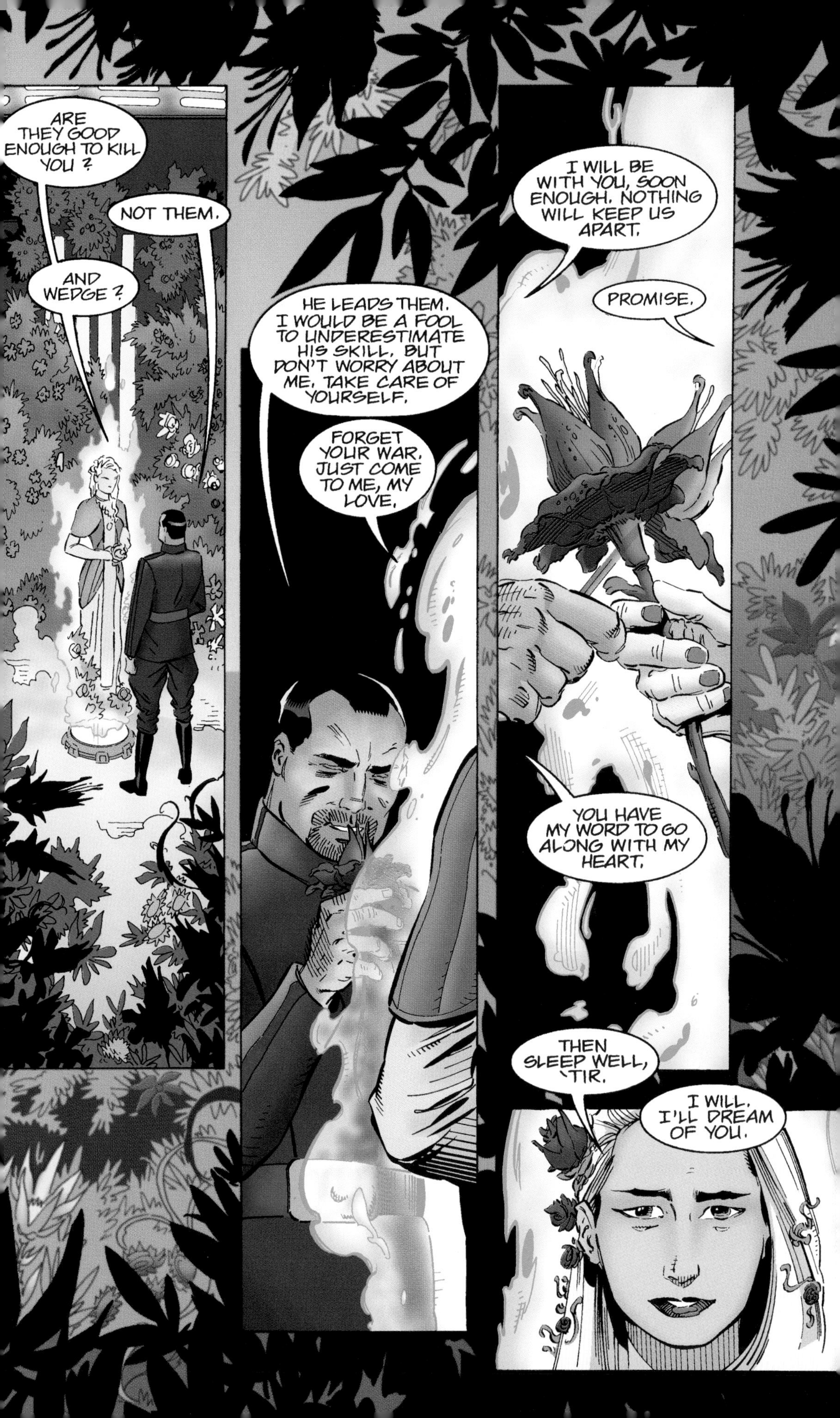
ARE THEY GOOD ENOUGH TO KILL YOU?
NOT THEM.
AND WEDGE?
HE LEADS THEM. I WOULD BE A FOOL TO UNDERESTIMATE HIS SKILL, BUT DON'T WORRY ABOUT ME. TAKE CARE OF YOURSELF.
FORGET YOUR WAR, JUST COME TO ME, MY LOVE.
I WILL BE WITH YOU, SOON ENOUGH. NOTHING WILL KEEP US APART.
PROMISE.
YOU HAVE MY WORD TO GO ALONG WITH MY HEART.
THEN SLEEP WELL, 'TIR.
I WILL. I'LL DREAM OF YOU.

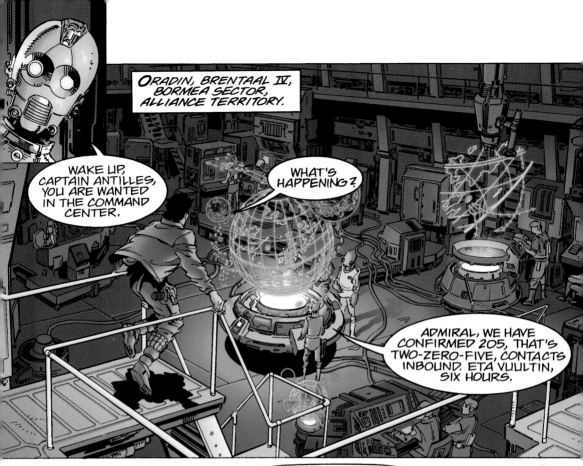

ORADIN, BRENTAAL IV, BORMEA SECTOR, ALLIANCE TERRITORY.

WAKE UP, CAPTAIN ANTILLES, YOU ARE WANTED IN THE COMMAND CENTER.

WHAT'S HAPPENING?

ADMIRAL, WE HAVE CONFIRMED 205, THAT'S TWO-ZERO-FIVE, CONTACTS INBOUND. ETA VUULTIN, SIX HOURS.

THIS ARMADA HAS ARRIVED FROM CORUSCANT TO EVACUATE THE PLANET'S WEALTHIER CITIZENS, WE SUSPECT, SHUTTLES ARE ALREADY LIFTING FROM VUULTIN TO MEET THEM.

GREAT. WE'LL GET VUULTIN WITHOUT BLOODSHED.

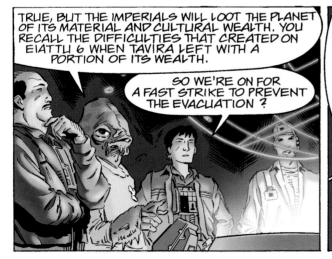

TRUE, BUT THE IMPERIALS WILL LOOT THE PLANET OF ITS MATERIAL AND CULTURAL WEALTH. YOU RECALL THE DIFFICULTIES THAT CREATED ON EIATTU 6 WHEN TAVIRA LEFT WITH A PORTION OF ITS WEALTH.

SO WE'RE ON FOR A FAST STRIKE TO PREVENT THE EVACUATION?

SOME FOLKS IN THE PROVISIONAL COUNCIL THINK BRENTAAL'S ELITE WILL BUY FREEDOM WITH ALLEGIANCE, WHICH WOULD BE VERY USEFUL IN TOPPLING PESTAGE.

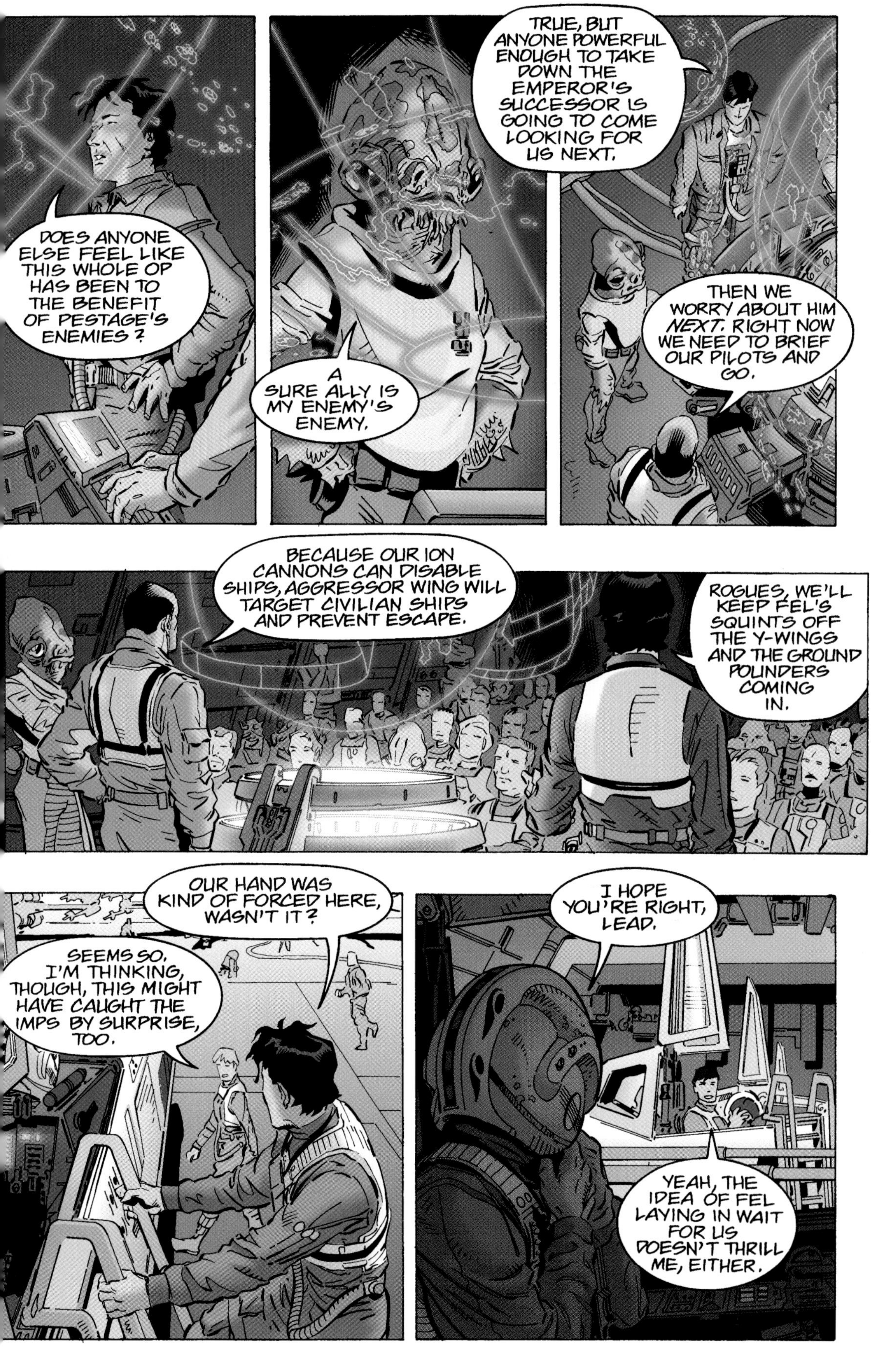
DOES ANYONE ELSE FEEL LIKE THIS WHOLE OP HAS BEEN TO THE BENEFIT OF PESTAGE'S ENEMIES?
A SURE ALLY IS MY ENEMY'S ENEMY.
TRUE, BUT ANYONE POWERFUL ENOUGH TO TAKE DOWN THE EMPEROR'S SUCCESSOR IS GOING TO COME LOOKING FOR US NEXT.
THEN WE WORRY ABOUT HIM *NEXT*. RIGHT NOW WE NEED TO BRIEF OUR PILOTS AND GO.
BECAUSE OUR ION CANNONS CAN DISABLE SHIPS, AGGRESSOR WING WILL TARGET CIVILIAN SHIPS AND PREVENT ESCAPE.
ROGUES, WE'LL KEEP FEL'S SQUINTS OFF THE Y-WINGS AND THE GROUND POUNDERS COMING IN.
OUR HAND WAS KIND OF FORCED HERE, WASN'T IT?
SEEMS SO. I'M THINKING, THOUGH, THIS MIGHT HAVE CAUGHT THE IMPS BY SURPRISE, TOO.
I HOPE YOU'RE RIGHT, LEAD.
YEAH, THE IDEA OF FEL LAYING IN WAIT FOR US DOESN'T THRILL ME, EITHER.

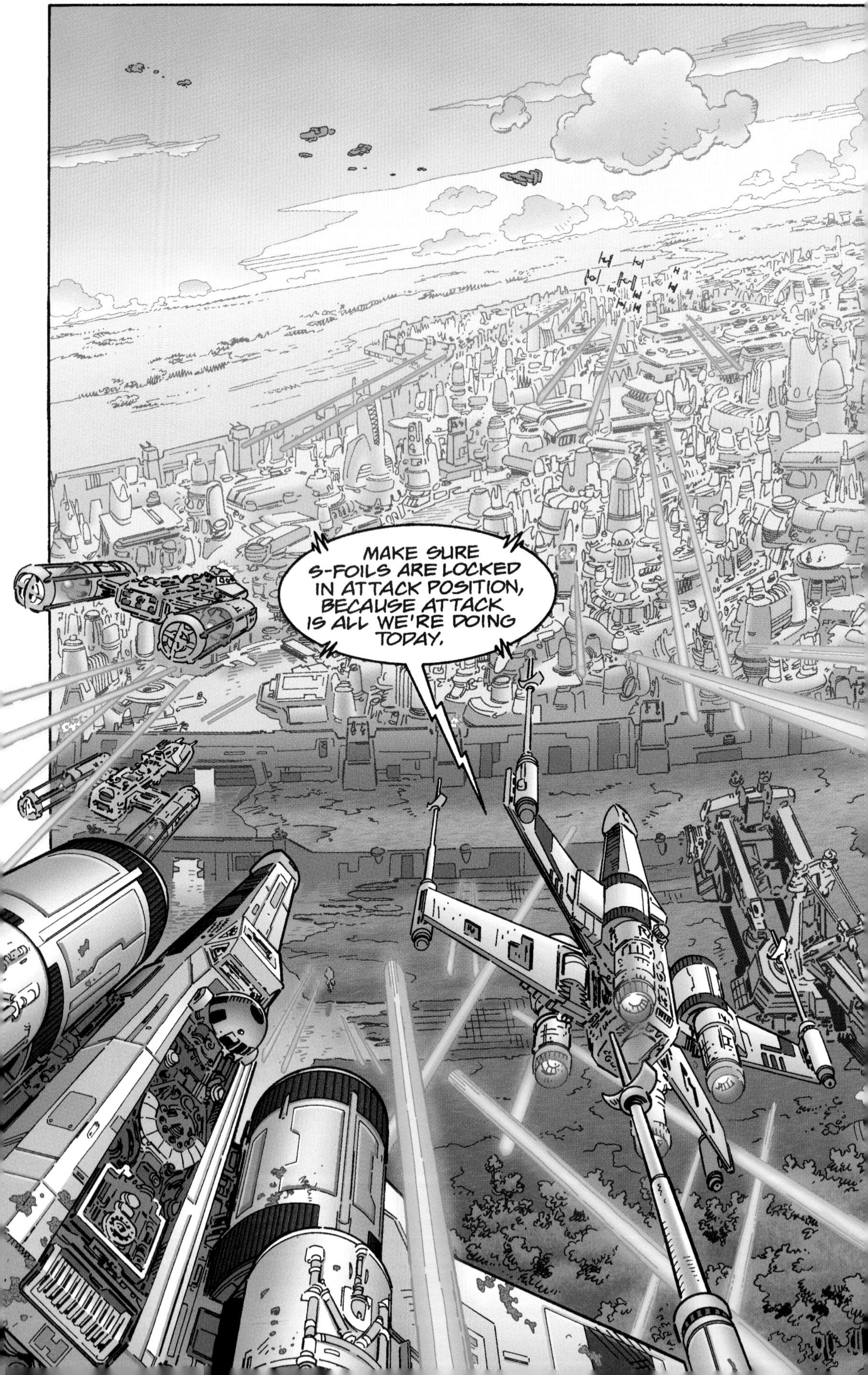
MAKE SURE S-FOILS ARE LOCKED IN ATTACK POSITION, BECAUSE ATTACK IS ALL WE'RE DOING TODAY.

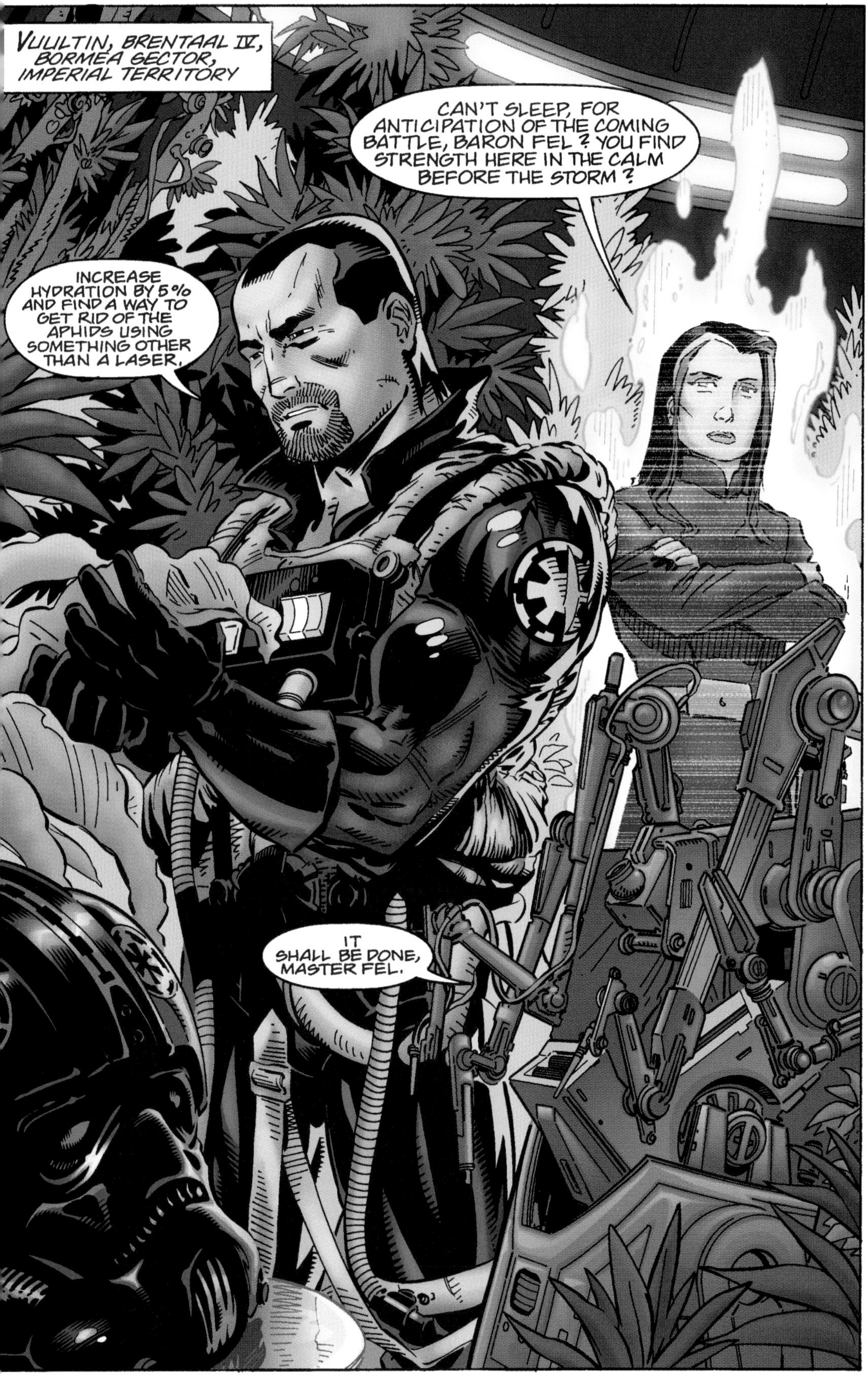
VUULTIN, BRENTAAL IV, BORMEA SECTOR, IMPERIAL TERRITORY
CAN'T SLEEP, FOR ANTICIPATION OF THE COMING BATTLE, BARON FEL? YOU FIND STRENGTH HERE IN THE CALM BEFORE THE STORM?
INCREASE HYDRATION BY 5% AND FIND A WAY TO GET RID OF THE APHIDS USING SOMETHING OTHER THAN A LASER.
IT SHALL BE DONE, MASTER FEL.

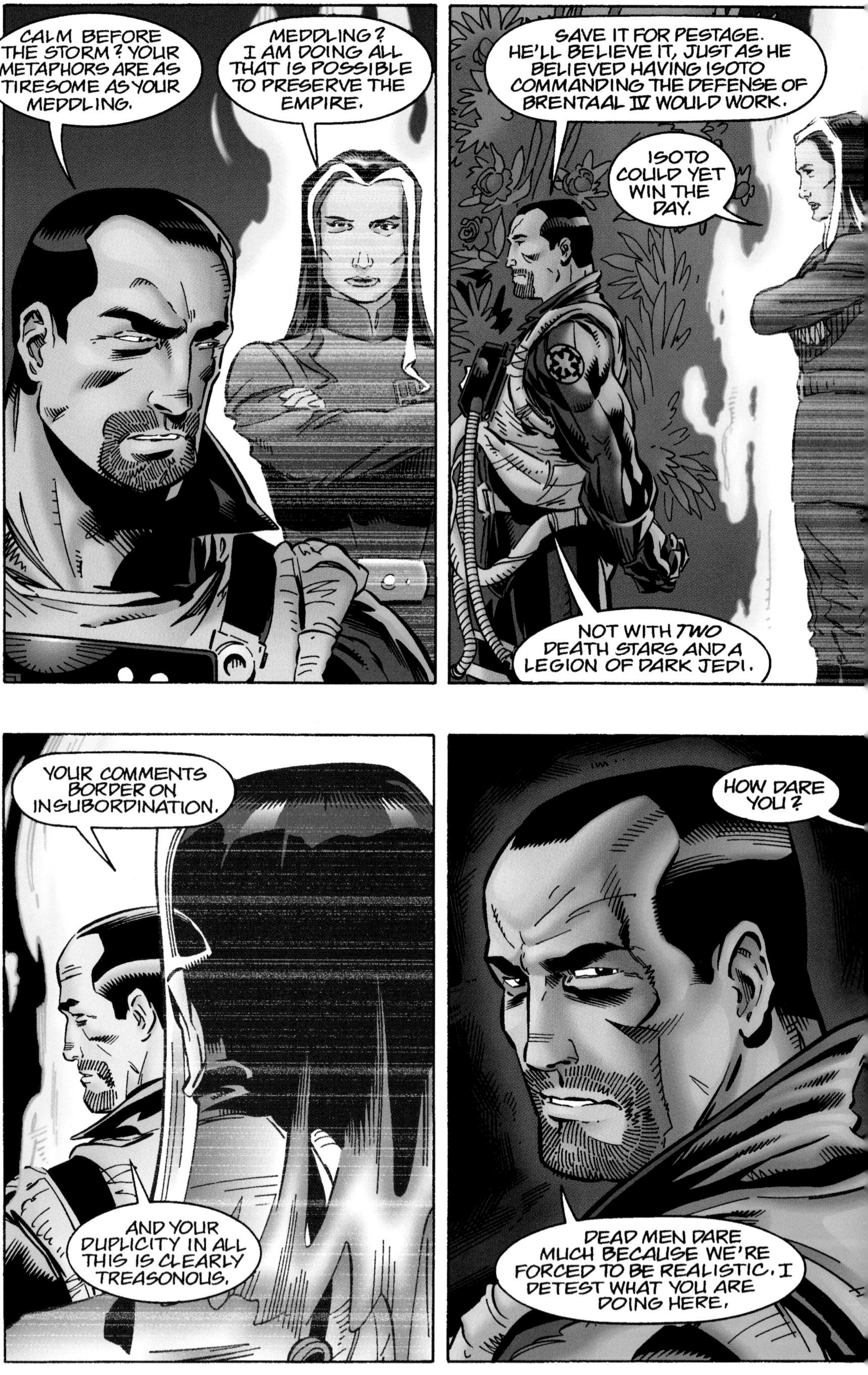
CALM BEFORE THE STORM? YOUR METAPHORS ARE AS TIRESOME AS YOUR MEDDLING.
MEDDLING? I AM DOING ALL THAT IS POSSIBLE TO PRESERVE THE EMPIRE.
SAVE IT FOR PESTAGE. HE'LL BELIEVE IT, JUST AS HE BELIEVED HAVING ISOTO COMMANDING THE DEFENSE OF BRENTAAL IV WOULD WORK.
ISOTO COULD YET WIN THE DAY.
NOT WITH *TWO* DEATH STARS AND A LEGION OF DARK JEDI.
YOUR COMMENTS BORDER ON INSUBORDINATION.
AND YOUR DUPLICITY IN ALL THIS IS CLEARLY TREASONOUS.
HOW DARE YOU?
DEAD MEN DARE MUCH BECAUSE WE'RE FORCED TO BE REALISTIC. I DETEST WHAT YOU ARE DOING HERE.

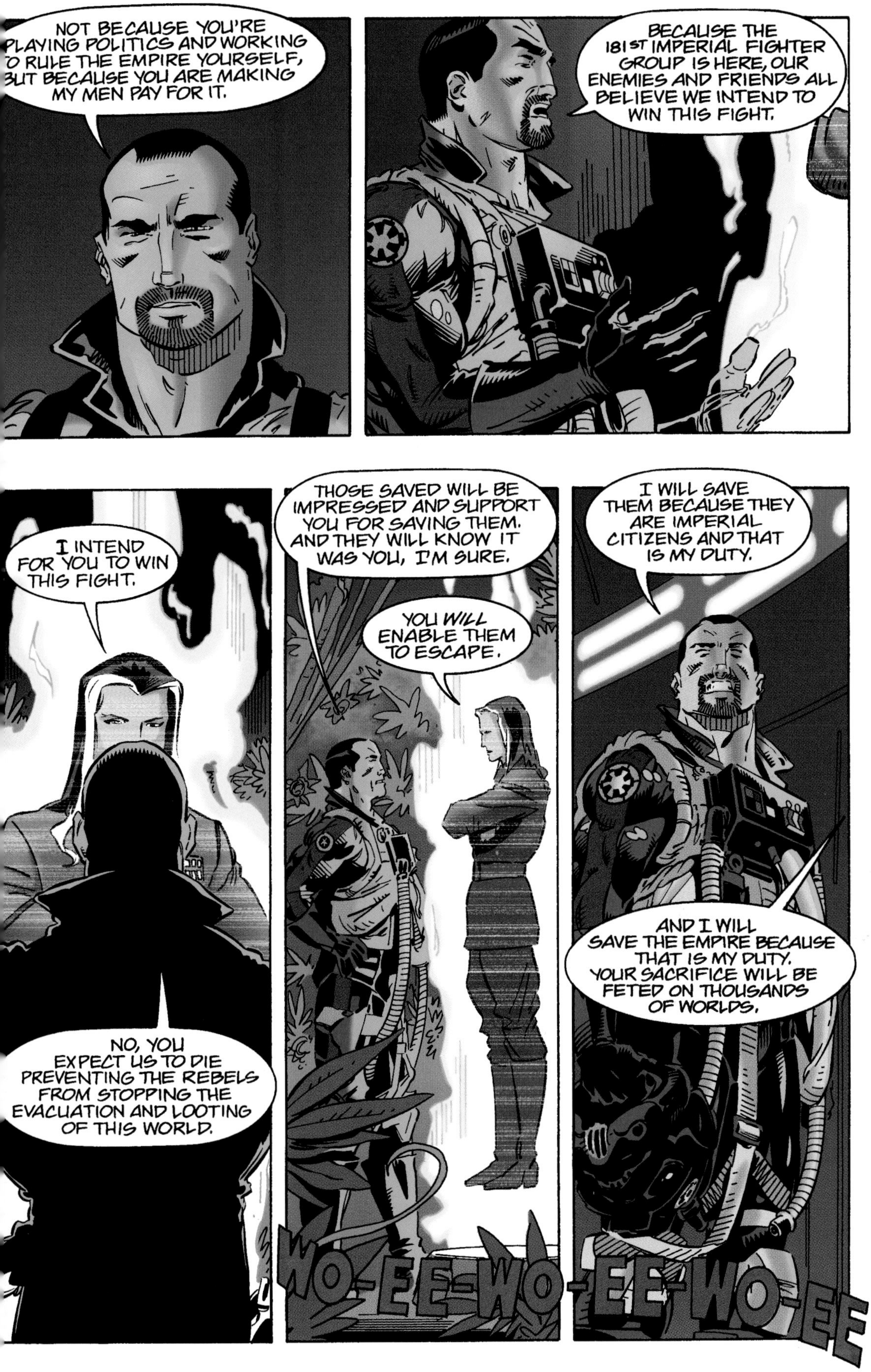
NOT BECAUSE YOU'RE PLAYING POLITICS AND WORKING TO RULE THE EMPIRE YOURSELF, BUT BECAUSE YOU ARE MAKING MY MEN PAY FOR IT.
BECAUSE THE 181ST IMPERIAL FIGHTER GROUP IS HERE, OUR ENEMIES AND FRIENDS ALL BELIEVE WE INTEND TO WIN THIS FIGHT.
I INTEND FOR YOU TO WIN THIS FIGHT.
NO, YOU EXPECT US TO DIE PREVENTING THE REBELS FROM STOPPING THE EVACUATION AND LOOTING OF THIS WORLD.
THOSE SAVED WILL BE IMPRESSED AND SUPPORT YOU FOR SAVING THEM. AND THEY WILL KNOW IT WAS YOU, I'M SURE.
YOU WILL ENABLE THEM TO ESCAPE.
I WILL SAVE THEM BECAUSE THEY ARE IMPERIAL CITIZENS AND THAT IS MY DUTY.
AND I WILL SAVE THE EMPIRE BECAUSE THAT IS MY DUTY. YOUR SACRIFICE WILL BE FETED ON THOUSANDS OF WORLDS.
WO-EE-WO-EE-WO-EE

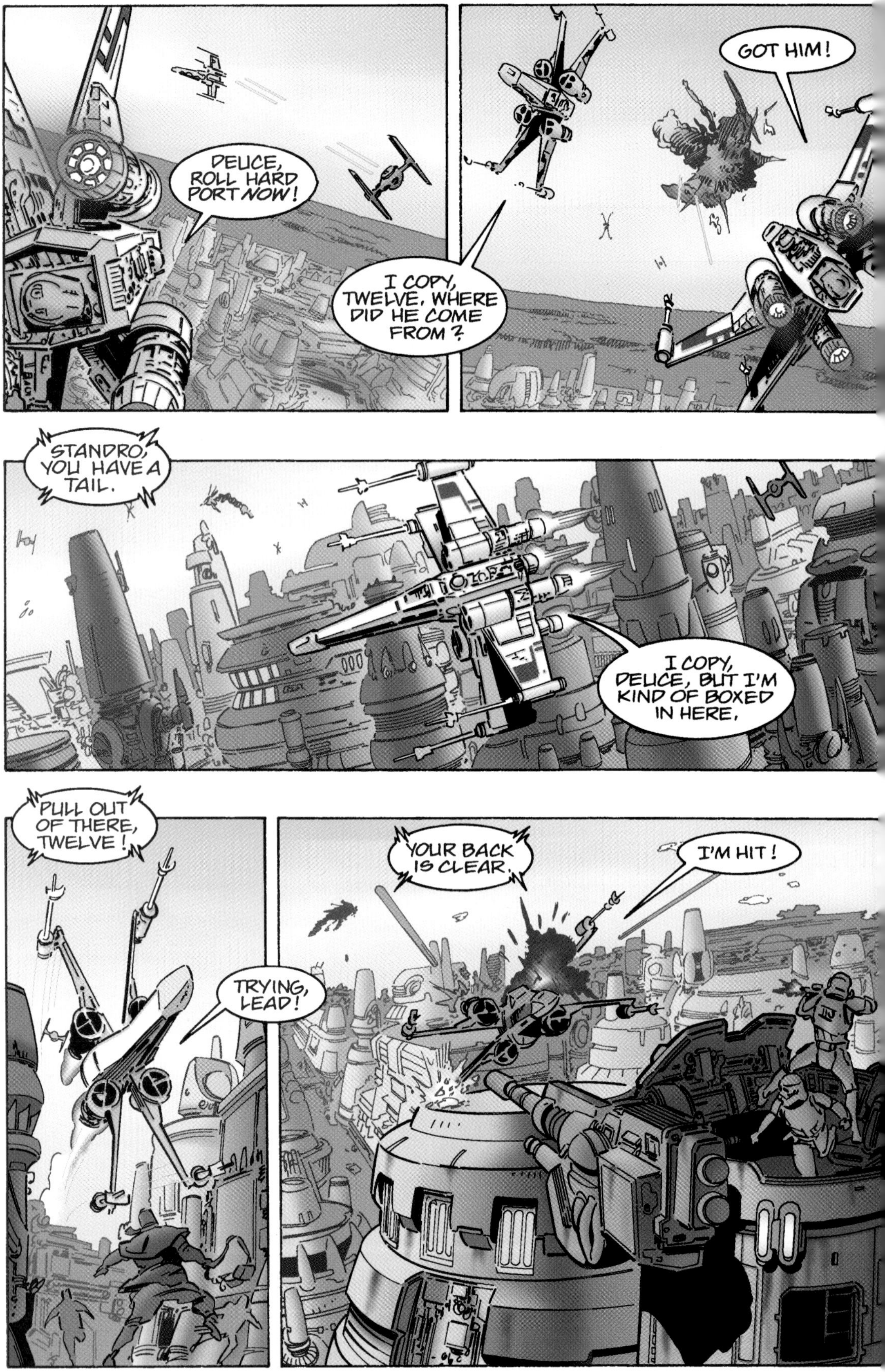
DELICE, ROLL HARD PORT NOW!
I COPY, TWELVE, WHERE DID HE COME FROM?
GOT HIM!
STANDRO, YOU HAVE A TAIL.
I COPY, DELICE, BUT I'M KIND OF BOXED IN HERE.
PULL OUT OF THERE, TWELVE!
TRYING, LEAD!
YOUR BACK IS CLEAR.
I'M HIT!

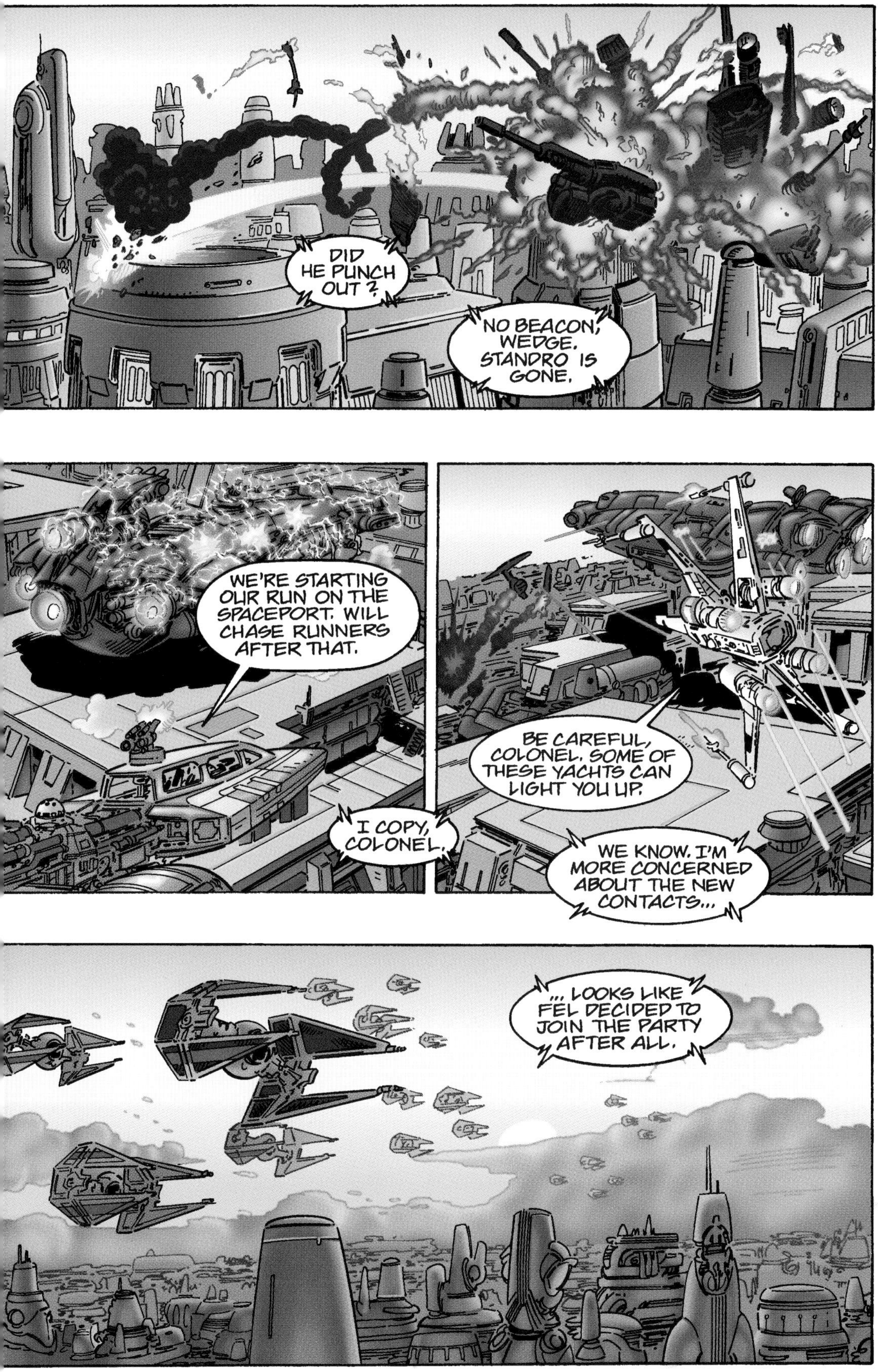
DID HE PUNCH OUT?
NO BEACON, WEDGE. STANDRO IS GONE.
WE'RE STARTING OUR RUN ON THE SPACEPORT. WILL CHASE RUNNERS AFTER THAT.
I COPY, COLONEL.
BE CAREFUL, COLONEL. SOME OF THESE YACHTS CAN LIGHT YOU UP.
WE KNOW. I'M MORE CONCERNED ABOUT THE NEW CONTACTS...
... LOOKS LIKE FEL DECIDED TO JOIN THE PARTY AFTER ALL.

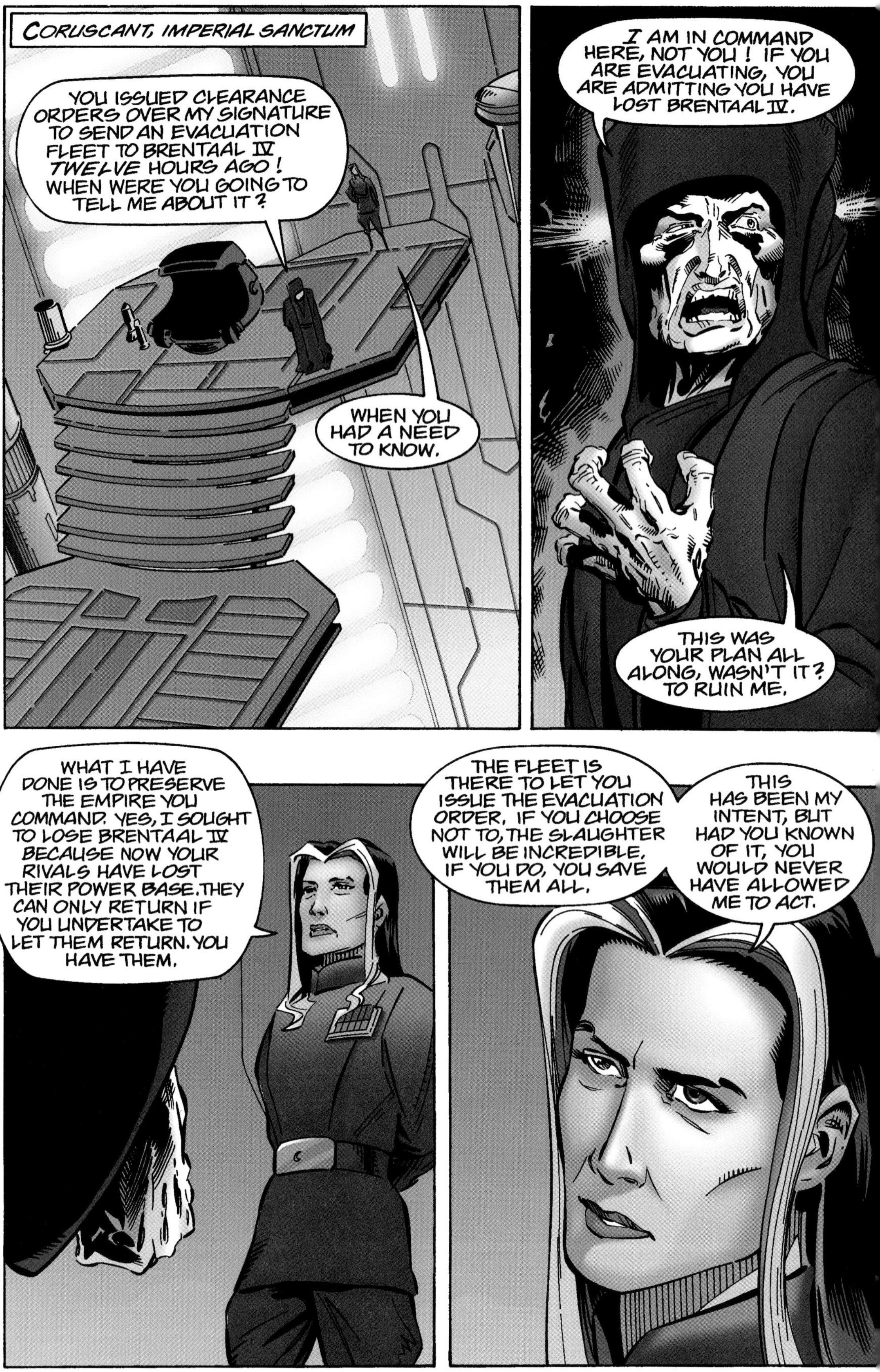
CORUSCANT, IMPERIAL SANCTUM
YOU ISSUED CLEARANCE ORDERS OVER MY SIGNATURE TO SEND AN EVACUATION FLEET TO BRENTAAL IV TWELVE HOURS AGO! WHEN WERE YOU GOING TO TELL ME ABOUT IT?
WHEN YOU HAD A NEED TO KNOW.
I AM IN COMMAND HERE, NOT YOU! IF YOU ARE EVACUATING, YOU ARE ADMITTING YOU HAVE LOST BRENTAAL IV.
THIS WAS YOUR PLAN ALL ALONG, WASN'T IT? TO RUIN ME.
WHAT I HAVE DONE IS TO PRESERVE THE EMPIRE YOU COMMAND. YES, I SOUGHT TO LOSE BRENTAAL IV BECAUSE NOW YOUR RIVALS HAVE LOST THEIR POWER BASE. THEY CAN ONLY RETURN IF YOU UNDERTAKE TO LET THEM RETURN. YOU HAVE THEM.
THE FLEET IS THERE TO LET YOU ISSUE THE EVACUATION ORDER. IF YOU CHOOSE NOT TO, THE SLAUGHTER WILL BE INCREDIBLE. IF YOU DO, YOU SAVE THEM ALL.
THIS HAS BEEN MY INTENT, BUT HAD YOU KNOWN OF IT, YOU WOULD NEVER HAVE ALLOWED ME TO ACT.

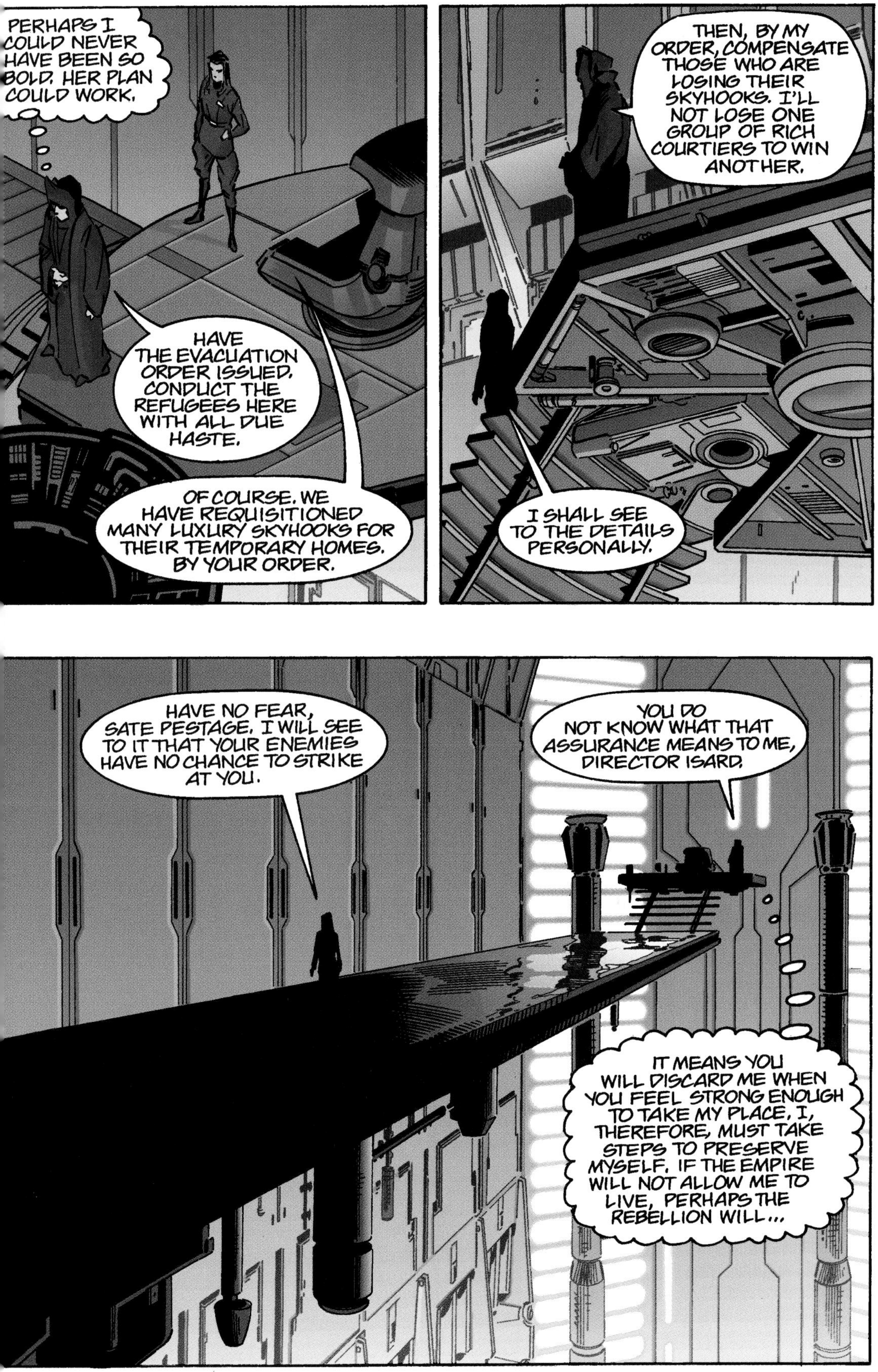
PERHAPS I COULD NEVER HAVE BEEN SO BOLD. HER PLAN COULD WORK.
HAVE THE EVACUATION ORDER ISSUED. CONDUCT THE REFUGEES HERE WITH ALL DUE HASTE.
OF COURSE. WE HAVE REQUISITIONED MANY LUXURY SKYHOOKS FOR THEIR TEMPORARY HOMES. BY YOUR ORDER.
THEN, BY MY ORDER, COMPENSATE THOSE WHO ARE LOSING THEIR SKYHOOKS. I'LL NOT LOSE ONE GROUP OF RICH COURTIERS TO WIN ANOTHER.
I SHALL SEE TO THE DETAILS PERSONALLY.
HAVE NO FEAR, SATE PESTAGE. I WILL SEE TO IT THAT YOUR ENEMIES HAVE NO CHANCE TO STRIKE AT YOU.
YOU DO NOT KNOW WHAT THAT ASSURANCE MEANS TO ME, DIRECTOR ISARD.
IT MEANS YOU WILL DISCARD ME WHEN YOU FEEL STRONG ENOUGH TO TAKE MY PLACE. I, THEREFORE, MUST TAKE STEPS TO PRESERVE MYSELF. IF THE EMPIRE WILL NOT ALLOW ME TO LIVE, PERHAPS THE REBELLION WILL...

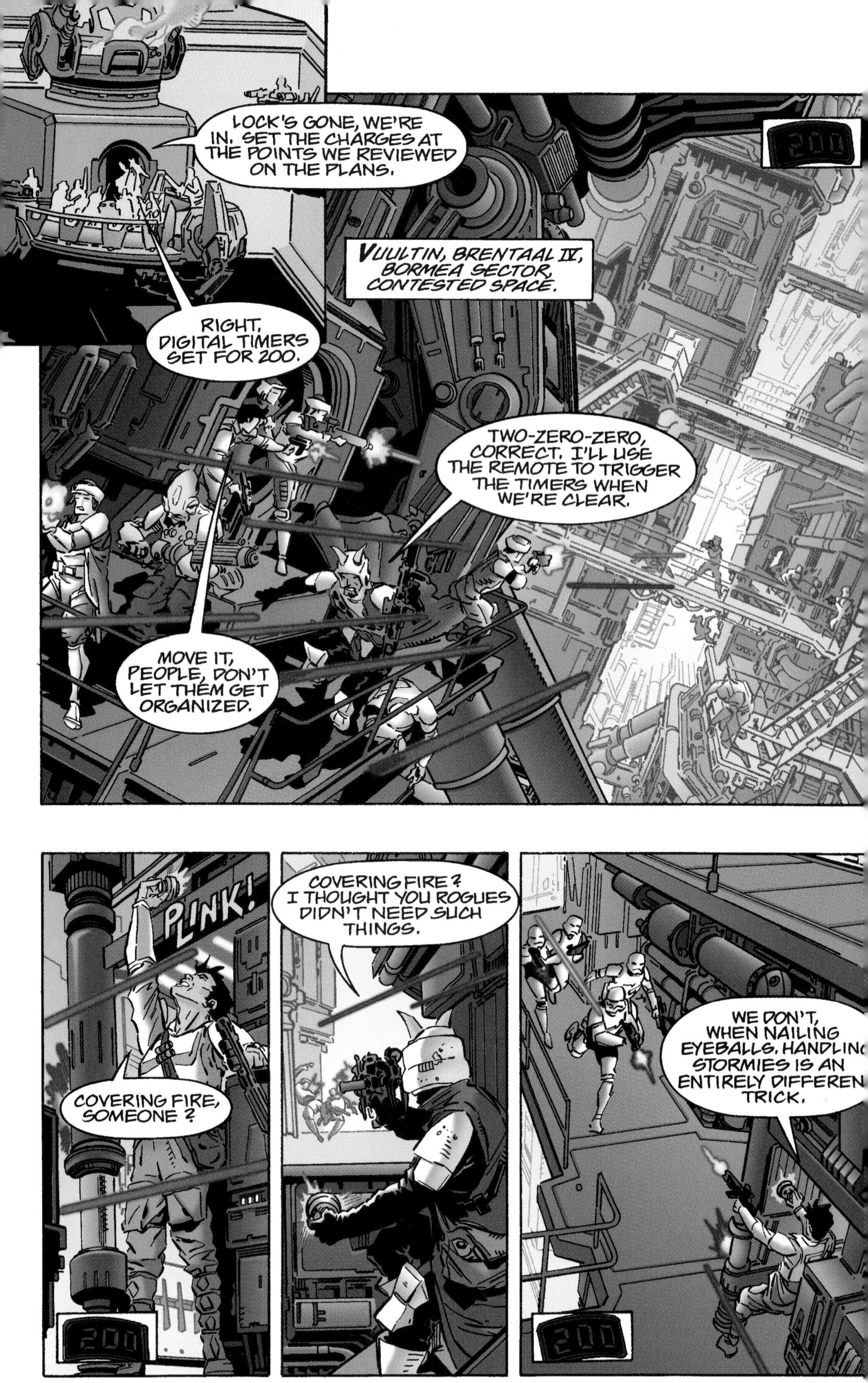
LOCK'S GONE, WE'RE IN. SET THE CHARGES AT THE POINTS WE REVIEWED ON THE PLANS.
200
VUULTIN, BRENTAAL IV, BORMEA SECTOR, CONTESTED SPACE.
RIGHT, DIGITAL TIMERS SET FOR 200.
TWO-ZERO-ZERO, CORRECT. I'LL USE THE REMOTE TO TRIGGER THE TIMERS WHEN WE'RE CLEAR.
MOVE IT, PEOPLE, DON'T LET THEM GET ORGANIZED.
PLINK!
COVERING FIRE, SOMEONE?
200
COVERING FIRE? I THOUGHT YOU ROGUES DIDN'T NEED SUCH THINGS.
WE DON'T, WHEN NAILING EYEBALLS. HANDLIN STORMIES IS AN ENTIRELY DIFFEREN TRICK.
200

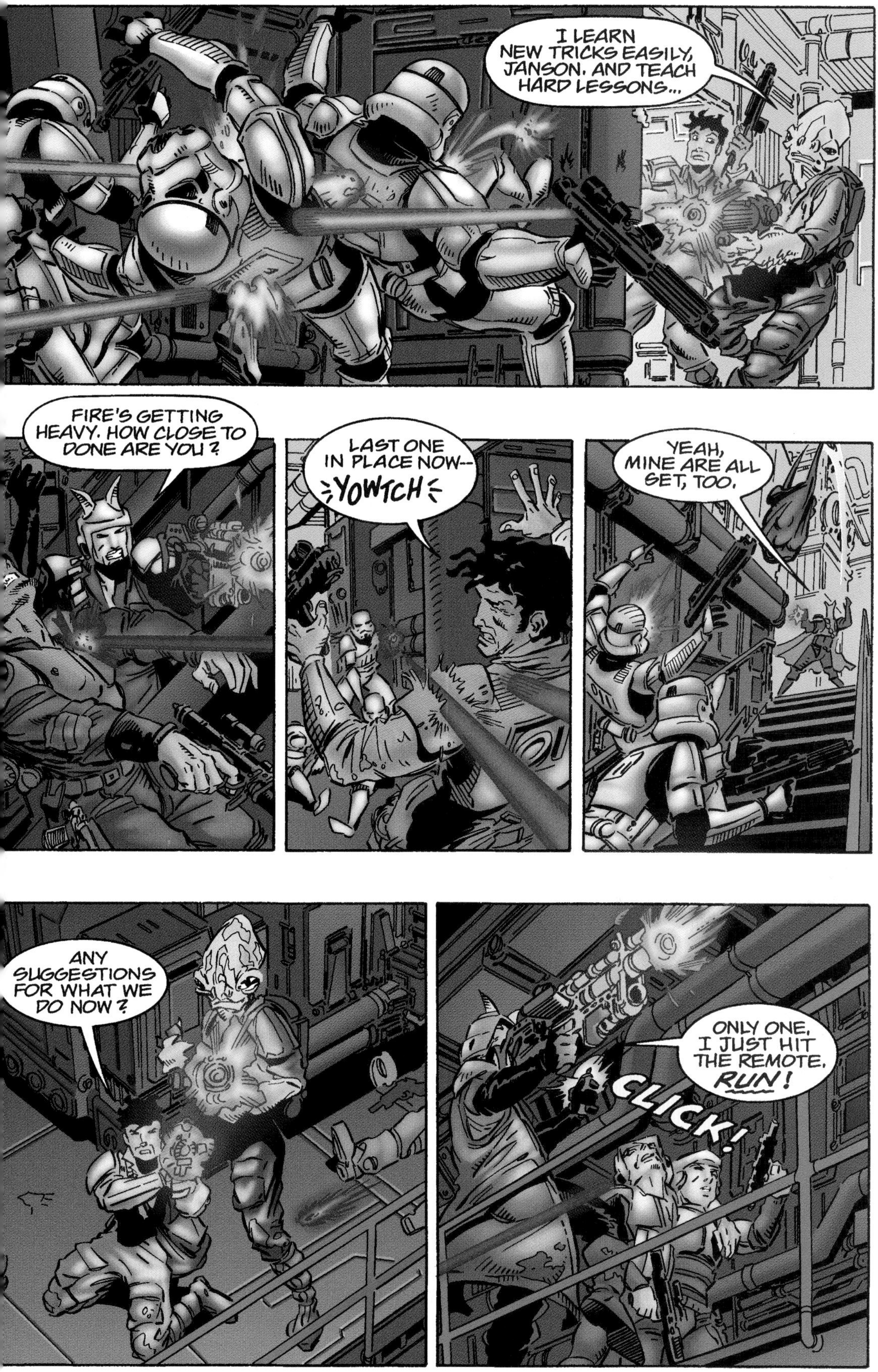
I LEARN NEW TRICKS EASILY, JANSON. AND TEACH HARD LESSONS...
FIRE'S GETTING HEAVY. HOW CLOSE TO DONE ARE YOU?
LAST ONE IN PLACE NOW--
YOWTCH
YEAH, MINE ARE ALL SET, TOO.
ANY SUGGESTIONS FOR WHAT WE DO NOW?
ONLY ONE. I JUST HIT THE REMOTE. RUN!
CLICK!

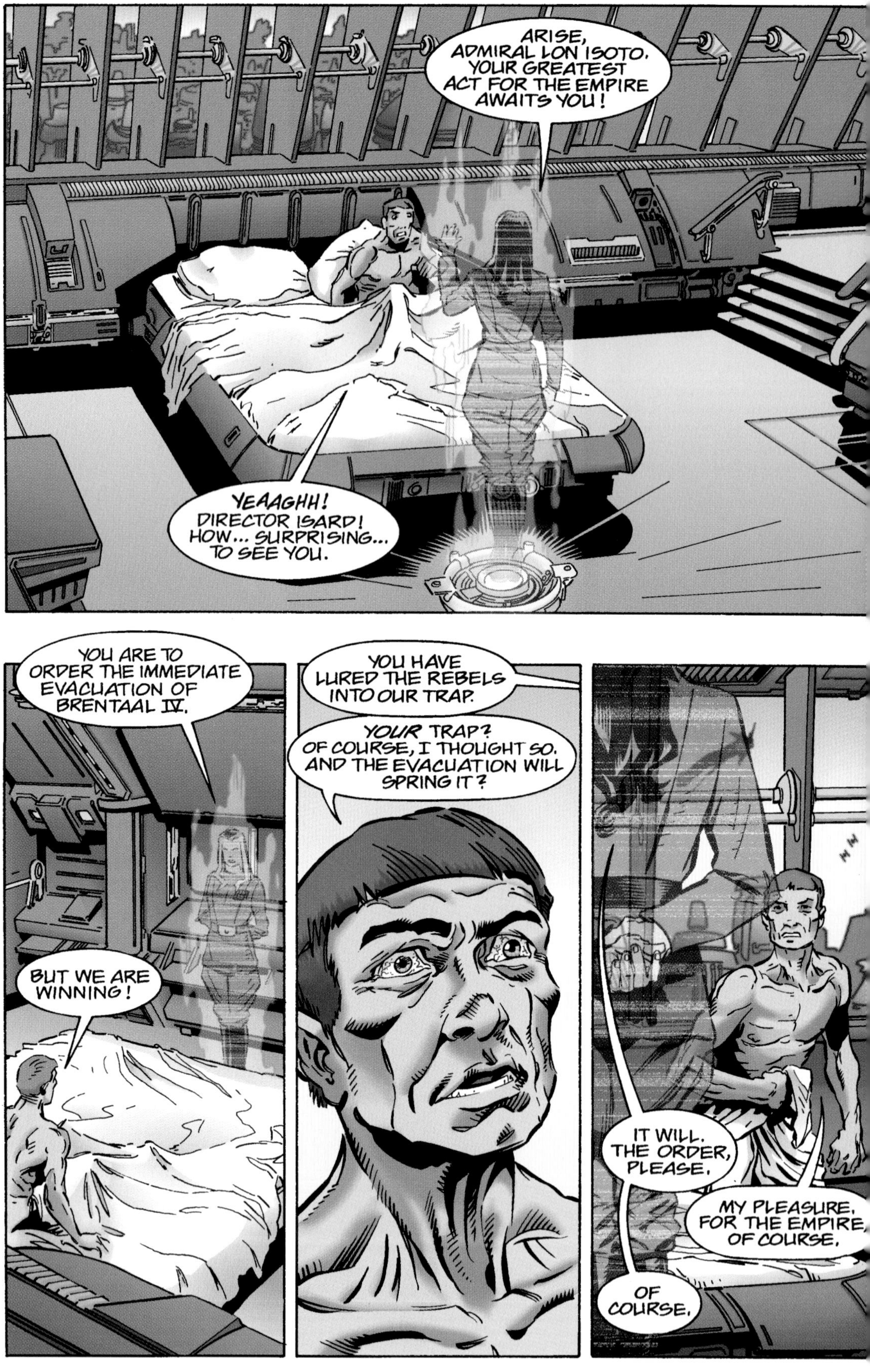
ARISE, ADMIRAL LON ISOTO. YOUR GREATEST ACT FOR THE EMPIRE AWAITS YOU!
YEAAGHH! DIRECTOR ISARD! HOW... SURPRISING... TO SEE YOU.
YOU ARE TO ORDER THE IMMEDIATE EVACUATION OF BRENTAAL IV.
BUT WE ARE WINNING!
YOU HAVE LURED THE REBELS INTO OUR TRAP.
YOUR TRAP? OF COURSE, I THOUGHT SO. AND THE EVACUATION WILL SPRING IT?
IT WILL. THE ORDER, PLEASE.
MY PLEASURE. FOR THE EMPIRE OF COURSE.
OF COURSE.

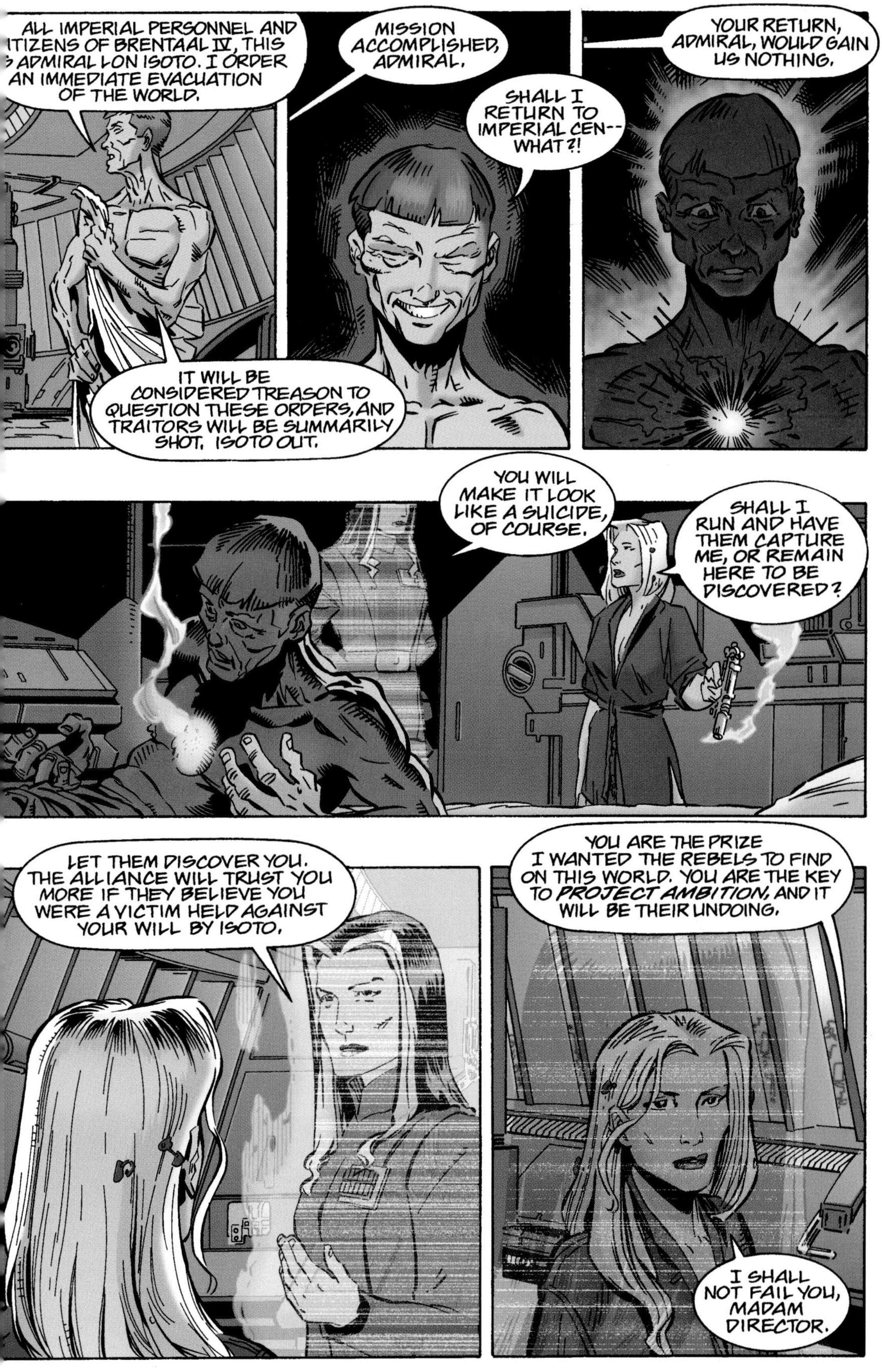
ALL IMPERIAL PERSONNEL AND ITIZENS OF BRENTAAL IV, THIS S ADMIRAL LON ISOTO. I ORDER AN IMMEDIATE EVACUATION OF THE WORLD.
IT WILL BE CONSIDERED TREASON TO QUESTION THESE ORDERS, AND TRAITORS WILL BE SUMMARILY SHOT. ISOTO OUT.
MISSION ACCOMPLISHED, ADMIRAL.
SHALL I RETURN TO IMPERIAL CEN-- WHAT?!
YOUR RETURN, ADMIRAL, WOULD GAIN US NOTHING.
YOU WILL MAKE IT LOOK LIKE A SUICIDE, OF COURSE.
SHALL I RUN AND HAVE THEM CAPTURE ME, OR REMAIN HERE TO BE DISCOVERED?
LET THEM DISCOVER YOU. THE ALLIANCE WILL TRUST YOU MORE IF THEY BELIEVE YOU WERE A VICTIM HELD AGAINST YOUR WILL BY ISOTO.
YOU ARE THE PRIZE I WANTED THE REBELS TO FIND ON THIS WORLD. YOU ARE THE KEY TO *PROJECT AMBITION*, AND IT WILL BE THEIR UNDOING.
I SHALL NOT FAIL YOU, MADAM DIRECTOR.

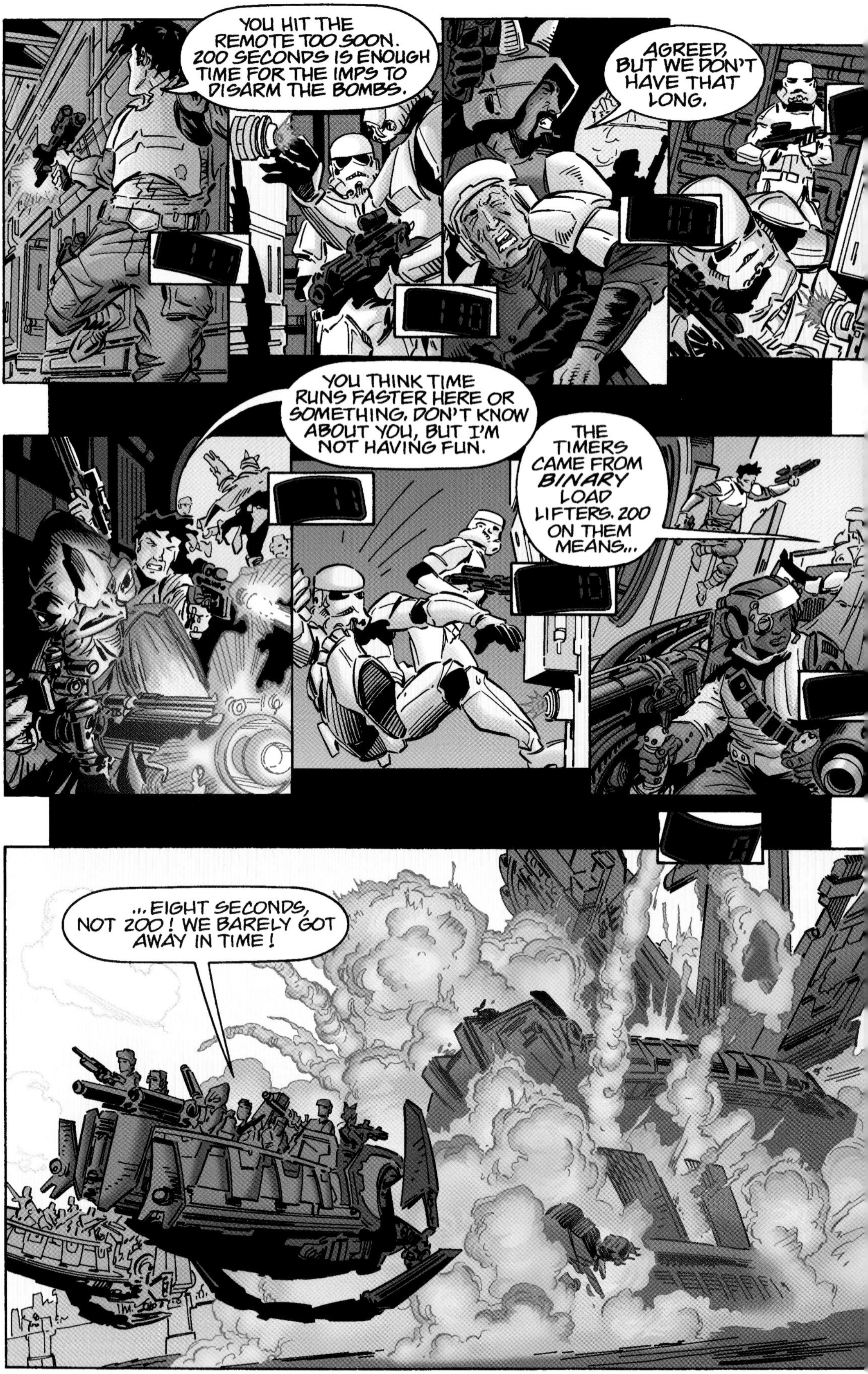
YOU HIT THE REMOTE TOO SOON. 200 SECONDS IS ENOUGH TIME FOR THE IMPS TO DISARM THE BOMBS.
AGREED, BUT WE DON'T HAVE THAT LONG.
YOU THINK TIME RUNS FASTER HERE OR SOMETHING. DON'T KNOW ABOUT YOU, BUT I'M NOT HAVING FUN.
THE TIMERS CAME FROM BINARY LOAD LIFTERS. 200 ON THEM MEANS...
...EIGHT SECONDS, NOT 200! WE BARELY GOT AWAY IN TIME!

LEAD, LOOKS LIKE EVERYTHING ON THE PLANET GOT CLEARED FOR VERTICAL.
NOTED. CONCENTRATE ON THE SQUINTS.
NINE, YOU HAVE A PAIR COMING AFT PORT. BREAK LEFT.
AT THEM, EIGHT?
AS ORDERED.
ONE DOWN. HELP KEYIS, NINE!
ON HIM, BUT TOO LATE! *SITHSPAWN*!

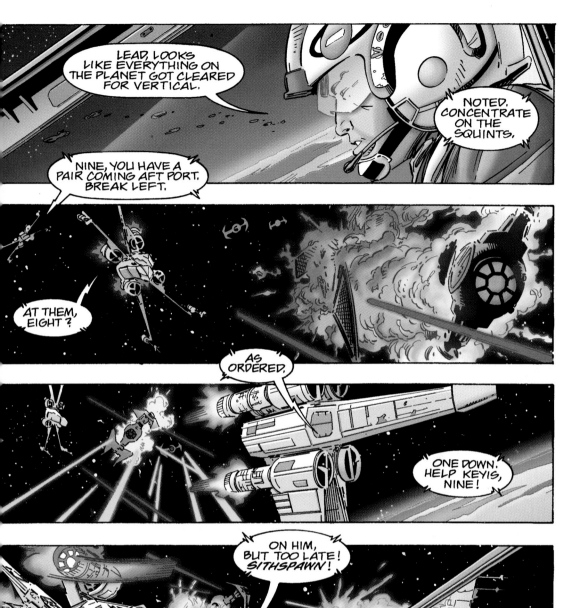

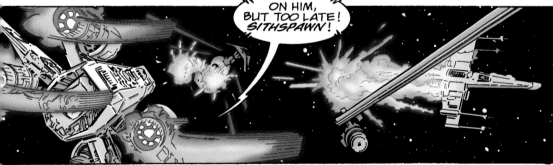

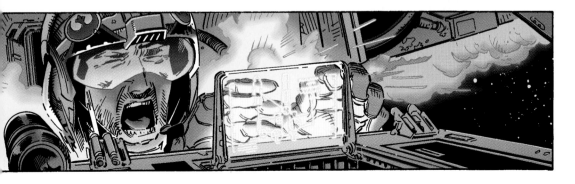

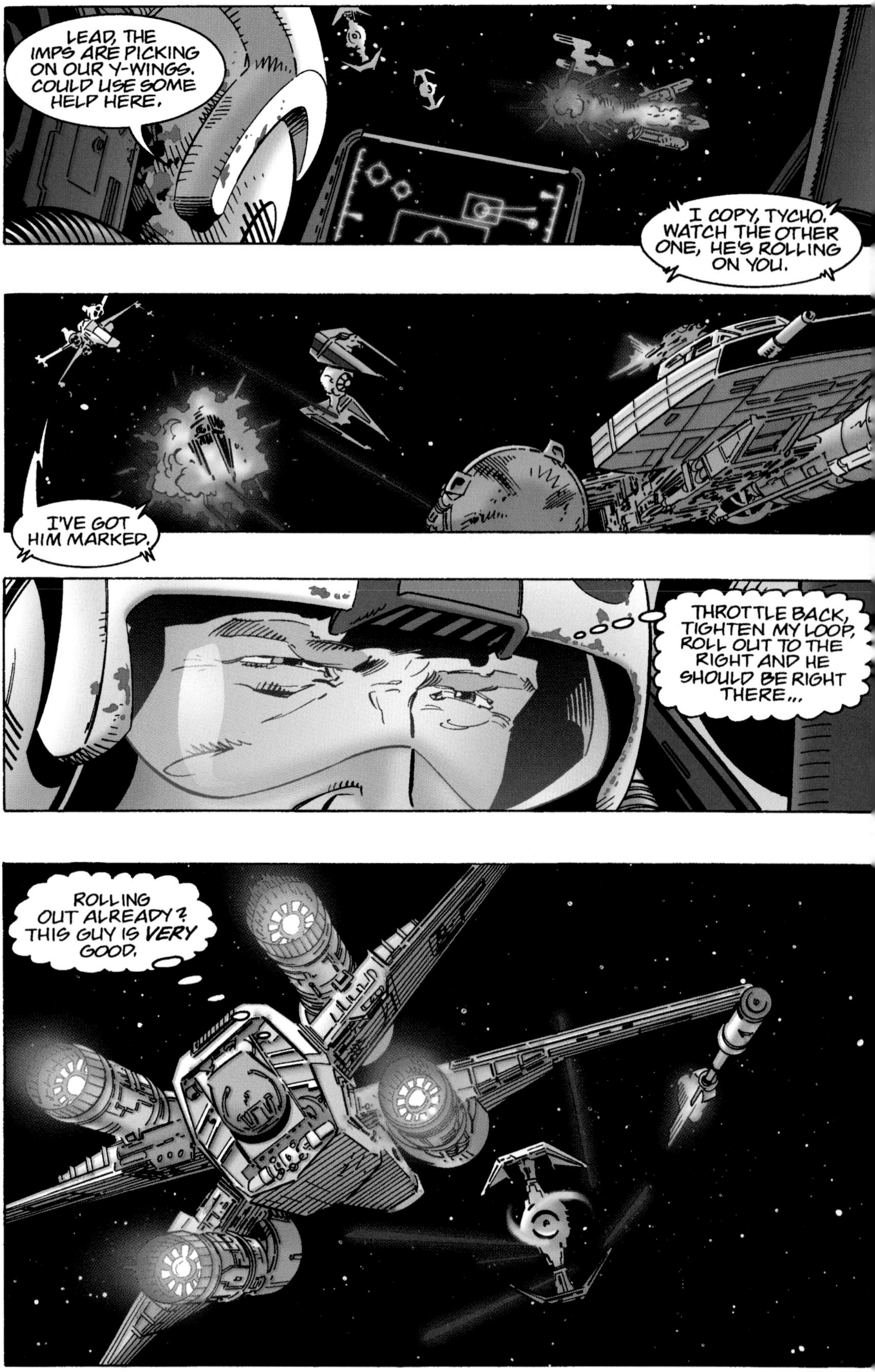
LEAD, THE IMPS ARE PICKING ON OUR Y-WINGS. COULD USE SOME HELP HERE.
I COPY, TYCHO. WATCH THE OTHER ONE, HE'S ROLLING ON YOU.
I'VE GOT HIM MARKED.
THROTTLE BACK, TIGHTEN MY LOOP, ROLL OUT TO THE RIGHT AND HE SHOULD BE RIGHT THERE...
ROLLING OUT ALREADY? THIS GUY IS VERY GOOD.

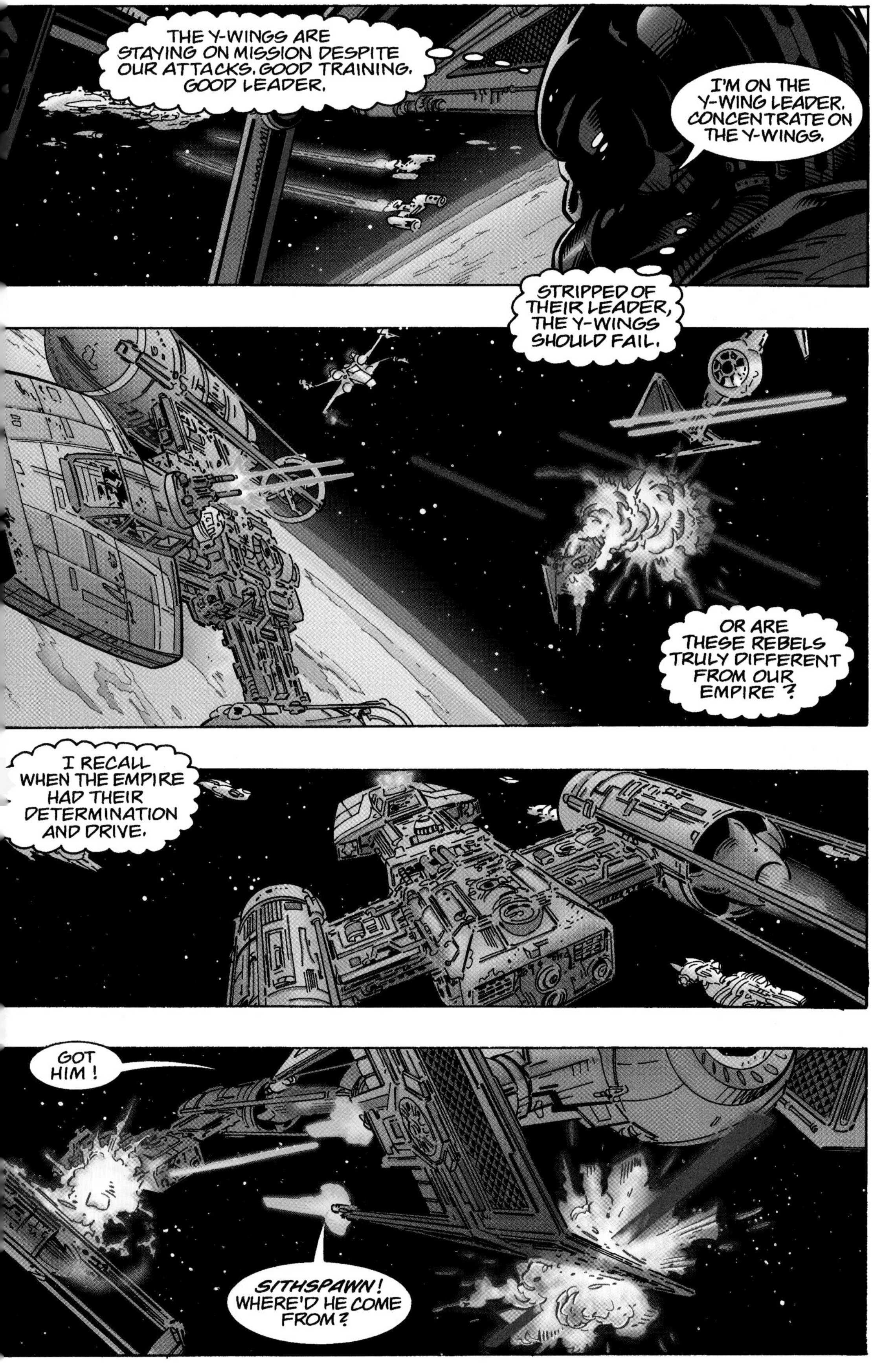
THE Y-WINGS ARE STAYING ON MISSION DESPITE OUR ATTACKS. GOOD TRAINING. GOOD LEADER.
I'M ON THE Y-WING LEADER. CONCENTRATE ON THE Y-WINGS.
STRIPPED OF THEIR LEADER, THE Y-WINGS SHOULD FAIL.
OR ARE THESE REBELS TRULY DIFFERENT FROM OUR EMPIRE ?
I RECALL WHEN THE EMPIRE HAD THEIR DETERMINATION AND DRIVE.
GOT HIM !
SITHSPAWN! WHERE'D HE COME FROM ?

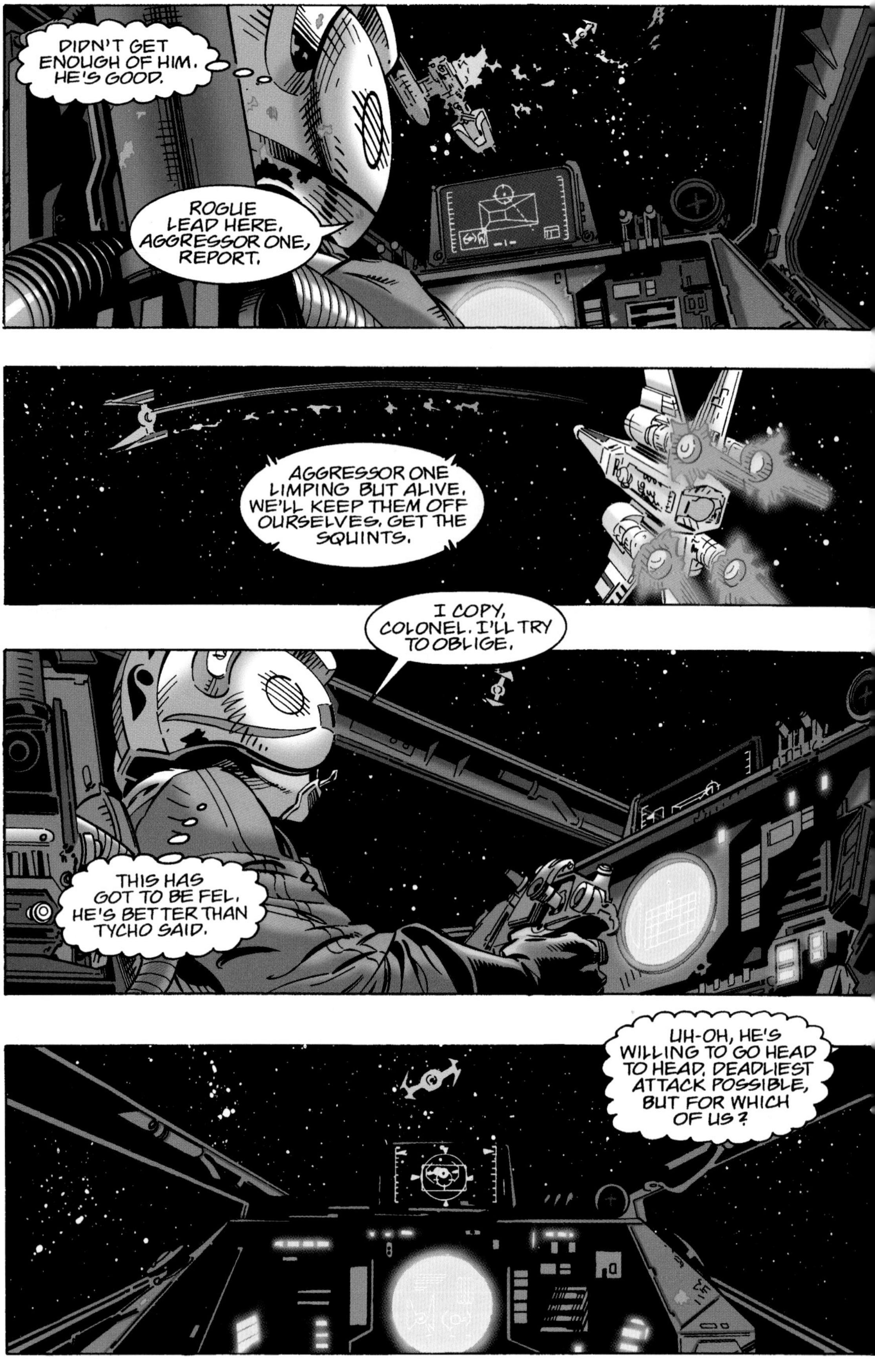
DIDN'T GET ENOUGH OF HIM. HE'S GOOD.
ROGUE LEAD HERE, AGGRESSOR ONE, REPORT.
AGGRESSOR ONE LIMPING BUT ALIVE. WE'LL KEEP THEM OFF OURSELVES. GET THE SQUINTS.
I COPY, COLONEL. I'LL TRY TO OBLIGE.
THIS HAS GOT TO BE FEL. HE'S BETTER THAN TYCHO SAID.
UH-OH, HE'S WILLING TO GO HEAD TO HEAD. DEADLIEST ATTACK POSSIBLE, BUT FOR WHICH OF US?

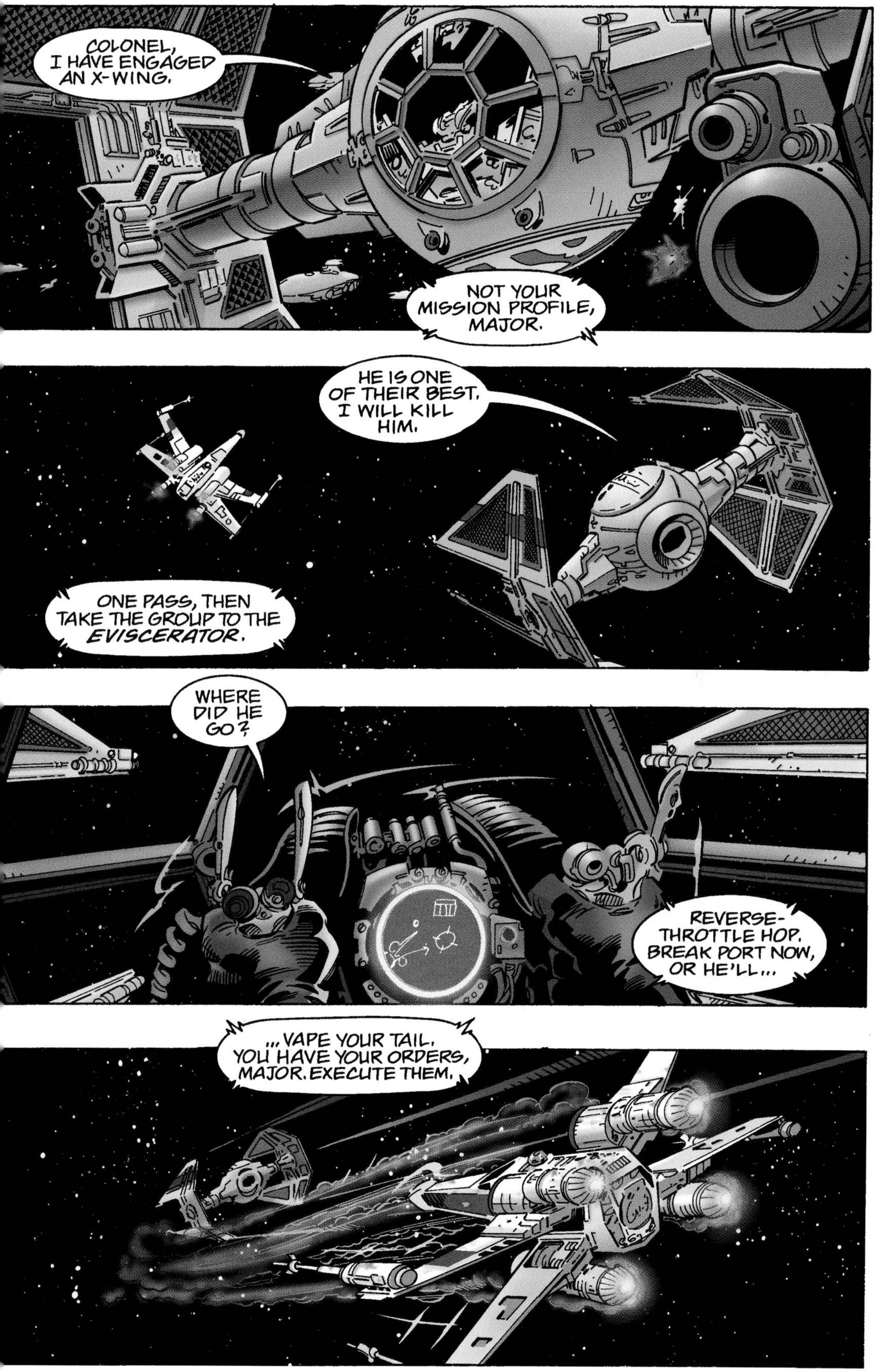
COLONEL, I HAVE ENGAGED AN X-WING.
NOT YOUR MISSION PROFILE, MAJOR.
HE IS ONE OF THEIR BEST. I WILL KILL HIM.
ONE PASS, THEN TAKE THE GROUP TO THE *EVISCERATOR*.
WHERE DID HE GO?
REVERSE-THROTTLE HOP. BREAK PORT NOW, OR HE'LL...
...VAPE YOUR TAIL. YOU HAVE YOUR ORDERS, MAJOR. EXECUTE THEM.

CAN'T SEE FOR THE SHIELD SCATTER.
WHERE IS HE? WHERE IS HE?
BREAK TO PORT, LEAD. LOOK FOR HIM STARBOARD.
THANKS, PLOURR.
THEY'RE RUNNING, WEDGE, TO THE SAFETY OF THE FLEET.
LET THEM RUN. HERD THE HEAVY MASS FREIGHTERS BACK TOWARD THE Y-WINGS.
COPY, LEAD. WANT HELP WITH YOUR FRIEND?
NEGATIVE, TYCHO. JUST STOP THE LOOTERS.
BELOW?! HOW DID HE GET THERE?
BETTER START FLYING LIKE YOU EARNED YOUR REP, WEDGE, OR YOU'LL BE JUST ANOTHER DEAD HERO.

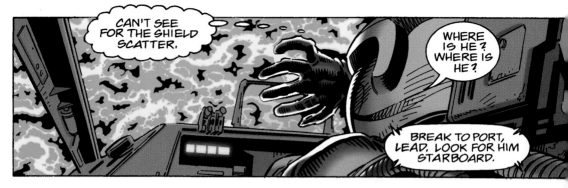

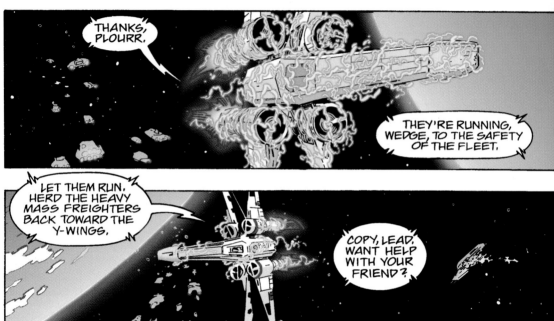

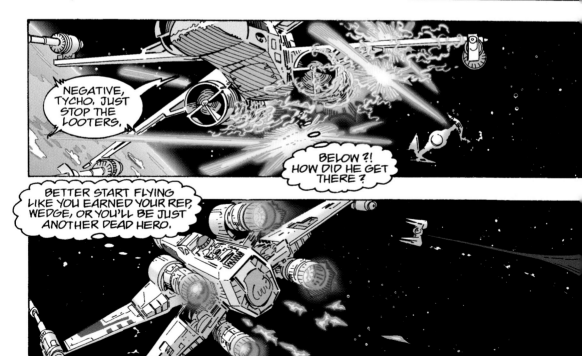

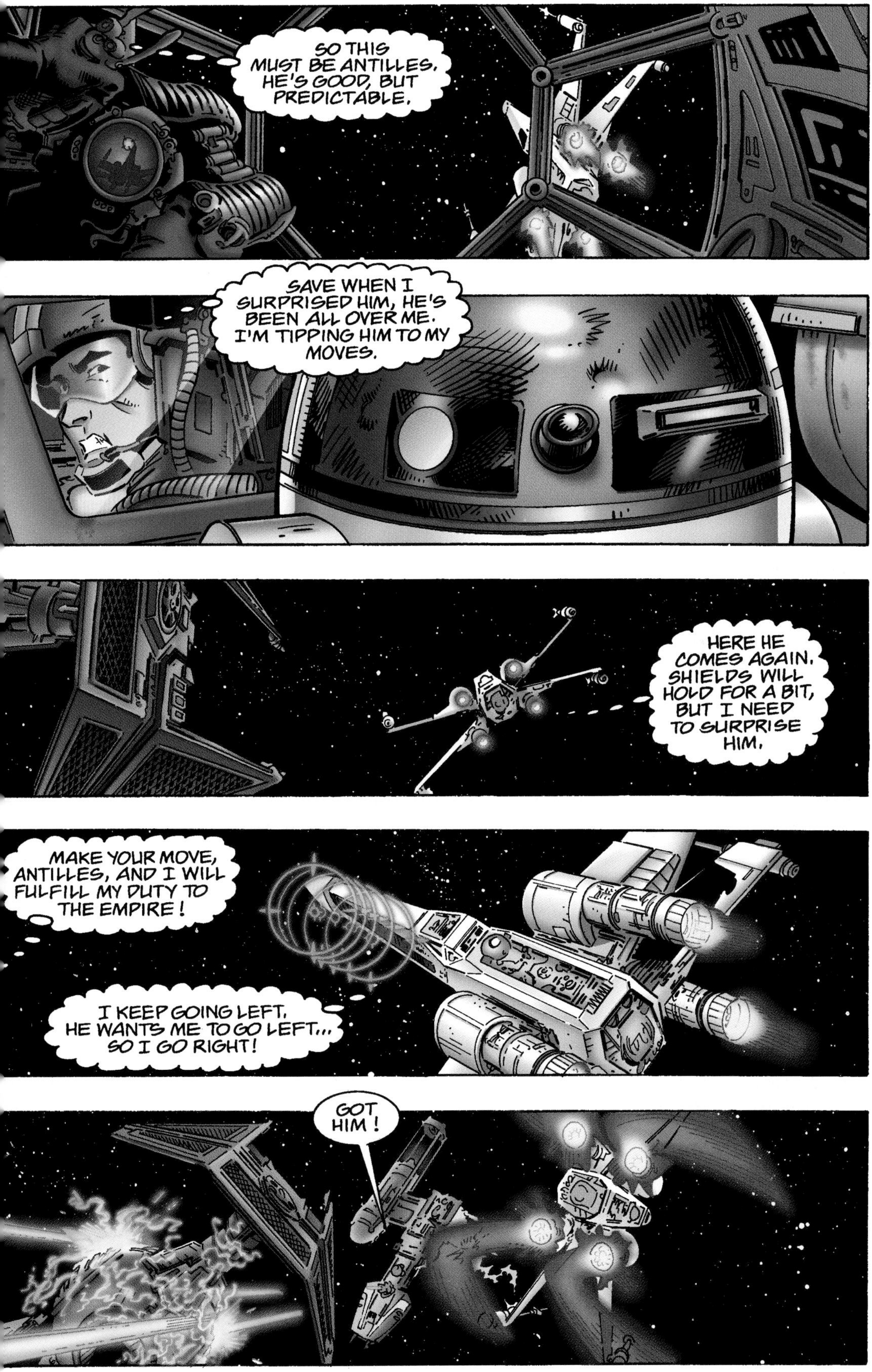
SO THIS MUST BE ANTILLES. HE'S GOOD, BUT PREDICTABLE.
SAVE WHEN I SURPRISED HIM, HE'S BEEN ALL OVER ME. I'M TIPPING HIM TO MY MOVES.
HERE HE COMES AGAIN. SHIELDS WILL HOLD FOR A BIT, BUT I NEED TO SURPRISE HIM.
MAKE YOUR MOVE, ANTILLES, AND I WILL FULFILL MY DUTY TO THE EMPIRE!
I KEEP GOING LEFT. HE WANTS ME TO GO LEFT... SO I GO RIGHT!
GOT HIM!

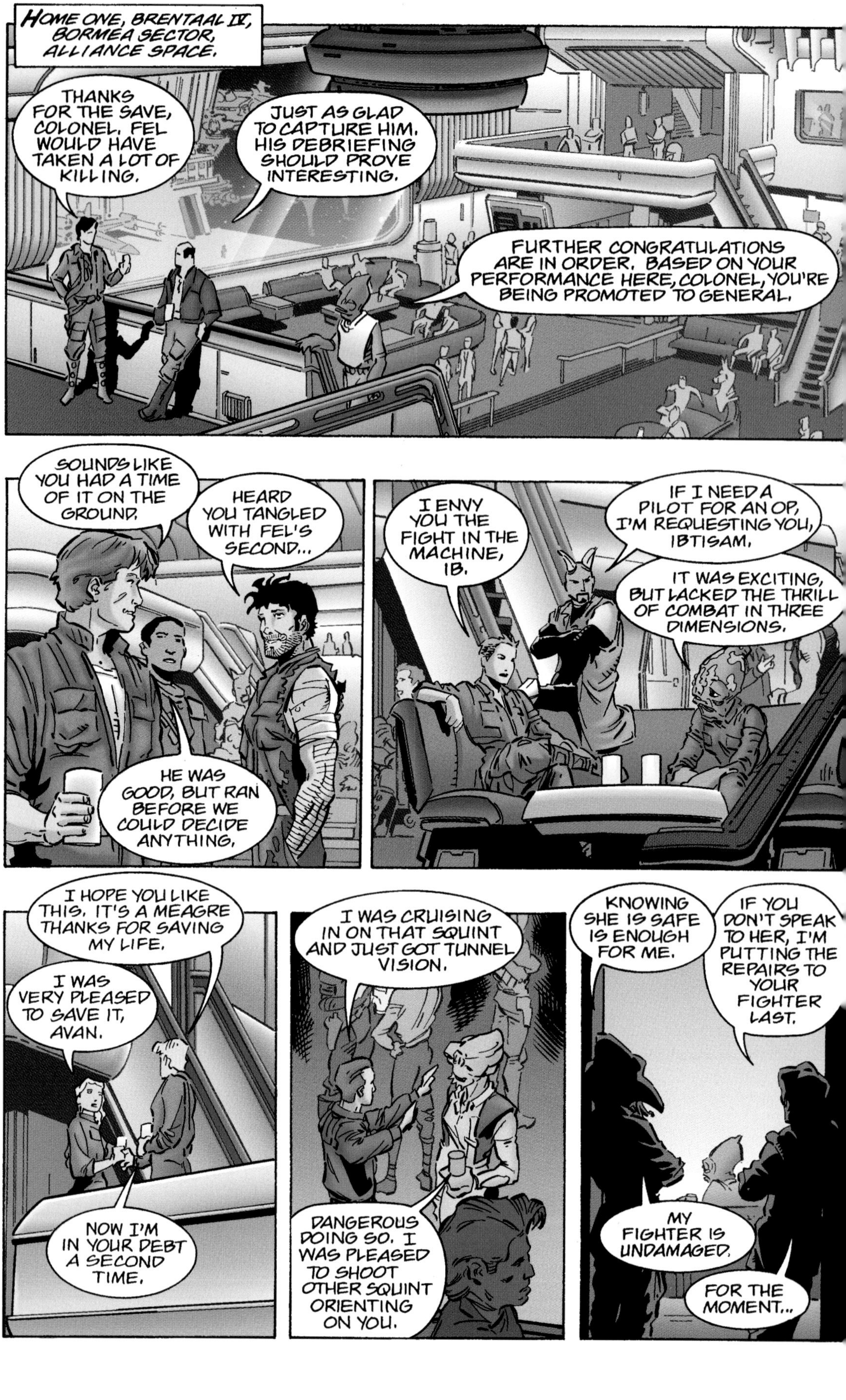
HOME ONE, BRENTAAL IV, BORMEA SECTOR, ALLIANCE SPACE.
THANKS FOR THE SAVE, COLONEL. FEL WOULD HAVE TAKEN A LOT OF KILLING.
JUST AS GLAD TO CAPTURE HIM. HIS DEBRIEFING SHOULD PROVE INTERESTING.
FURTHER CONGRATULATIONS ARE IN ORDER. BASED ON YOUR PERFORMANCE HERE, COLONEL, YOU'RE BEING PROMOTED TO GENERAL.
SOUNDS LIKE YOU HAD A TIME OF IT ON THE GROUND.
HEARD YOU TANGLED WITH FEL'S SECOND...
HE WAS GOOD, BUT RAN BEFORE WE COULD DECIDE ANYTHING.
I ENVY YOU THE FIGHT IN THE MACHINE, IB.
IF I NEED A PILOT FOR AN OP, I'M REQUESTING YOU, IBTISAM.
IT WAS EXCITING, BUT LACKED THE THRILL OF COMBAT IN THREE DIMENSIONS.
I HOPE YOU LIKE THIS. IT'S A MEAGRE THANKS FOR SAVING MY LIFE.
I WAS VERY PLEASED TO SAVE IT, AVAN.
NOW I'M IN YOUR DEBT A SECOND TIME.
I WAS CRUISING IN ON THAT SQUINT AND JUST GOT TUNNEL VISION.
DANGEROUS DOING SO. I WAS PLEASED TO SHOOT OTHER SQUINT ORIENTING ON YOU.
KNOWING SHE IS SAFE IS ENOUGH FOR ME.
IF YOU DON'T SPEAK TO HER, I'M PUTTING THE REPAIRS TO YOUR FIGHTER LAST.
MY FIGHTER IS UNDAMAGED.
FOR THE MOMENT...

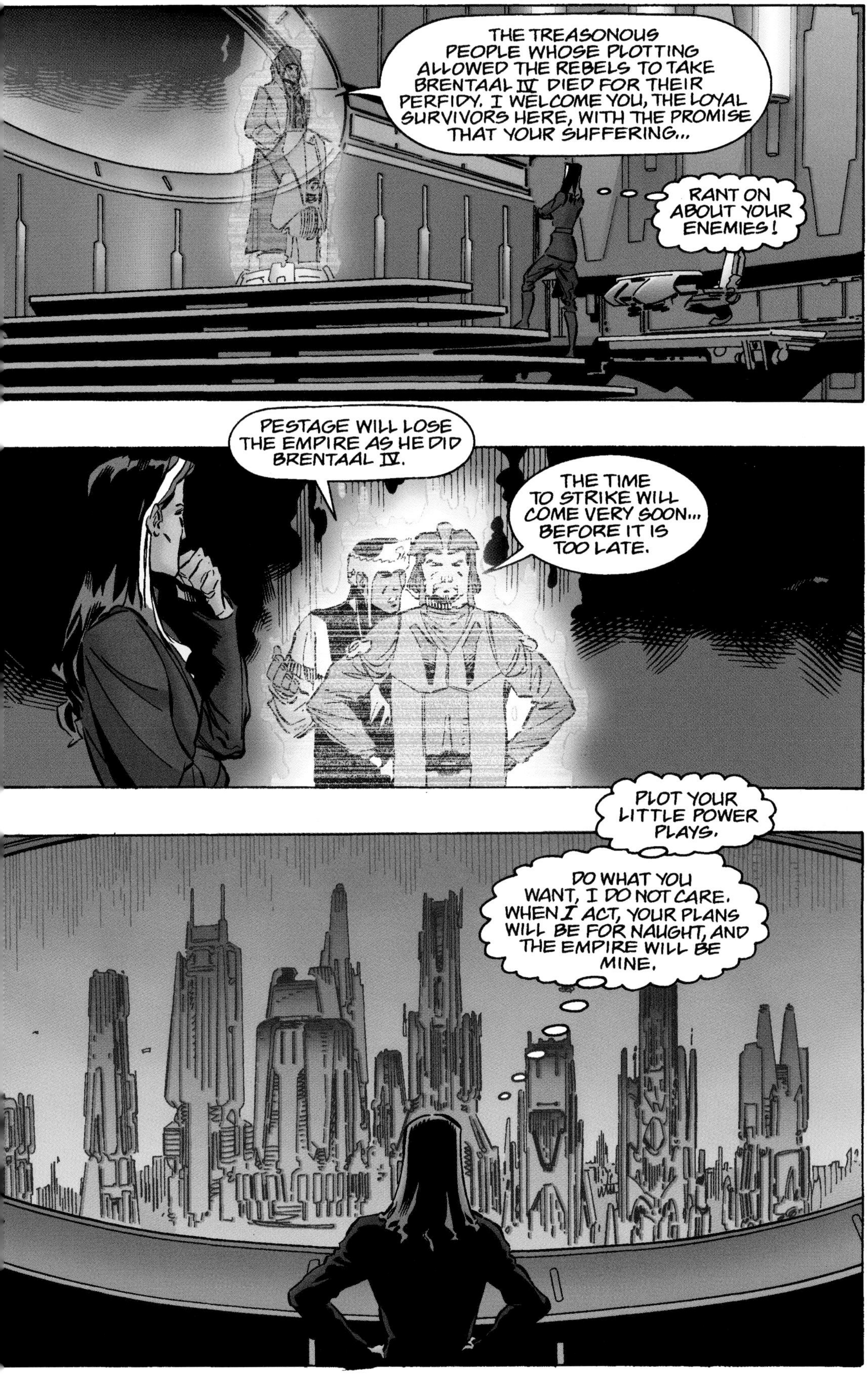
THE TREASONOUS PEOPLE WHOSE PLOTTING ALLOWED THE REBELS TO TAKE BRENTAAL IV DIED FOR THEIR PERFIDY. I WELCOME YOU, THE LOYAL SURVIVORS HERE, WITH THE PROMISE THAT YOUR SUFFERING...
RANT ON ABOUT YOUR ENEMIES!
PESTAGE WILL LOSE THE EMPIRE AS HE DID BRENTAAL IV.
THE TIME TO STRIKE WILL COME VERY SOON... BEFORE IT IS TOO LATE.
PLOT YOUR LITTLE POWER PLAYS.
DO WHAT YOU WANT, I DO NOT CARE. WHEN *I* ACT, YOUR PLANS WILL BE FOR NAUGHT, AND THE EMPIRE WILL BE MINE.

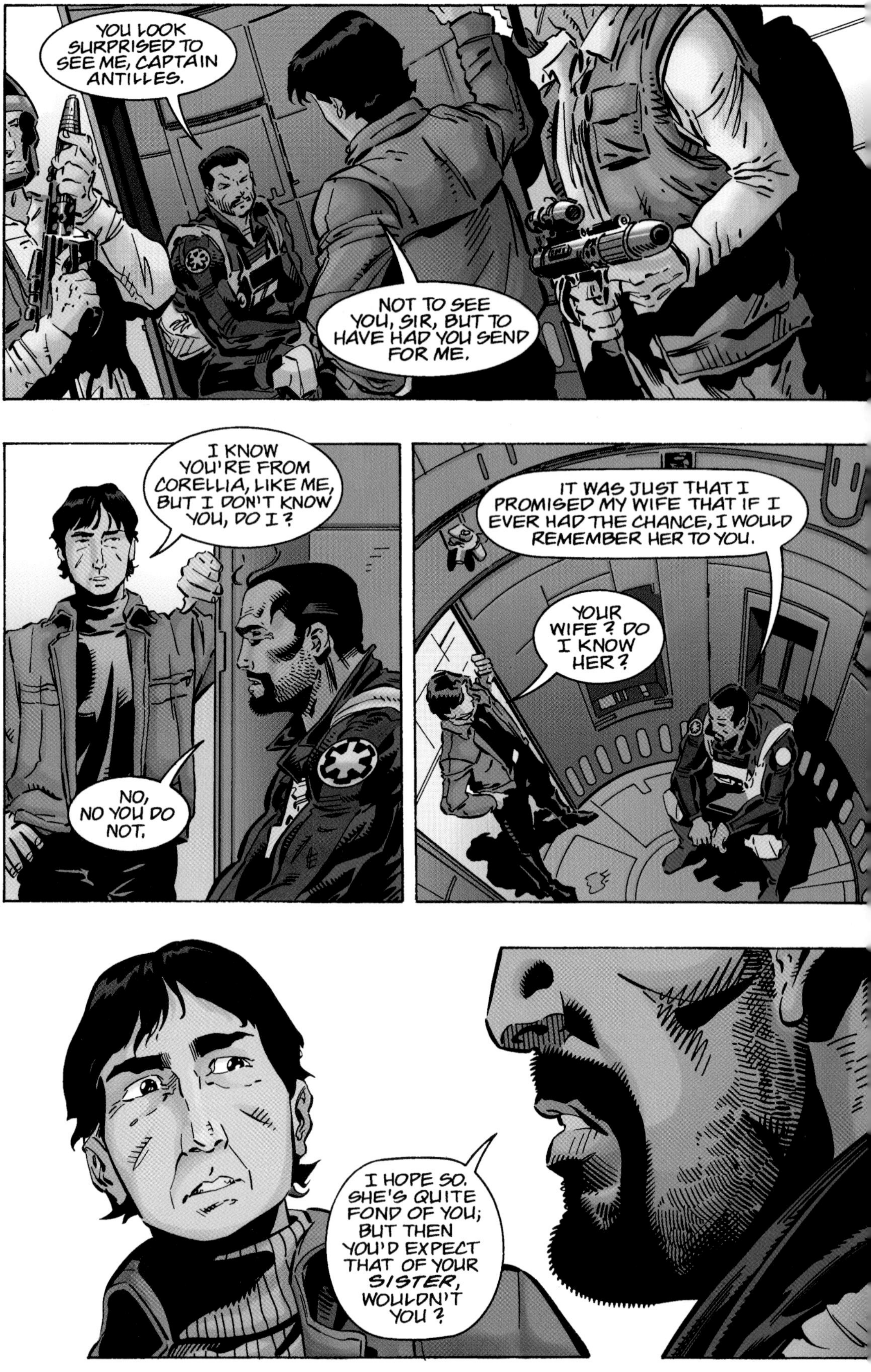
YOU LOOK SURPRISED TO SEE ME, CAPTAIN ANTILLES.
NOT TO SEE YOU, SIR, BUT TO HAVE HAD YOU SEND FOR ME.
I KNOW YOU'RE FROM CORELLIA, LIKE ME, BUT I DON'T KNOW YOU, DO I?
NO, NO YOU DO NOT.
IT WAS JUST THAT I PROMISED MY WIFE THAT IF I EVER HAD THE CHANCE, I WOULD REMEMBER HER TO YOU.
YOUR WIFE? DO I KNOW HER?
I HOPE SO. SHE'S QUITE FOND OF YOU; BUT THEN YOU'D EXPECT THAT OF YOUR SISTER, WOULDN'T YOU?

Michael A. Stackpole

Michael A. Stackpole is an award-winning game and computer game designer, and the author of five *Star Wars* novels: the first four *X-Wing Rogue Squadron* novels and *I, Jedi*. His sixth *Star Wars* novel, *Isard's Revenge*, will be published by Bantam Books in 1999. Mike marks the creation of Baron Fel for this series, and being able to script the books, as two of the high points of his *Star Wars* career.

John Nadeau

X-Wing Rogue Squadron fans are very familiar with the work of penciller John Nadeau. Few other artists have been able to capture so well the original "hardware" look of George Lucas' vision. John's highly detailed style appeared in *Aliens: Cargo* and *Aliens: Colonial Marines* before he signed on to Rogue Squadron, his work being featured in four story arcs—*Battleground: Tatooine*, *The Warrior Princess*, *In the Empire's Service*, and *Mandatory Retirement*. Not limited to *X-Wing* missions in the *Star Wars* universe, John has also served admirably on *Boba Fett: Enemy of the Empire*. An aspiring filmmaker, John one day hopes to utilize on the big screen the cinematic storytelling skills developed in comics.

Jordi Ensign

Jordi Ensign first began her professional comics career while still in high school, producing work for AC Comics. After college, Jordi pencilled *Hard C.O.R.P.S.* and *The Second Life of Dr. Mirage* for Valiant before teaming with high-school classmate John Nadeau as inker on *Aliens: Colonial Marines* and furthering their collaboration on *X-Wing Rogue Squadron*. No stranger to hardware, Jordi is an avid motorcycle enthusiast.

STAR WARS

X-WING ROGUE SQUADRON

IN THE EMPIRE'S SERVICE

GALLERY

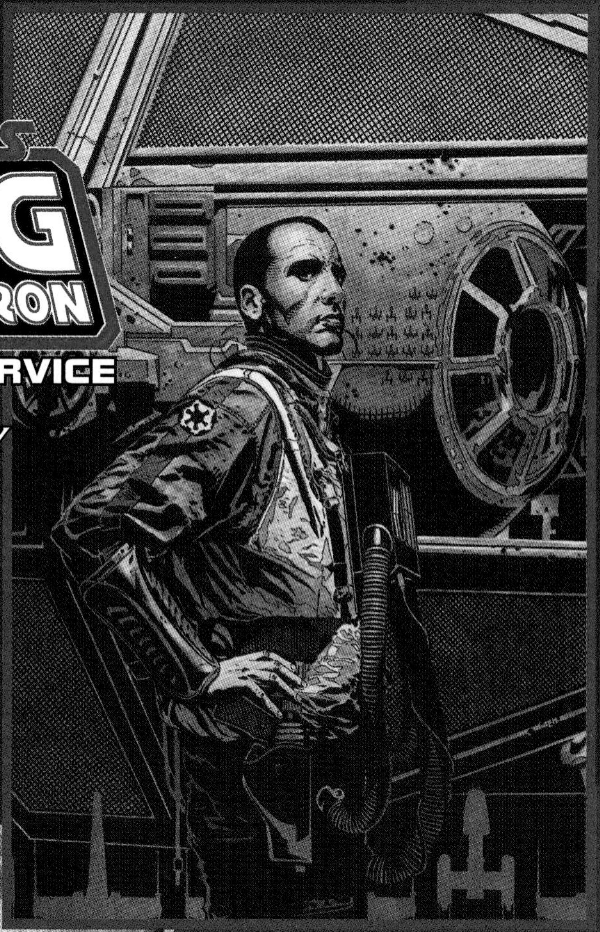

Timothy Bradstreet

John Nadeau

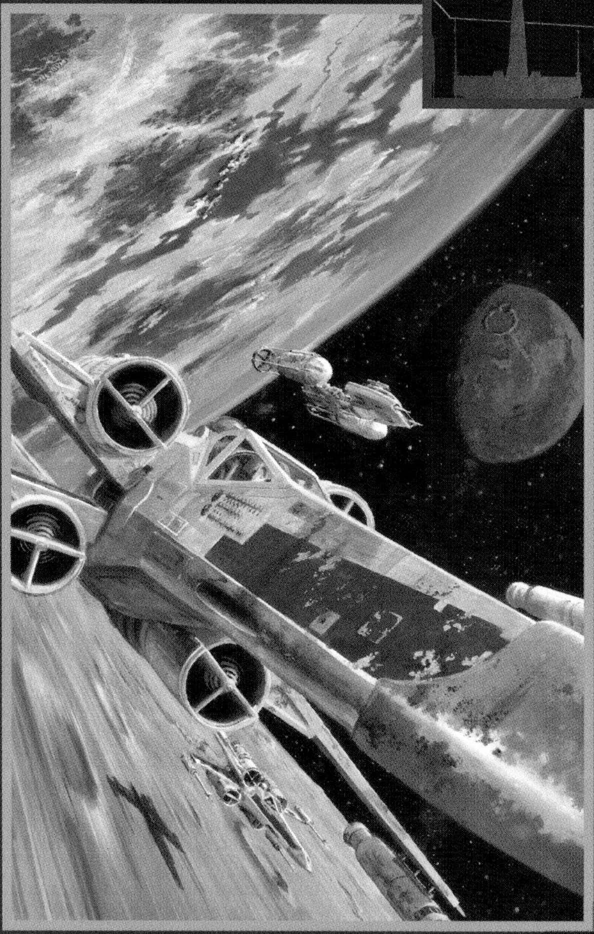